Hating THE PLAYER

CAMPUS *Wallflowers*

BOOK TWO

USA TODAY BESTSELLING AUTHOR

REBECCA JENSHAK

ISBN: 978-1-951815-40-0

Rebecca Jenshak
www.rebeccajenshak.com
Cover Design by Lori Jackson Designs
Editing by Edits in Blue and Fairest Reviews Editing Services
Proofreading by Sarah at All Encompassing Books

Hating THE PLAYER

"If I loved you less, I might be able to talk about it more." —Jane Austen

Chapter
ONE

Violet

"**Y**OU'RE GOING CAMPING?" JANE COMES INTO MY ROOM as I'm throwing all the essentials into my backpack for an impromptu trip.

"You could sound a little less surprised. I've camped before."

"Really?"

"Once. Kind of. We stayed in a camper. Just one night. I hated it."

Jane laughs and tosses her platinum blonde hair over one shoulder.

"But that was years ago. Maybe I'll be more in tune with nature in my old age. Plus, it will be nice to get away for the weekend." My gaze drifts out my bedroom window to the house next door. Cars are already parked out front and the faint rhythmic beat of the bass pumps from the backyard. The telltale signs of the beginning of a party.

I live in an off-campus house with three friends: Jane, Dahlia, and Daisy. Our neighbors, basketball players on Valley U's nationally ranked team, know how to throw a party. It'd be far less annoying if we didn't have to deal with the constant noise, trash thrown into our yard, and cars blocking our driveway. And if *he* didn't live there.

"It will be better than staying here all weekend by myself. Plus, Daisy asked, and since she and Jordan got back together, we haven't spent as much time together."

My roommate fights a smile. "I am so sorry I won't be there to see it."

"What are your plans while visiting your family?" I ask.

"It's my parents' twenty-fifth wedding anniversary. They're having a little party at the house tomorrow night." She shrugs one shoulder. "I'd rather watch you try to tackle nature."

"Well, keep your phone on. I might need to phone a friend."

Daisy bursts into my room with a smile splashed across her face in almost cartoon-fashion. "Who's ready for a great weekend?"

"Yay!" I try for enthusiastic, but I'm a smidge nervous.

"It's going to be fun," she insists. "Did Dahlia already leave?"

"Yeah. She had to go meet the bus for her golf tournament, but she said to tell you to keep a close eye on that one." Jane points at me.

"I will be fine."

"Mhmmm." Jane stands and hugs me, then Daisy. "All right. I have to go or I'm going to miss my flight. See you on Sunday! Hope you're in one piece."

"Ha, ha," I call to her back.

When she's gone, Daisy aims her excited grin right at me. "Are you ready for this?"

We're the first to arrive at the campsite on top of Mount Loken. Jordan's friends are on their way, but while we wait, we start to unload the SUV. I'm the only single person attending this little weekend getaway with Daisy and Jordan and two other couples, but I was promised my own tent, and I brought a book and some old magazines. I'm going to treat the next two days like a nature spa weekend. I'll hike, read, sketch, maybe meditate. And if that fails, I have a portable charger for my phone and Jane's Hulu login.

Honestly, though, it doesn't look so bad. There are bathrooms and showers nearby, and a grill for cooking. I can totally do this.

"Jenkins is bringing his extra tent, so I'll set that up when he gets here. Do you want to be next to us?" Jordan asks as he starts to put up his and Daisy's tent.

"How about a tent or two away. I want to be able to drown the two of you out with headphones."

Chuckling, he says, "You got it."

"Perfect." I still when Daisy grabs a stack of blankets. "Oh crap. Was I supposed to bring my own blankets and pillows?"

Daisy laughs softly.

"We can spare a blanket or two, and I'll ask the guys if anyone has a pillow you can use," Jordan says.

"Thank you."

He smiles. "No problem."

He gets back to work putting up their tent while Daisy and I unload everything else.

"You're boyfriend's not so bad."

"He's the best," she sing-songs.

Jordan's roommate and teammate, Liam, and his boyfriend, Cole, arrive next. As soon as we've all said our hellos, the next car comes into view.

I go back to unloading supplies, but seconds later, Daisy gasps beside me.

I swivel around and follow her gaze to Jenkins and his girlfriend, Taylor. I start to ask what the big deal is, but then I see him. *Gavin.*

He steps out of the car and scans the campsite. His sunglasses keep me from seeing his eyes, but I can tell the second he spots me. He stills and his jaw drops. I quickly look away.

"What the hell is he doing here?" I keep my voice low, but my heart hammers loudly in my chest. I can feel him still staring this direction.

"I don't know," she says, panic clear in her tone. "I promise. I had no idea he was coming. Jordan said he had a date or something."

I came all the way up the mountain to get away from my neighbor, and here he is, invading my spa-nature-getaway. Freaking figures.

"Do you want to go? I can ask Jordan to take us back, or maybe Uber comes up here?"

I appreciate her concern, but I am not letting Gavin run me off. I was here first.

"It's fine. I'll just avoid him for the next forty-eight hours."

How hard could that be?

I'm successful in my *stay the hell away from Gavin* plan for the first few hours. I hike with Jordan and Daisy, and he goes, well I don't know, but somewhere that isn't with us.

It's later, when the sun is setting and we gather to make dinner and hang out, I find myself sitting across from him.

He has a bottle of Jager in hand and he's barely said a word to anyone. I doubt hanging out with me was in his weekend plans either. The thought makes me feel slightly better.

Not to worry. It's turning into couples' island out here, and I am not about to sit around and watch them get handsy.

"We should play cards or something," Liam says, looking around the circle.

That's my cue.

"I think I'm gonna go to bed." I fake a yawn.

I say goodnight, and Jordan tosses me his keys, so I can grab my backpack from his SUV. I breathe a sigh of relief as I walk away. I did it. I survived a day in nature (okay, fine, it's only been a few hours) and I managed to avoid a confrontation with Gavin.

After I wash my face and change clothes in the campsite bathroom, I head back to my tent. There's a small lantern hanging from the center of the tent that puts off enough light for me to see as I get situated. I pull my hair up into a messy bun, eye the blanket and pillow Jenkins must have dropped off for me, *thank you very much*, and am generally feeling like a badass when something rustles at the front of the tent.

"H-ello?" My voice trembles on the word.

No answer. *Oh god, what if it's a mountain lion or a bear?*

I take a step backward. The tent isn't all that big and there is nowhere to go or hide. I glance around for something—anything—to use for protection. I grab my book from the front pocket of my backpack and hold it out in front of me as Gavin moves into the space with me.

Oh, hell no.

Chapter
TWO

Violet

GAVIN LEONARD IS THE WORST.

There are a lot of reasons why, but right now, it's because he's standing half-naked in front of me inside *my* tent, holding the T-shirt he just took off in one hand. His brow furrows as he scans my body from head to toe.

I drop the book and cross my arms over my chest, acutely aware that I'm not wearing a bra under this flimsy tank top. And why did I have to pack my Powerpuff Girls sleep shorts? *Groan.*

"What are you doing in here?" As if it isn't bad enough that I got stuck on a couples' camping trip, where we're the only two not coupled up, but now he has the gall to waltz into my tent after dark. He nearly gave me a heart attack. I thought he was a bear. Truthfully, I might have preferred a bear over him.

"This is *my* tent. Why are you in it?" His deep, husky voice skates over my skin.

I take absolutely no offense to the disdain dripping from his every word. It would be shocking for him to find me in his tent. *If* it were his tent.

"I think maybe you had a little too much Jager tonight. Jenkins told me I could use it this weekend."

When Daisy threw out the last-minute invite to come this weekend, I almost said no. The outdoors isn't really my thing, but I wanted to show Daisy how much I love and support her. When she started dating Jordan, hockey player and party connoisseur, I was skeptical. She's my cousin and my absolute favorite person, and I didn't want to see her get hurt like I had in the past.

Anyway, I judged Jordan and assumed the worst, but thankfully he keeps proving me wrong. And it's really good to see Daisy so happy.

Now I think I should have just told her how glad I was to see her happy and maybe baked her a cake instead of traipsing up a mountain and camping for two nights with a bunch of couples. And *him*.

Gavin brings a hand up to his forehead and pushes back the dark locks. His tone is laced with annoyance and indifference—a combination that irks me like none other—as he says, "I'm not nearly drunk enough for this."

He points, and I follow the line of sight to a rolled up sleeping bag, blanket, and pillow in the corner. "See. My stuff is right there."

"I thought Jenkins dropped those off for me." My face heats. *Oh crap. This can't be happening.* "I was promised my own tent this weekend."

And there's no way I'm sharing it with this guy of all people. I'd rather sleep outside.

"Be my guest," he says, making me realize I said that last part out loud.

"No. You should sleep outside. Maybe a bear will eat you."

"You wound me," he says dryly. Then instead of turning around, he bulldozes farther in.

"Hey." I place a hand on his chest and regret it immediately. I've successfully avoided shirtless Gavin for a year. And now I remember why. His body is insane. He's lean and muscular. He's almost too pretty to believe he can do such savage things on a basketball court. His hair is thick and disheveled. Not messy. It has more of the *I'm hot and don't need to waste my time with things like brushes or hair gel* vibe.

Our friends poke their heads out of their tents to see what the commotion is about. *Oh great, we've attracted a crowd.* I march out with Gavin on my heels. Since it's Jenkins' tent, I look to him to back me up.

The humorous glint in his eye makes a pit form in my stomach. He's trying hard to fight a smile. "Yeah, sorry, I forgot."

"You forgot?!" I glare at him. "Forgot what exactly?"

"I promised you the tent before I knew that Gavin was coming, but it's actually his tent. I forgot to tell you that you guys would have to share."

In what world would Jenkins think that I'd be okay with sharing a tent with Gavin? My dislike for him isn't a secret.

"See?" Gavin says and heads back inside the tent.

"Oh no, get out of there." Blood roars in my ears as I follow him. "This changes nothing."

"You'd kick me out of my own tent?" He unrolls his sleeping bag and lies down on top of it. "This tent is big enough for both of us. You won't even know I'm here."

"Doubtful." I run through different scenarios. I'm thirty minutes from my house with my own bedroom that is guaranteed to be Gavin-free, but I have no car, and it's doubtful any of my friends are down for a late-night trip up the mountain to rescue me.

"Three hundred and sixty-five days since our last incident," I mutter.

His lips curl in amusement. "Keeping track?"

"I was being flippant. You know like, 'it's been five days since a safety incident in the warehouse.'"

He snorts. "Funny."

"I'm not trying to be funny, and I definitely don't keep track of anything related to you. And there is absolutely no way you and I are sharing a tent." My voice rises in panic with every word.

He turns over on his side. He has a tattoo on the inside of his forearm. It's new, and I can't make out the words in the near darkness of the tent. "Well, I'm sure Daisy and Jordan will let you crash with them."

I love my cousin, and I'm really happy that things between them are going so well, but I don't need a front-row view of just how well it's going. I can hear it just fine from two tents down.

"Can't you stay with Jenkins?"

"Definitely not. It's his first sleepover with Taylor. They're not going to be doing a lot of sleeping, and I am beat."

He looks up to where I'm still standing in the doorway of the tent. Over a year ago, Gavin and I hung out, talked, or whatever you want to call it. I was a bright-eyed freshman and so taken with the handsome, college basketball star. Our "whatever" only lasted for three weeks, which I know in the grand scheme of things seems insignificant, but it was enough time for me to fall for him and to offer up my v-card. All that to say, I might be a little extra salty when it comes to all things Gavin.

"No. This can't be happening."

A beat passes before he gets to his feet, far more gracefully than one would expect of someone so tall.

"Fine. I will sleep outside." He rolls up the sleeping bag and grabs his blanket and pillow.

I bite my lip to keep myself from stopping him. I feel the tiniest bit bad, but I can't bring myself to tell him not to go.

After he disappears outside, I walk over to zip up the tent for the night and catch sight of him, rolling out the sleeping bag next to the fire. I feel another twinge of guilt but I easily dismiss it. He'll be fine. He's bigger than just about anything out in these mountains. And really, it isn't even *that* cold, I think as I shiver.

"Vi?" Daisy calls, stepping out of her and Jordan's tent. She glances from me to where Gavin is settling into his sleeping bag and then pulls a sweatshirt over her head as she jogs over to me. "I am so sorry." Following me into the tent, Daisy gives me a sympathetic smile. "I feel awful about this entire trip. I swear I had no idea he was going to be here or that the extra tent was his."

"Just my luck, right?" I blow out a long breath and sit on the hard floor. Gavin took my sleeping bag, blanket, and pillow. Or, technically, I guess they are his, but I thought they were mine for tonight and now I have nothing.

"Does Jordan still have extra blankets and pillows in his SUV?"

"I think so. If not, you can take one from our tent. Want me to go check?"

"No, I can do it. Go have fun. One of us should be enjoying this."

She sticks out her bottom lip in a pout and reaches over to squeeze my arm. "I'm sorry."

"Ignore me. I'm being dramatic. I'll be fine."

She hugs me and then stands. "If you need anything, anything at all, just yell. Night, Vi. See you in the morning."

Chapter
THREE

Violet

I WAIT A GOOD THIRTY MINUTES, UNTIL I ASSUME GAVIN will be sleeping, before creeping out of the tent in flip flops for Jordan's SUV.

Holy moly, it gets cold up here at night. I move as quickly as I can, rubbing my bare arms as I walk. When I reach the vehicle, I open the cargo door and find one, lone blanket. It'll have to do. I hug it to my chest and rush back. The campsite is dark and quiet. Everyone must be all banged out for the night.

I'm six feet from the tent when a scratching noise stops me in my tracks. I hold my breath and wait to see if it comes again. When it does, I whimper and then sidestep, moving closer to where Gavin is sleeping by the fire.

"Gavin!" I whisper-screech.

"What?"

"I heard something."

"Don't worry. If they know what's good for them, they'll eat me first." He doesn't so much as open his eyes.

The scratching noise starts up again and my heart races as I weigh my chances of sprinting to the tent safely. That's when I see it—the flaps hanging open. Oh my god, I didn't close them when I left. What if there's an animal inside?

"O-okay, you can come in the tent," I say, and nudge him lightly with a foot.

One of Gavin's eyes opens for the briefest of seconds. "Worried about me?"

"No," I say quickly. "But maybe staying in pairs is a good idea."

"You'll be fine, Vi. It's probably just a raccoon or something."

I love how he says that like running into a raccoon would be perfectly fine. Raccoons are scary, and I'd like not to encounter one in the dark, thanks.

"I think it's in the tent."

"How would it get in the tent?" His dark eyes open and he gives me his full, albeit sleepy, attention.

"I went to Jordan's SUV to get a blanket. You took mine. Or yours. I needed a blanket and now there is a wild animal in my tent. Your tent. Oh my god, please just help me." My voice is bordering on a whine and I'm full-blown freaking out.

"Relax," he says and stands. His arm brushes mine. He pulled on sweats and a hoodie since I last saw him and he's so warm and calm, so I don't move away. He takes a step and I fall in behind him, staying close. He walks over to a chair and un-zips his backpack.

"Are you getting a weapon?" I ask as he rummages in the front pocket.

He turns with his phone in hand and the flashlight shines in my eyes. I hold up a hand to block the light, but I can still see his smug grin.

"Why would I have a weapon in my backpack?"

12

"I don't know. I've never camped before. I have no idea what people bring."

He shakes his head, and I follow close again, my hands resting lightly on his lower back. I feel safer with him leading the way, but then I also can't see anything, and not being able to see is terrifying.

He stops, and I run into the back of him, heart pounding. I squeeze my eyes shut and cling to him. The blanket in my hands acts as a barrier between us, but I can still feel the warmth pouring off him. He smells like smoke and dirt, but it doesn't repulse me like I wish it would.

"What is it? A wolf?"

"I don't see anything." The light moves across the dark horizon.

"Did you check the tent?" I ask, still using him as a human shield.

"It's all clear," he says.

Clutching at his sweatshirt, I peer around him slowly. He shines the light into the tent to show me there's nothing in there except my backpack and cell phone.

I release him and step out from behind him on shaky legs. "We must have scared it off."

"We?" His brows lift.

"Fine. You." I look around at the black sky. The moon is a tiny sliver up there tonight and the stars are hiding, making this campsite seem even darker than I imagine it would on a clear night. I don't want to think about what is out there lurking around us.

A shiver rolls up my spine.

"You need more than a flimsy blanket out here." His gaze drops to the one I'm still holding.

"This is all that was left in Jordan's SUV." I clutch the thin blanket to my chest, feeling very protective of it. It's not its fault it wasn't made for outdoor adventure.

Somewhere in the distance, an animal howls. I rush into the tent, fully aware that Gavin is laughing at me.

"All set?" he asks as he angles his body to leave.

I bite the corner of my lip. There is no way I'm going to get any sleep tonight.

"Maybe you should stay in the tent," I say, not quite meeting his dark gaze.

His only reaction is a slight raise of one brow.

"Because it's cold, and if you get eaten then people will probably blame me."

"I'll be fine," he assures me and takes a step away.

"No. Wait," I call. I take a breath before continuing, "Please will you sleep in here? I don't want to be alone."

"And you thought of me? How sweet." Sarcasm drips from his words. He lets the tent flap fall closed and disappears.

Ugh.

"Jerk," I mutter and lie down. I unfold the blanket and pull it over me. It covers about half of my body, but if I curl up into the fetal position, it's perfect. It isn't like I'm going to be able to sleep anyway, so I'll just try not to freeze to death tonight. *Goals: they're important.*

I'm just settling in when Gavin ducks inside with all his stuff.

Wordlessly, he zips us in. The sound sets a new type of anxiety spreading through me. I'm alone in a tent with Gavin. Did I mention he's the worst?

He sets his backpack in the corner and unrolls the sleeping bag as far away from me as he can get.

The three feet between us isn't far enough. Outer space isn't far enough. With Gavin, there is no empty space between us. Every molecule is charged and agitated.

I toss and turn. My toes keep slipping out from the bottom of my trusty blanket.

And I can hear him breathing. Does he have to breathe so loud?

I'm moving onto my other side when an object collides with my face. I start to yell, but then realize it's his blanket. *Ohhhh.* It's so warm, a happy groan escapes, and I can't even pretend like I'm going to turn it down.

"Do you want to use the other one?" It would probably cover half his legs, but it's something.

He turns away from me, giving me his back, and puts his pillow over his head. "Go to sleep, Violet."

Chapter
FOUR

Violet

I WAKE UP IN A COCOON OF WARMTH.

I start to roll over only to realize several things at once. Number one, I'm trapped by a heavy arm tossed over my middle and there's no longer three feet of distance between me and Gavin. Number two, he's hard or has a flashlight in his sweats, and three, did I mention he's hard?!

My movement must have woken him because he pulls his arm away in a flash and rolls onto his back.

"Sorry," he says, voice full of gravel.

"It's fine," I squeak. *Totally* fine. I jump up, taking the blanket with me and wrapping it around my body as I move to my backpack. Instead of pulling out what I need, I loop the bag over one shoulder and head outside. I don't care what time it is or how dark it is, I will brave the wild animals to get out of this awkward situation.

Thankfully, the sun is up. In the light of day, it seems silly that I was so freaked out last night. It's peaceful up here. Serene, even. Jenkins and his girlfriend, Taylor, are already out at the fire.

"Morning," Jenkins says, lifting a coffee mug. He has the ghost of a smirk on his face.

"Morning," I reply, ignoring the heat creeping into my cheeks. So we slept in the same tent and spooned, we still hate each other. I head off toward the bathrooms to shower and change.

By the time I get back, everyone else is up. Daisy and Jordan are sharing a chair. She sits on his lap and cuddles into his chest. They really are the cutest. Liam and his boyfriend, Cole, are cooking something in a pot over the fire, while Gavin sits off to the side by himself. Much like he did yesterday.

I drop my stuff in Jordan's SUV, so I won't have any more tent run-ins with Gavin later and then join the group.

Jordan holds out a mug filled with hot coffee to me. I take it with a murmured thanks.

"What's the plan today?" I am eager to go off in groups. Yesterday, I spent most of the day hiking with Daisy and Jordan, and more importantly, avoiding Gavin.

We're leaving first thing tomorrow morning, so I just need to survive twenty-four more hours. We'll get off this mountain and go back to hating each other from a distance. Or, well, I guess not too much distance since we're neighbors, but a couple of thick walls between us ought to do nicely and keep us from killing each other.

"I'm not feeling well today," Daisy says. Her voice is raspy. "I'm going to hang back at least this morning."

The look Jordan gives her, the look Jordan *always* gives her, tells me there's no way he's going anywhere without her.

"We're going to hike to the fishing lake," Liam says, and he and Cole share a grin.

Jenkins glances at Gavin before saying, "The three of us talked about walking up to the ski resort. They keep the lift going and the views are killer."

"There's also a cute little restaurant up there and a fudge shop," Taylor adds.

My stomach growls. All that hiking yesterday has me famished, but I don't really know Taylor or Jenkins that well. And Gavin, well, I know him *too* well.

"You should go, Vi," Daisy urges, then adds, "if you want."

"I don't want to leave you if you're feeling sick."

"I'm okay. I think sleep will help. If I get to feeling better, I'll text you, and we'll come meet up with you."

All eyes are on me. Is there a polite way to say I'd rather stay here and read a book?

"Sure," I say finally, "I'll come."

After last night, I think I can handle a short walk with Gavin.

The "short" walk to the ski resort turns out to be over two miles at a steady incline. Jenkins and Taylor are walking ahead of us, holding hands and flirting, while Gavin and I pull up the rear. He's behind me, which is unnerving, because I swear I can feel him watching me.

But the weather is beautiful, and it really is pretty amazing up here, looking down on Valley and being surrounded by trees that reach up high into the sky and have more green than in all of Phoenix, where I grew up.

I pull off my sweatshirt and tie it around my waist. There's a great lookout spot, where a few cars are parked, and people are taking pictures. Jenkins and Taylor stop for a few kissing selfies, and I pull out my phone to take one of myself.

"I could take it if you want," Gavin offers.

I hesitate, but hand over my phone.

He looks up over the screen. His eyes are shielded with Ray-Bans, but I still somehow know his eyes are twinkling with humor.

"Try to look happier. You're standing in front of a gorgeous view, and you look like you just shoved someone over the ledge."

"Oh, I wish," I tease, but I pull out my best fake smile, one that I've honed over more than a decade of school photos.

He hands it back and then we stand together at the metal railing, looking out.

"You were imagining pushing me off, weren't you?"

"No, too many witnesses."

He chuckles softly and then angles his body, his hip resting on the railing as he faces me. "About last night—"

I hold up a hand to stop him from continuing. "It's fine."

The sun suddenly blazes a thousand times hotter at the memory of waking up in his arms with his sizable dick pressed against my ass.

"Are you guys ready?" I ask, passing Jenkins and Taylor, and taking off toward the ski resort. I don't wait for their answer.

I lead us to the top, stretching my short legs and pumping my arms. I'm panting and sweating when we get there. We pass a restaurant and gift shop before reaching the ski lift. As promised, it's running and there's already a line of people waiting. The weather is perfect—blue skies, sun shining bright with a slight breeze.

We get tickets for the lift and Gavin and I end up side by side once again while we wait. I can't seem to escape him.

At the front of the line, he holds out his hand, letting me go ahead of him.

This whole day was one terrible idea, and being trapped thirty feet in the air with my nemesis unequivocally proves that I should have stayed back at the campsite.

"I thought you had a date this weekend?" I ask, in a tone I was hoping sounded conversational, but it comes out accusatory.

"Didn't work out." He stares straight ahead. "Sorry I ruined your weekend."

It's true if I'd known he was going to be here, I wouldn't have come, but we do share friends, now that Daisy and Jordan are dating, so it's getting hard to predict when we might run into one another these days. Plus, the whole neighbors' thing. Over forty thousand people are enrolled at Valley University, but he's the only one I seem to run into everywhere I go.

Since things ended between us, Gavin has dated plenty of girls. 'Dating' might be too strong of a word, but there have been no shortage of girls waiting in line to keep him company.

He's the captain of Valley U's nationally ranked basketball team, not at all hard to look at, unfortunately, and he can be sort of charming when he wants to be.

"What about you? Are you dating anyone?" He taps a pinkie finger on his thigh.

"No, not right now." Not since him, actually. Not because I've been secretly pining away for him or anything. Read: Gavin is the worst. School is hard for me, so I have had to study my butt off the past two semesters to keep my grades up.

After the lift ride, we walk to the gift shop together and then split up inside. I buy two pounds of fudge in varying flavors and then take my bag out front and sit on the curb to sample the goodness. I bite into a square of chocolate and groan happily. It melts on my tongue and chases away some of my irritation from this morning.

"So, Jenkins and Taylor want to walk up to some scenic spot."

I jump at Gavin's voice; he's stealthy for such a tall guy.

"Okay." I start to grab my stuff and get up, but Gavin shakes his head.

"They want to go alone."

My shoulders slump. "Well, that's not very friendly."

"It's their first trip together," he says, as if it were him that had brought a girl up here, he would want to spend every minute alone, too. It makes me wonder what it would have been like to come up here with him when we were "whatever-ing."

"Are we supposed to wait here for them or…"

He shrugs. "We could walk back or grab food, whatever you want."

What I want is to not have to spend more time alone with Gavin. It's too weird. Even when he's not being the absolute worst, I know, deep down, he's the worst.

I hold out the fudge as a peace offering. Like him or not, I'm stuck with him a little longer.

At the plea of my stomach, I opt for food before we head back to the campsite. The restaurant is busy, and they seat us at the bar. Two girls, possibly Valley students, though I don't recognize them, are seated on the opposite side of Gavin.

I see them eyeing us up, trying to decide if he's single or taken. At some point, they must decide he's fair game, or just don't care, because they start talking to him.

I scarf down the burger and fries while Gavin picks at his food and makes new friends. It's too loud and I'm too hungry to try and eavesdrop, but I can read the body language just fine. The girl closest to him, smiles up at him like he's the best thing since cashmere. Why does everyone treat jocks like they're God's gift to the universe?

The four of us pay for our food at the same time. Now that I'm fed, I am ready to get back to the campsite and check on Daisy, then take a nap in the hammock Liam set up behind his and Cole's tent.

The words, "Us too," catch my attention, and I look up to find Gavin glancing at me with a stare that can only be described as worried.

"Oh my gosh!" the girl exclaims. "What are the odds that we're staying at the same campsite?"

There aren't that many campsites on Mount Loken, so I'd say the odds are good, but I keep my mouth shut as the four of us head down the mountain. I use all my new food energy (and the downhill momentum) to stay ahead of them. Leave it to Gavin to pick up two girls at lunch, while eating with me.

About halfway back, I have to slow down. My feet are killing me. Gavin falls into step beside me. "Are you okay?"

"Fine." I pick up the pace again.

"Jesus, you're fast when you're angry."

"How can you tell I'm angry?"

"I just can, but why are you angry?"

"I'm not." I'm annoyed and tired, and I just want to be alone. "It isn't like I could tell them no, they can't walk back with us," he whispers.

"It's fine, Gavin."

"About last night," he starts.

"Oh my gosh, this again?" I stop and face him. "I get it. You're a dude and you couldn't help it. I think you're the worst. You think I'm the worst. Your dick just didn't get the memo."

His mouth closes, and his jaw flexes. "Yeah. Right. You're the worst."

I hate to admit it stings a little to hear him say it out loud, even if I already know it's how he feels.

"Let's just get back to the campsite and we can go our separate ways. Me, to take a nap, and you, to do whatever you want with those two girls."

"Got it," he clips.

We make it back down in almost half the time it took us to get up the mountain.

"Come with us," the girls beg Gavin, when it's time to go our separate ways.

"Yeah," he agrees. His tone is playful and fun. He looks right at me as he says, "Sounds more fun than going back to my tent."

I don't wait around to watch. With a small wave, I head straight to my tent. Or Gavin's tent. Whatever.

Chapter
FIVE

Gavin

Y OU'RE THE WORST?! I HEAR MYSELF SAYING IT OVER
and over again in my head. God, what a dick thing to
say.

Sure, I was just repeating her words, but she's earned the
right to say shitty things to me.

Being around Violet brings out some primal, barbaric side
of me. I want her, but since I can't have her, I end up acting like
a giant asshole.

I followed Tracy and Lori, the girls we met at the top of the
mountain, back to their camp. At least being here, I can't put my
foot in my mouth around Violet, but the truth is, I have no desire to hang out with these girls.

They seem nice enough, they're even kind of hot, but I'm
not getting naked with either one (or both) of them.

I stay long enough for them to introduce me to some more

of the friends they're camping with this weekend and to drink the beer they offer me, but as soon as the can is empty, I crush the aluminum in my hand and get to my feet. "Thanks for the beer, but I should get back."

"What? No way," Tracy says, and wraps her long, slender fingers around my wrist.

"Sorry. My friends will be expecting me."

"We should merge our parties, and all hang out together."

"Yeah, maybe."

"Go get them and come back," she insists.

Smiling, I nod my agreement. I already know my friends aren't interested in that. They're all coupled up and just want to spend time with the people they came with instead of a bunch of random strangers.

I knew Violet was going to be here. She's most of the reason I canceled my date and tagged along with Jenkins and Taylor. I thought maybe it would be an opportunity for us to hang out and bury the hatchet, so to speak. We live next to each other; our friends are dating. I could think of any number of reasons to cease fire with her, but so far, all I've done this weekend is give her a million more reasons to keep hating my guts.

When I get back to camp, Jordan is the only one I see. He pulls a water from a cooler by the fire pit and stands tall. "Hey. You're alive."

I arch a brow in question.

"With you and Vi spending the morning together, death seemed like a distinct possibility. Did you really have a threesome with some girls you met on the ski lift?"

"What?" I shake my head. "Definitely not. Is that what she said?"

He lets out a soft chuckle. "I'm sure I'm leaving out some details, but that was the gist of it."

"No. I didn't hook up with anyone." I curse under my breath

and wonder if I should have. Maybe a threesome is just the thing to obliterate Violet from my brain. "Is she around?"

"She was. I think she might have gone on a hike with Liam and Cole."

I pull a beer from the cooler, have a seat in one of the chairs around the fire pit, and try to calm the irrational part of me that wants to go find her and clear the air. I'd probably do more damage than good. Nah, I think I'll just get good and drunk until I'm numb to it all.

Jordan's still standing, body angled toward the tent, where I imagine his girl is holed up.

"How's Daisy?"

"Better, but I don't think she's going to be drinking tonight." He lifts the bottle in his hand. "I should get this to her. When everyone gets back, we should have a chill night. Cook, hang out, maybe play some cards?"

I smile. Jordan doting on someone still catches me by surprise. He wasn't big on relationships until he met Daisy, and now, he's got this permanent dopey grin, acting like he's Doctor freaking McDreamy. I'm thrilled for him, but it's trippy. "Sounds good."

He still hesitates to leave me.

I jut my chin in that direction. "Go check on your girl, man. I'm gonna drink this and then crash for a bit."

He walks off, and I take my beer and head toward the hammock behind Liam and Cole's tent. It's turned muggy out, making my clothes stick to my skin.

I slept like shit last night. It took me forever to fall asleep, knowing Violet was only a few feet away. I have no idea how I ended up curled up next to her, but her skin is just as soft as I remember. And her hair. How does it always smell so good?

When the hammock comes into sight, I chug the remainder of my beer, toss it on the ground to pick up later, and pull my T-shirt over my head. I'm kicking off my shoes and about half a second from sinking into the hammock, when it sways and Violet's head pops up. "What are you doing here?"

"I was coming to nap. What are you doing here?"

"Same." She lies back down and closes her eyes. "Occupied. Sorry."

She doesn't look or sound sorry.

"I'm tired, Vi. I don't want to fight."

"Who's fighting?"

God, she's so frustrating. I push the hammock to get her attention.

"Get out or I'm getting in with you."

Her eyes open and flash with anger. "You wouldn't."

"Wouldn't I?"

She doesn't move, and I push the netting down with one arm until she rolls toward me.

"Last warning, Violet."

She steadies herself. "I was here first."

"And I'm tired and you already claimed *my* tent as yours."

"It's too hot in the tent."

There is no graceful way to get into a hammock and I'm six foot six anyway, so grace isn't really in my repertoire. I dive in butt first. Violet's small body rolls under me. My head is at her feet, and it occurs to me too late that I'm within striking distance. She doesn't kick me, but one of her knees gets awfully close to my balls.

"Oh my god, you're all sweaty." Her smooth legs tangle with mine as she tries to escape.

"Stop thrashing or you're going to knock both of us on our asses."

"Good."

A crack of thunder has us temporarily freezing but then she's back to kicking and screaming, trying to get away from me.

"For the love of god, woman, cut it out."

I glance up at the dark clouds as drops of rain start to fall. "It's going to rain."

"It *is* raining," she says, just as the pellets of water pick up speed. Her white T-shirt is dotted with water spots and another drop sits on her lashes.

We both make a move to get out at the same time.

Note: there's also no graceful way to get out of a hammock.

"Just, hold still for a second," I say.

She actually complies for a change, and I pick her up by the waist and set her on the ground in front of me.

Her lips part. Violet has great lips. Full and soft. The bottom one always sticks out in a pout, and I can remember all too well what it felt like to have that mouth all over me.

"You manhandled me," she says, straightening her clothes.

I step out of the hammock next to her. The rain comes down hard now, silencing everything else as it pelts leaves and structures all around us.

"You're welcome."

We take off running toward the tent. I get there first and hold it open for her to step inside. Her T-shirt is see-through at this point, but I don't let my gaze linger there. I stare out into the campground and can barely see the other tents.

I zip us in and sit down. "I don't think we're going anywhere for a while."

She shivers. I grab my backpack and pull out a shirt. I left mine outside, along with my shoes. I pull it over my head and glance at Violet. She hasn't moved except to hug her knees against her chest.

"Do you have dry clothes in here?"

She gives her a head a small shake. "I put my bag in Jordan's vehicle this morning."

I stare at her while I try to decipher the intent behind that.

"I didn't want to have any more tent run-ins with you," she says, without meeting my gaze.

27

A laugh builds in my chest, breaking free in a rough chuckle. "How's that working out for you?"

The rain doesn't last long, but it leaves a chill in the air and the ground is soaked around the campsite. As we emerge from the tent to check on the others, Violet keeps on my hoodie. It comes down past her shorts like a dress. Looks way better on her than me.

Everyone's made it back, so we pull out everything that's left of our food for the trip and decide to hang out in my tent. It's the largest and least crowded with stuff since Violet and I are tiptoeing around each other.

I have a bottle of Jager in one hand and a can of beer in the other. We're playing cards, but the mood is different tonight. We're all tired, not really interested in getting drunk or partying. Daisy's feeling better, but she sits between Jordan's legs and leans back against his chest. He's barely touched his beer, and his interest in the cards is only second to kissing his girl.

Jenkins and Taylor are even worse. They're full-on making out between hands of poker.

"Let's play something else," Liam says after I take the pot.

I scan the circle. "Any suggestions?"

Taylor extracts herself from Jenkins long enough to offer up one. "Truth or dare."

I wait for someone to shoot it down. Looks like I'm gonna have to be the bad guy.

"No."

"Why not?" Jenkins asks. He pulls back the tent flaps and a gust of cold air blasts through the space. "Nothing else to do."

"Because you're gonna dare me to kiss your bare ass or something, and I haven't had nearly enough to drink." I lift the bottle and let more of the dark liquid spill down my throat.

"I've never?" he counters.

I shake my head.

"Two truths and a lie," Violet says. She's sitting across from me, pulling on the strings of my hoodie, wrapping them around her delicate fingers.

Everyone agrees and she goes first. "I'm allergic to blackberries." She pauses and takes a sip of her beer. "It took me two times to pass my driver's test." Another small pause. "I don't like French fries."

"The first one is a lie," Taylor says.

Jenkins nods his agreement. Daisy smiles but doesn't guess.

"Everyone likes French fries," Liam says.

"Yeah, that one is the lie." Cole points a finger at her.

"I'm gonna go with the blackberries." Jordan watches Daisy's face for confirmation, but she gives nothing away.

Violet grins and then everyone looks to me. She fidgets under my gaze.

"It didn't take you two times to pass your driver's test."

"Who is right?" Jenkins asks.

Daisy laughs. "It took her *three* times."

Violet lets her gaze hold with mine and her brown eyes narrow. We continue around the circle, hitting Taylor, then Jenkins, but before it gets to me, someone suggests we brave the cold and sit by the fire one last time.

In the morning, we're heading home, and it'll be back to school, back to practices, back to reality.

"I didn't tell you the driver's license story," Violet says as she comes to stand next to me. We're huddled close to the fire as Liam gets it going. "Are you stalking me or something?"

I huff a laugh. "No."

I abandoned the Jager in the tent and now I'm wishing I hadn't.

"Did Daisy tell you?"

"No one told me."

"Then how did you know?"

I face her. "I can tell when you're lying."

"Bullshit." She rolls her eyes and brings her hands in front of her body to rub her palms together.

"I'm serious. It's in the rhythm of your words. You talk faster when you're nervous or excited, or telling a lie. Your eyes widen too."

"Mhmm. Sure. I think you just got lucky."

"You don't believe me?" It's more a statement than a question. I can tell she doesn't. "Fine. Let me try again."

"And if you get it wrong?"

"I won't."

"But if you do, I get the tent tonight and you have to find somewhere else to sleep. And I'm keeping your blanket."

"And if I win, where are you going to sleep?"

"I'll crash with Daisy and Jordan."

"Fine."

She lifts her chin defiantly. Her first words make me suck in a breath. "I lost my virginity to a jerk who pretended to be super into me."

I swallow the acid burning my throat.

"A week later I found him in bed with my roommate."

Every word is a physical blow.

"And finally, the same jerk crashed my weekend camping trip with friends while continuing to hook up with every girl that crosses his path."

I want to tell her that they're all lies, or at least not the complete truth. I *was* super into her. I don't even remember getting in that bed with her roommate, and I didn't hook up with those girls today, but I know it won't matter. I fucked up. Irrevocably.

So, instead of fighting with her, I take a step away. "You can have the tent."

Chapter
SIX

Gavin

S UNDAY AFTERNOON, I'M BACK HOME, LYING IN BED
scrolling through my phone, when my teammate, buddy,
and roommate, Noah Anderson, appears in the doorway.

"Knock, knock," he says as he does just that on the open door.

"Hey." I drop my phone to my chest. "How was the weekend?"

"Good. Killer party at the football house last night. How was
camping?" He says the word like it's an absurd weekend activity.

"It was nice to get away, but I'm glad to be back." As soon as
I say the words, I wonder if they're true. I'm back but no closer to
getting Violet to forgive me.

"And right in time for more drama." A smirk that's part concern and part humor crosses his face, and he lifts his phone to show
me a news headline I recognize all the way across the room. "Saw
Mommy and Daddy are fighting again. Want to talk about it?"

I clench my jaw and give my head a shake. "Definitely not."

The other reason I wanted to get away this weekend—to avoid the never-ending media coverage of my parents ongoing drama. He's quiet a beat, giving me time to reconsider. Noah's a great roommate, a lot of fun, and just an all-around good guy. Outside of Jenkins, he's my closest teammate. "Shoot some hoops then?"

"Yeah. Give me five."

He steps out of my doorway, and I grab my phone to reread the article. Words like rumors, cheating, and divorce catch my eye and make my head want to explode. My dad, retired NBA all-star Anthony Leonard, allegedly cheated on my mom, a well-respected women's college basketball coach, for the entirety of their marriage. I say allegedly, but I know at least some of it's true. How much? I'm not sure.

I could ask my dad, but we're not exactly on speaking terms. I thought after the divorce, things would calm down with the media, but it's been months since it was finalized, and still, every time he or my mom pops up in the news for something completely unrelated to their relationship, the headlines reappear. It never fucking stops. A constant reminder that my dad is a cheating piece of shit. Like father, like son.

I toss my phone to the end of the mattress, clench my hands into fists. I wish punching something would help. Instead, I get to my feet. My gaze goes straight to the window next to my bed. My view looks over the fence to our neighbors—to Violet. She's in her room, unpacking from the looks of it. I linger, watching her for a few seconds longer.

Her mouth moves like she's singing along with music. Her black hair falls past her shoulders and she's wearing a tank top and short shorts. Violet's stunning always, but the glimpses of her like this are my favorite.

She stills as if she can feel me watching her, and then looks right at me. I don't look away. Couldn't even for a million dollars. Violet lifts a middle finger in my direction and then turns on her heel and goes back to ignoring me.

Practice Monday afternoon is a light scrimmage in preparation for our game against Oregon tomorrow night.

Coach Reynolds paces the sideline, watching us move up and down the court. He hasn't said a word in at least ten minutes. He's quieter than any other coach I've had, more patient. At the beginning of the season, he was a little more in our faces, but now, he sits back and lets us play, make mistakes, and figure out how to get ourselves back on track.

As the captain of the team, I respect his style and the trust he gives me.

After another five minutes of play, he blows the whistle and walks out to the middle of the court.

We huddle up around him.

"Leonard, Jenkins, that was a nice passing rush to end things. All around, not bad at all for a weekend off. This is it. The final push. We've got Oregon tomorrow, Stanford on Friday, and then the PAC-12 tournament next week. Make sure you are getting enough sleep and fueling your body right."

"Does beer count?" someone asks, and we all laugh.

Coach Reynolds shakes his head, a knowing grin on his face. He was a college basketball player, too, and he doesn't pretend like he doesn't know what happens on off nights and weekends.

"If you want to be dragging ass up and down my court, then by all means, go out and party as much as you want. I've got plenty of bench for you to sit on." He laughs lightly. "All right, boys. Get out of here. See you tomorrow."

Noah catches me as we're walking to the locker room. "Hideout?"

"Coach literally just told us to get some rest."

"We will, but we have to eat, right?" He slaps me on the shoulder. "See you there."

The Hideout is a local restaurant with a big bar area. It's the unofficial Valley U hangout. The place to go if you want to drink, be seen, and potentially not go home alone.

Jenkins, Noah, and Tommy are already at a booth in the bar area when I arrive. These three are my roommates. We live together in an off-campus house that was built for basketball players, aptly named The White House because it's big and white, across from the arena where we practice and play games. The house has been handed down over the years to upper classmen and starters, and is well-known for all the legendary parties that have been thrown there.

"I wasn't sure you were going to make it," Tommy says, and slides an empty glass in my direction. He is always ready to drink, always ready for just about anything, really. He's out the rest of the season with an ankle fracture, so I'm not about to get on his case. We're having a good season. The past two years, we haven't made it into the NCAA championship tournament, and it's the only thing on all our minds this year. Get there, dominate, and win.

"Someone has to make sure you three make it home." I take the pitcher, sitting in the middle of the table, and pour myself a beer.

Tommy slings an arm along the back of the booth and smirks at me. "I heard you spent the weekend fighting with our neighbor."

"Not exactly."

"Bullshit," Jenkins says.

"Well, no more than usual."

"She's hot, I get it, but can you stop pissing her off?" Tommy asks. "She yelled at me yesterday because some girls that came over parked in front of their house."

Jenkins whistles through his teeth. "She's very touchy about the parking situation."

"That's because people are always blocking their driveway for parties and stuff." I find myself defending her. She isn't wrong, though. On nights when we have parties, cars line the street, parking anywhere they can find a spot. It gets out of control. I wouldn't want to live next door to us either.

"Well, could you just fix it? I know she's like half my size, but I'm injured, and she scares me." Tommy gives a little involuntary shudder.

"Yeah," I say with a chuckle. I'll get right on that. Like I haven't been trying to get Violet to stop hating me for the past year.

Chapter **SEVEN**

Violet

TUESDAY AFTERNOON, DAHLIA AND I WALK ACROSS campus to our fashion design class. It's my last and most favorite class of the day.

"There's a basketball game tonight," she says as we pass a group of girls in blue Valley U T-shirts cut to show off their midriffs.

I hum a short sound of annoyance. It's almost impossible to be oblivious to the happenings of the basketball team. Their games are widely attended; even last year, it was standing room only when their record wasn't great. This year, they're winning a lot and the excitement level is hard to ignore.

Dahlia bumps my hip with hers. "Tell me the part again about how you made him check the tent for a wild animal."

I cringe. When Daisy and I got back Sunday, we spent a lazy evening chilling with our roommates, Dahlia and Jane, and of course, Gavin showing up and crashing our weekend was a hot topic. "It was so embarrassing."

"Yes, maybe, but he did it. He still likes you."

Her words, however ridiculous, still spread a rush of heat down my neck. "Oh, please. Did you not hear the part where he went off with two girls we met at the ski lodge?"

"I heard it all *six* times you mentioned it," she says as she lifts a brow in challenge.

Okay, so I might be a little stuck on that. Not because I think he's doing anything wrong by hooking up with whomever he wants, but because it annoys me just a teensy tiny bit how easily he seems to go from one girl to the next. It reminds me of how quickly he moved on from me, and that is a wound that hasn't quite healed.

We get to class and take our seats as Professor Richards walks in.

"Good afternoon," she says, and sets her Marc Jacobs purse on the desk she never uses. She prefers to pace the front of the room in her designer outfits and stilettos, basically using our classroom as her personal runway. Her short, grey hair is styled to perfection, as usual, and her lips are a classic red.

She worked as a buyer for several luxury stores in Beverly Hills before retiring and moving here. I love her eye for fashion. A lot of people that work in the business don't live it themselves. They hide behind store bought cotton tees while designing or working with these gorgeous creations. Even though there's nothing wrong with it, it's just always struck me as unusual. I'm sort of somewhere in the middle. I love to create historical pieces, gowns, corsets, long-flowing skirts, etc. I do break out my designs on special occasions or, more often, for a fun night in with my roommates, but for every day, I'm much more practical.

But not Professor Richards. I think she'd rather die than be seen in a T-shirt. She wears mostly dresses, sometimes fierce pantsuits. She's sort of my idol.

"I have been approached about a unique, and frankly

unprecedented, opportunity for this class." She stops pacing and faces us. "A friend of mine is a stylist for a well-known actress and singer. You might have heard of her, Penelope Hart?"

She cracks a grin at the collective gasp heard around the room. Dahlia and I share an excited smile, and she mouths, "No way!"

"Penelope is about to go on a summer tour. The winning design will be the showcase piece—"

I don't hear anything else she says. My mind races with possibilities and visions of Penelope wearing one of my creations. The fact that she's always on the best-dressed lists, and designers fight to have her wear them on the red carpet makes this is an opportunity I could only dream about.

Goosebumps dot my arms and excitement flows through me in waves. Exhilaration, followed by adrenaline, and then panic. I have to win.

Dahlia moves her chair closer. "I can't believe this."

The room is buzzing with chatter as everyone gets to work.

"I think I blacked out. Are there any limitations or guidelines on what we can create?"

Dahlia shakes her head. "No, but she said to keep in mind that it will be on stage and she needs to be able to walk, possibly dance, in it."

"And what is our deadline?"

My friend laughs. "You really did black out. Mid-April."

"Oh my gosh, that is no time at all."

"For something like this, I agree. Designs are due as soon as we come back from spring break, so really, we only have this week, unless you want to spend your vacation doing homework."

"I'm not going anywhere. I have to win this. Can you imagine?"

"I can't," she says. "You're really going to stay here over break to work on this?"

I nod. "I was only planning on going home. My parents will understand."

"Jane and I already booked our hotel at the beach."

"Maybe you'll get some inspiration while sipping umbrella drinks and watching the waves."

"I hope so. This is way out of my comfort zone."

Dahlia and I might both be fashion design majors, but our style is night and day. Literally. She's all about daywear. Comfort meets fashion. I have no doubt that, someday, she's going to be revolutionizing the basic T-shirt and charging like two hundred dollars apiece. Or maybe she'll combine her love of golf and fashion and do athletic wear. Whatever she does, it's going to be amazing. But I understand her hesitancy with this assignment.

"I think you could do a really amazing jumpsuit or skirt and blouse combo that would knock her socks off. You understand the movement of clothes when being active better than most of us. Channel that."

She smiles and taps her pencil on the table. "That gives me an idea."

While Dahlia gets to sketching, I get lost in possibilities. I pull out my phone and type in Penelope Hart. Hundreds of images pop up from her red carpet appearances, her social media, and her magazine cover shoots.

As we near the end of the hour, Professor Richards comes around to check on each of us. When she gets to me, she glances at the blank page before me.

"I don't know which direction to go," I say. "She's never worn anything like the Victorian era gowns I like to make."

"There's a first for everything."

"She wears a lot of bold colors, which isn't really what I do either."

"You've done your homework and that's great, Violet, but I would focus less on what she has worn and more on the present."

I chew on the corner of my lip. "You mean like current trends?"

"That and her latest album. What's it about? What is she trying to say? Who is she?"

My brain feels like it's going to explode.

Professor Richards continues, "What type of garments might she want to wear to represent the theme of the tour?"

"I haven't listened to it," I admit. I know a couple of her songs. They're what my mom would call angry girl music. Penelope sings a lot about heartache, unrequited love, breakups, and standing on your own. She captures teenage angst like none other.

"I'd start there."

After class, Dahlia and I rush back to the house.

Jane and Daisy are in the living room. I already texted them the news on my way back because I have zero chill.

I fling my backpack on the couch and stand in the middle of the living room as I tell them every detail of the assignment, Dahlia filling in the parts where I blacked out.

"What kind of outfit are you going to design?" Daisy asks both of us.

Dahlia shakes her head. "No clue."

"No idea either. I need to listen to her latest album, maybe see if there's a set list for her tour, so I can get a vibe on the songs she typically closes the show with. I have so much to do. Should we order takeout tonight?"

My friends share a look.

"What?"

"We're going out tonight," Daisy says.

I start to object, but then try to remember the last time my cousin suggested a girls' night.

"Why? What's going on?"

"Jane is singing at The Hideout."

"What?!" Dahlia and I exclaim in unison.

Jane beams from ear to ear. "Eric's band has a gig there and Mackenzie has a bad head cold, so I'm only filling in."

Although Jane is a music major, she rarely sings in public. I've heard her belt it out in the shower though, and I know she's great.

"Congratulations. This is amazing. Yes, of course I will be there. Maybe you could shake it a bit, give me some ideas for my design."

"Oh, you know it. Penelope doesn't have anything on me."

The Hideout is already packed when Dahlia, Daisy, and I get there. Jane came early with the band to warm up.

"There's Jordan," Daisy says, and takes off to the table he has saved for us. It's a good thing he did because they've removed a lot of the tables and chairs on one side to make room for the band and it's standing room only. I dressed up tonight, feeling inspired by Penelope, and Jane's big night, and these heels were not made for standing.

I laugh when I spot Jane. She's rocking a tight spandex dress and gold heels. The heels match big, gold hoops in her ears, and her hair is in a high ponytail.

"Holy crap, she looks stupid hot," I say as we take our seats.

"You are not the only one that noticed." Dahlia points to a group of guys standing at the bar, openly checking her out.

The only people that aren't staring at her, are the ones watching the basketball game. I make the mistake of glancing at the large flatscreen behind the bar, just as the camera pans to Gavin standing at the free throw line. His chest rises and falls as he catches his breath, sweat making his dark hair stick to his forehead. He pulls off sweaty jock better than I'd like to admit. The ref bounces him the ball, and he cradles it in his giant palms while staring up at the hoop.

I look away before he shoots, but the applause in the bar tells me everything I need to know.

The band starts up soon after, and I forget all about Gavin and the game. Mostly.

Jane is amazing. Eric's band does mostly nineties covers, and her voice is perfect. Honestly, I've only heard Mackenzie once and she's not bad, but Jane brings the house down. People are singing along, clapping after every song, dropping tips in a guitar case in front of her; they're completely captivated by our friend.

It's more than an hour into their set, during a No Doubt cover, that I get an idea for a sketch. I don't have a pad of paper, so I go up to the bar and grab a stack of napkins. A server lets me borrow a pen.

While Jane sings, I sketch. It takes several tries to get the idea in my head down on the napkin, but even when I do, something still isn't right. I hate when that happens. I see it so clearly in my head, but on paper, it just isn't working.

Several songs later, I ball up the napkin and toss it to the empty spot next to me. Daisy and Jordan disappeared up to the bar for more drinks and Dahlia ran outside for a phone call from her mom.

"Let me guess, some guy had the audacity to give you his number." Gavin pulls out the chair next to me and sits.

He smells like soap and his hair is combed back neatly, no longer sweaty or stuck to his forehead like on the TV.

"What?" I ask, a little dumbstruck. I truly loathe the effect he has on me.

He lifts the napkin in two long fingers and starts to unfold it.

"Not a number," I say as I grab it. "I was working on a design."

He nods.

A guy passes him and offers congratulations. Then another.

"I guess that means the team won?"

"You didn't watch?"

"No, I was here."

His gaze flits to all the TVs around the bar.

"I was here for Jane," I clarify.

"I heard she was singing tonight."

Jenkins and Noah take seats across from us.

"Hey, Violet," Jenkins says.

"Hey." I wave.

Noah smiles but doesn't speak. I think my table just got taken over by the jocks. Figures.

"I think I'm gonna get another drink." I stand and walk to the bar.

Daisy is standing between Jordan's legs and he has both arms wrapped around her waist.

"How much longer do you think they'll play?" I ask and nod toward Jane.

"She's been going for a long time," Daisy says. "Probably not much longer. Why?"

"I'm anxious to work on my design."

"And to get away from a certain basketball player," Jordan adds, grinning and looking past me to where Gavin sits.

"Yes, that too. They waltzed in and took over our table."

"I, uh, told Gavin I was saving a spot for them." He manages to look apologetic and amused at the same time. "You know, because it's so crowded."

"Right." Why did Daisy have to fall for a jock?

My cousin gives me a pitying smile and then stands straighter and mumbles, "Incoming."

I feel him behind me before he speaks to the bartender over me. "Can I get a Corona Extra?"

Reluctantly, I take a step to the side to let him into the circle.

"Congrats on the win," Jordan says, and then tells the bartender to put the beer on his tab.

"Thanks. When do you guys play next?"

"Thursday, away game in New Mexico." Jordan smiles. "I love this time of year. Eat, sleep, hockey."

Daisy turns to stare at him.

"And kiss my hot girlfriend, of course." He takes her mouth as if to prove the point.

They get lost in each other, which happens often. Gavin gets his beer, and we stand awkwardly next to each other. People are looking at us, more specifically him. He's a big deal on campus: likeable, talented, and a little intimidating—the perfect mixture for jock royalty.

Gavin takes a step closer to me. "Hey, uh, is Jane dating anyone?"

Anger pricks up my spine. "Jane, as in my roommate?"

"As in the girl singing ten feet away." He gives me a weird look.

Oh my god. I can't believe him. The audacity. Hooking up with my ex-roommate and ex-friend Bailey wasn't enough for him? Now he wants to go out with Jane?! Is he going to work his way through everyone close to me?

I wish it didn't hurt every time he finds a new way to crush my heart, but no matter how hard I try, I can't make myself immune to him.

"No, she's single, but don't even think about it. Stay away from me and my roommates," I say, and then turn on my heel, moving as far away from him as possible.

Chapter
EIGHT

Gavin

"**W**ELL?" NOAH ASKS AS I GET BACK TO THE TABLE. "She's single," I mutter. "And thanks a lot. Now Violet thinks I want to ask Jane out."

He and Jenkins burst out laughing.

"Why didn't you just tell her you were asking for Noah?"

"She didn't give me much of a chance." I tip the beer bottle back, letting the cool liquid slide down my throat.

Violet's standing near the door, hugging Daisy. A second later, she and Dahlia leave. Perfect. Not only did I offend her, but I also ran her off.

My buddies and I only stay for one beer. It's been a long day and we have another game Friday and then a tournament next week. I love the rush of the end of the season, but it is exhausting.

The following night, Jenkins and I head to the bowling alley to meet up with Jordan and Liam, who are already waiting for us.

"Sorry," I apologize as I pull on my team shirt, "Coach had us watching film pretty late tonight."

"No worries," Liam says. "I already got us set up and ready to go."

The four of us: me, Jenkins, Liam, and Jordan started bowling together our freshman year. We all lived in the dorms across the hall from each other and became quick friends.

Since Liam and Jordan both play hockey, it's nice to get out and shoot the shit with guys that get it but aren't teammates. As the captain, I feel a certain pressure to be an example. But not here. Jenkins has seen me do some really dumb shit, so have the other two. They all get it, which makes it nice to just kick back once a week and catch up with them.

"How have you been? I barely got to talk to you last night." Jordan takes the seat next to me after his frame.

"That's because you were sucking face with your girl."

He smiles.

"Things are good," I say.

"Bullshit. You look stressed. Is it about the latest blow up with your parents in the news?"

I clamp my mouth shut.

"Okay, not talking about that. Got it." Jordan nods his head. "Let's talk girls then. Specifically, did you really hit on Jane?"

"Oh my god." I throw my hands up exasperated. "I was asking for Noah. Violet flipped out before I could explain. And why does she care anyway? She fucking hates me."

He shakes his head and lets out a low whistle through his teeth. "You two sure know how to get under each other's skin."

"It's like the less I want to piss her off, the more I end up doing it." I blow out a breath. "I think maybe I should just cut my losses and steer clear. She's never going to forgive me."

"Have you really tried?" he asks.

"What do you mean? Of course I have."

"Have you said the words, 'I'm sorry?'" Liam asks.

Suddenly, everyone's looking at me.

"What is this?" I ask.

"We just want you to be happy," Jenkins says.

Perfect. I'm a pity case. These three are all coupled up, and suddenly, I'm a project.

"I apologized a million times last year."

"Maybe you should try again now that some time has passed." Jordan shrugs one shoulder.

"Yeah," Liam agrees. "Should we spitball some ideas?"

"I'm fine," I say. "I'm fine. She's fine. Everyone is fine. Leave it be."

"One more fine and I won't believe you." Jordan smirks.

"It's your turn," I grit out.

He just smiles at me.

As we pull into the driveway of the White House after bowling, I get a call from my mom. I wait until I step out of the car to answer, "Hey."

Jenkins goes inside, but I linger in the driveway.

"How have you been?" she asks.

"Good. You saw we won last night?"

"I did." I can hear the smile in her voice. "We did too."

"I know. I caught the highlights."

"One step closer. Maybe if I win a national tournament, my son might come visit and help me celebrate."

I laugh at the tiny dig. It's hard to get away from school during the season. Even during breaks, there are games or practices. Same for her. Though I can admit that part of the reason I haven't been home much in the past few years is to avoid dealing with her and my dad. He moved out a long time ago, but it's just all too freaking weird still.

As if she knows exactly what I'm thinking, she asks, "Have you talked to your father?"

"No, but I caught his interview in *Men's Health*."

For all the shit that he's pulled, it still surprises me how considerate my mom is of him. She always makes sure I'm calling him, encourages me to have a relationship with him. I can tell you for sure that when I talk to him on the phone, he doesn't waste any breath on asking me if I've heard from my mother.

Though, she's a lot more consistent in calling, so maybe there's a reason he doesn't bother to ask.

"I know he would like to hear from you," she says and sighs into the phone. "Just because things didn't work out with me and him, he's still your father, Gavin."

"I know." I run a hand through my hair, looking up into the dark sky. My gaze lingers on the window on the side of the house. Violet's window. I can't see her, but I know she's in there. I wonder what she's doing up there. Probably hatching a plan to set my house on fire.

"Gavin?" my mom says my name, recapturing my attention.

"I heard you. I will call him," I promise.

"Good. Now that we've covered that, how are your grades?"

As my mom and I chat, I continue to stand in the driveway. I don't even realize that I'm still staring at Violet's window until the light goes off. A minute later, the front door opens, and she comes out in shorts and a tank top.

"I gotta go, Mom," I say. "Good luck at your games this weekend."

"Thank you. You too."

As I hang up and pocket my phone, I walk toward Violet. Her gaze flicks up, and then her eyes widen when she sees me walking her way. She looks behind her like I might be coming to talk to somebody else. I fight a laugh. This freaking chick.

"Hey." I slow my steps when I reach her.

"Hiiii?" She draws out the word.

Now that I'm standing in front of her, I have no idea what to say.

Maybe I should just blurt out, 'I'm sorry.' Contrary to the

guys giving me shit about it, I have apologized. But once more couldn't hurt, right?

"About Jane, I wasn't asking for me. Noah wanted to ask her out."

She nods slowly. "Okay. Was that all? I'm heading on a food run."

"Late night studying?"

She doesn't answer.

"No, that wasn't all." I shift uncomfortably. "I also wanted to apologize."

She rears back like I'm about to strike. "For what?"

"Everything. I'm sorry about all of it."

She stands there. Maybe a little stunned. "Everything?"

"Yeah. Things didn't work out the way I hoped they would with us. I know that's my fault, and I'm sorry."

Her laugh is short and brittle. "You're sorry that you cheated on me or that I caught you?"

I'm at a loss for words. Of course, I'm fucking sorry. I've regretted it every day since.

"I never meant to hurt you, Violet. You were amazing. We had so much fun together. I don't even remember leaving with Bailey that night."

At the mention of her old roommate, she stiffens. "You know what? You can keep your apology. I don't want it, I don't need it, and I do not accept it."

Chapter
NINE

Violet

BY THE TIME FRIDAY AFTERNOON ROLLS AROUND, I AM cranky, and ready for everyone to leave. I was a little disappointed about staying here alone over spring break, but the closer it gets, the more I'm looking forward to blasting music, eating takeout, binge watching movies and hopefully coming up with a great idea for my project.

I've sketched no less than twenty designs but haven't loved any of them. This design has to be perfect. I'm never going to have this kind of opportunity again.

I hug Daisy goodbye. She and Jordan are spending the weekend at his parents' house before she goes with them to watch him play hockey. It's a whole *meet the parents'* thing that she's never really done with a guy, and it's adorable how nervous she is.

"They're going to love you," I reassure her. "And if they don't, call me and I will come get you and you can hang out with me."

I know she won't need me. Everyone loves Daisy. And if they don't, well, there's seriously something wrong with them.

Dahlia and Jane already left. They're driving to the beach for the week with plans to do nothing but lie in the sun and relax.

"Are you sure you want to stay here all by yourself?" Daisy asks. "You could come with us."

"Oh, I bet Jordan would love me crashing his weekend plans of nonstop sex." I can't help but laugh.

She blushes. "He would be fine with it."

He will do anything for her, so I know it would be fine if I really wanted to go with them.

"No," I say. "I am really excited about this. By the time you get back, I will have a fabulous dress design."

"I know you will." She hugs me again.

With the house to myself, I bring all my design stuff downstairs. Fabrics, sewing machine, my bust, colored pencils, tablet—every single thing. I spread out in the living room and let out a slow breath. *I can do this.*

I can finally start my week-long Jane Austen marathon. My plan is to watch all my favorites back-to-back as many times as it takes until I have a winning design. There is no better muse than a Jane Austen hero. Mister Darcy. Mister Knightley. Captain Wentworth. The latter is my absolute favorite. His passion for Anne after eight years is the thing of truly great love stories.

I begin with *Mansfield Park*. It's my least favorite, but that's like saying it's my least favorite of all my favorite foods. The bottom of the list is still fabulous.

Not a lot of sketching happens as I get pulled into the costumes and dialogue, and before I know it, I've crossed off the first movie and it's dark outside.

My stomach growls. After a quick scan of our kitchen, I pour a glass of wine and order takeout.

I put on *Emma* next but mute the TV and turn on subtitles. Maybe I need to go in a different direction for inspiration. I pull up Penelope's latest album on Spotify. With my wine in one hand, I move around the living room, listening to the lyrics and occasionally watching a favorite scene from the movie playing silently.

She has a way with words. Her lyrics dive into your deepest, darkest insecurities and serve them up in a bold, fun way. She does have some slower songs, but what people love most are the catchy, upbeat tunes.

As the last song is ending, there's a knock at the front door. I pull it open to a sweaty delivery guy. He hands me a brown bag with a heavy sigh.

"I had to park a freaking mile away," he mutters.

I lean forward to peer around the doorway. As I expected, cars line the street in both directions. My car is blocked in, and someone even had the gall to park in the empty spot next to my vehicle in the driveway.

Music, along with voices and laughter, blasts from the backyard of the White House.

"I'm sorry," I tell the delivery driver.

He hands over the brown bag with a frown, and I offer what I hope is an apologetic smile. I bet he spit in my food.

I take the bag inside and turn off my music. Apparently, I was blasting it pretty loud because now the party next door is all I can hear.

I turn on the next movie of the weekend and crank up the volume to drown out the noise next door. I love historical romance films. All of them really, but there's something about Jane Austen. It's the language and her strong heroines. And the way they always know exactly what to say to cut the hero to the quick. And, of course, he gives it right back while still being so very obvious to everyone but the heroine how much he cares for her.

Halfway through the food, my stomach cramps. I push it away and go into the kitchen for a glass of water. Staring out the window over the sink, I can see the lights in the backyard next door.

My mind goes to Gavin. Living next door to him has been

hard. Way harder than I thought. He hurt me. I thought I was tough enough to just get over it and pretend he doesn't exist, but that hasn't been easy.

A sharp pain wraps around my lower stomach. Wincing, I walk back into the living room and lie on the couch. I curl up in a ball while staring at the TV, barely seeing anything happening on the screen.

Not long after, a cold sweat breaks out over my body and my mouth waters. I run to the downstairs bathroom just in time to empty my dinner into the toilet bowl.

"He definitely spit in the food," I mutter as I walk back out to the couch. I don't even have time to get comfortable before the urgent desire to throw up again takes over.

When there is nothing left, I wobble out of the bathroom. The movie has ended, and the music next door sends a new rage vibrating through me.

"This is all his fault."

Anger and delirium push me out the door. I stalk across the yard toward the party. If I were thinking straight, I'd be aware that this is the first time I've stepped foot in the White House in over a year. Or that I'm knowingly walking into enemy territory.

But I'm not thinking straight.

I walk right in behind a group of people coming for the party. They shoot me a confused look, which reminds me I'm in cotton shorts and a tank top with flip flops. There's also a good chance I smell like barf.

From the front entryway, I can see that the party is mostly outside. I check the media room and kitchen on my way through the house, then do a lap around the yard. Gavin is usually easy to spot in a crowd. He's taller than most, and there's just something about him—I can always pick him out of a group of people. But I don't see him anywhere and my stomach is starting to ache again.

Finally, I spot Jenkins by the keg.

"Violet?" Both brows rise when he sees me. "Are you okay?"

I ignore the second question, aware that I look like a mess.

"Is Gavin here?"

"Uhh..." He works his jaw back and forth. I can tell he's holding back, but I'm not sure why.

I look to Taylor next to him.

"He went to his room," she says, and shoots Jenkins a rueful smile.

I spin on my heel.

"Wait, Violet," Jenkins calls. I don't stop.

Back in the house, I take the stairs up to the second floor. I've never been up here, but I know which direction to go since his bedroom window faces mine. The door also has the number thirty-one on it—his jersey number. It's as I'm staring at those numbers on his bedroom door that I start to reconsider, but it's too late to turn back now.

I knock twice on the door and wait. Nothing. I place my head closer and catch the faint sound of music playing inside.

That's odd. Why is he in here listening to music when there's a party outside?

I knock again and then turn the handle.

"Gavin?" My voice sounds reasonable and calm, considering I'm about to unleash my fury on him.

I push the door open farther and take two steps inside. I'm greeted with the sight of a redheaded girl straddling Gavin on his bed. She's topless, but it's his hands that get my attention. They're splayed out on her naked back with his long fingers caressing her skin.

"Oh, shit." I close my eyes and turn to flee, running into the side of the door on my way out.

"Violet?" Gavin's deep voice calls to me.

"Sorry." Ouch. I rub my arm as I try to get out of his room, but my head spins and my stomach rolls. Boy am I sorry. Of course, he was with a girl. *Stupid, stupid.*

If I didn't already feel sick, seeing that would have done the trick.

Bile creeps up my throat. *Oh no.*

Panic-stricken, I hold my breath and will myself to get it together and get home before I lose whatever's left in my stomach.

Gavin comes to me. He ducks his head, and those dark eyes scan me from head to toe. "Are you okay? You don't look so good, Vi."

"Gee thanks." I flail a hand in front of my face. "I'm fine. Sorry to have interrupted. *So sorry.*"

I wave awkwardly to the girl, holding an arm over her chest.

"You're not fine. You're pale and sweaty."

My stomach cramps and sweat beads up on my forehead. I try to leave, but his fingers circle my wrist.

"What are you doing here?"

"I came to yell at you."

"O-kay." He flashes me a half smile. His lips are swollen from kissing and his hair is messy. I hate him so much. "What about?"

"The delivery guy gave me food poisoning and it's all your fault."

I double over in pain and my legs wobble.

"Woah." His grip tightens.

I rip my hand free, but the movement sets me off balance and I have to hold on to the doorway to keep from falling.

"Ignore me. I'm just going to stand here for a minute until the pain subsides."

"Come on." He slides one arm under my legs and the other around my back to pick me up. I catch a whiff of perfume on his shirt.

"No," I mumble, squirming in his hold, "I don't need your help."

"You're sick."

"I already told you that. It's all your fault, by the way."

"That's what I hear."

"What are you doing? Where are you taking me?" I realize he's moved farther into his room. There's no sign of the boobalicious redhead. Nothing like vomit to ruin the mood.

"I'm just setting you on the bed. You need to chill for a minute and drink some water."

"Oh no, I am absolutely not getting in your bed."

"Vi—" he starts, exasperation in his tone.

And then I throw up on his chest.

Chapter
TEN

Gavin

VIOLET SITS ON THE EDGE OF MY BED WHILE I CHANGE into a clean T-shirt. Her gaze darts around the room. "I'm sorry your date left."

"It's fine." I take a seat beside her. Heat radiates off her body. I hold the back of my hand up to her forehead. "I think you have a fever."

She moves away from my touch. "It's food poisoning."

"Are you sure?"

"The delivery guy was mad he had to park so far away. He did something to the food to get back at me."

Now I understand why she blames me for this. "I don't think the delivery guy did this."

She moans.

"You need to rest. Do you want to hang here for a bit?"

"Why are you being so nice to me? I just yelled at you, scared off your date, and then threw up on your favorite shirt."

"You remembered my favorite shirt?"

"Probably the fever." Her brows draw together, and pain scrunches up her features. "I want to go home."

"Can I call someone for you?" I move to grab my phone from the desk.

"They already left. Everyone left."

Which brings up a good question, why then is Violet still in Valley?

I slide my phone into my front pocket. "I'll walk you."

"Okay." She slumps over and rests her head on my shoulder, and her eyes fall closed.

I lift her into my arms. Her not protesting tells me everything I need to know about how awful she feels.

She doesn't speak, or open her eyes, as I carry her home. The living room, which I've only ever seen from the doorway, is a disaster. I set her down and then follow her inside, stepping over fabric and sketch pads.

"Thanks." Her voice is so quiet I barely hear it.

"Can I get you anything?"

She lies on the couch and curls up into a ball, holding her stomach. "No. I just want to lie here until I die."

"Don't die on me. Then who would I fight with?"

"I'm sure you piss off lots of people on any given day. Pick one."

That isn't actually true. I get along with almost everyone. Sure, I've gotten into a few squabbles in my day—mostly on the basketball court, but otherwise, I'm a chill, friendly guy.

"There's no one I'd rather fight with than you, Vi."

"I'm good. Thanks for walking me home."

"Carrying you home, you mean?"

"You carried me?" She shakes her head. "That can't be right. I'd remember something like that."

"I must have dreamed it then," I say sarcastically.

She doesn't respond, just curls up tighter. I find a blanket tossed over the arm of a chair and cover her with it, then pick up the discarded food sitting in the middle of the floor. It smells fine, but I toss it just in case.

My pulse thrums quickly as I watch her. I think she dozed off. Her breathing is slow and steady, and she hasn't moved. Hopefully sleep will help. I glance at the door then back at her. I should go, but…

Before I can reconsider, I find the remote and take a seat on the opposite end of the couch, hitting play on a paused movie. I smile when I realize it's some historical flick. So very Violet.

She made me watch one of these with her once, before she hated my guts. Her eyes lit up and she couldn't resist quoting her favorite lines and interrupting to point out costumes she loved. I'm more of an action movie guy myself (give me Jason Statham and a fast car and I'm good), but that night was one of my favorite movie nights ever.

I'd never met someone like Violet before. From the very beginning she was just herself. Growing up with a famous dad, people (especially girls) sometimes get it in their head that being with me somehow makes them more important. I don't get it, but it's happened too many times to brush it off.

Those people have become easy to spot. They want to know all about my dad, what it was like growing up and going to games, and they beg me to tell them about all the other celebrities I've met. And the real giveaway, they don't share anything about themselves, or if they do, they're the biggest basketball fan ever and want to prove it with game stats and anecdotes about my father.

When I told Violet who my dad was, she shrugged and said, "That's cool, but I've never heard of him." That was that. She liked *me*, and I didn't realize how rare that was until then.

I watch the rest of the movie. Violet doesn't wake up or move, except to kick off the blanket.

When I try to place it back over her, she groans. "Too hot."

REBECCA JENSHAK

I take a better look at her. She's sweating and her cheeks are rosy. Leaning closer, I rest the back of my hand on her forehead. She definitely has a fever. I find the bathroom downstairs and look in the cabinet for a thermometer or medicine but come up empty.

Instead, I call my mom. She answers on the first ring.

"Gavin?"

"Hey," I whisper.

"Is everything okay? It's after one in the morning here."

Shit. "Sorry, I forgot about the time difference."

"It's okay. I was awake anyway. What's going on?"

"I'm with a friend and she's sick. I don't know if it's food poisoning or the flu, and I'm not sure what to do."

She's quiet a beat, and I pull the phone away from my ear to check that she's still there.

"Mom?"

"How high is the fever and how long has she had it?"

"A couple of hours, I think, and I'm not sure. I can't find a thermometer. She's sleeping now."

"You could try a cold compress on her forehead or a lukewarm bath, but if she's sleeping then that's probably the best thing. Make sure she drinks plenty of water when she does wake up."

"Thanks." I run a hand over my hair. "Anything else to look out for?"

"You sound worried. Who is she?"

"Can you save the interrogation?"

She laughs lightly. "Low-grade fevers are nothing to worry about. Rest is probably all she needs. Tylenol or Motrin if she's achy."

"Thank you." I blow out a breath. Violet goes into a coughing fit and my chest tightens with every hacking sound that comes out of her. "I better go. I'll call you tomorrow."

The coughing ends as I hang up, and Violet turns over on her back. I feel like I should be doing something. Just sitting here and watching her suffer is awful. Even in sleep, her face is pinched up in pain.

Something I hadn't thought to ask before I hung up with my mom—what the hell constitutes low-grade? What if Violet's is too high? I google fever concerns and the general consensus is death if it's too high, which sends me into a tailspin. I glance at the stairway. She might murder me if she wakes up and thinks I'm snooping around.

"Fuck it." I race upstairs and find the second floor bathroom and, thankfully, a thermometer and Tylenol.

I take it back down to the living room and rouse Violet.

She murmurs something I can't understand.

"I want to take your temperature and then you can go back to sleep."

I press the contraption to her forehead and press the button. It beeps several times. Violet's lashes flutter open, and those dark brown eyes lock on mine. "You're still here."

A number flashes on the small screen.

"One hundred and two," I say. "You are definitely sick."

"What gave me away?"

"Sick, but you haven't lost your dry humor."

Her gaze shifts to the TV. "Is it over?"

"Yeah. You want me to put it back on?"

"No. I'm working through a list. Least favorites first, so I don't mind that I slept through it." Her eyes close again. "Seriously, why are you still here? I don't need you to nurse me to health. Go back to your party and your half-naked girl. I feel better."

She starts coughing again, this time until her eyes start to water.

I grab her a glass of water and shake out two Tylenol. "You don't sound better. In fact, you sound worse."

She doesn't answer but takes the medicine and washes it down with water. Glass in hand, her body tilts toward me, and in slow motion, she drops her head into my lap. I quickly rescue the glass before it ends up all over her or me, or both of us.

"Is this you hoping to get me sick as payback?" I ask, as a lump lodges in my throat.

"Oh no." She shoots upright, her face instantly paling, and squeezes her eyes shut. "Woah. I moved too fast. I'm sorry I just got all up on you. I just sort of started falling and decided not to fight it."

"I was kidding, Vi. You threw up on me, so I think it's too late to worry about keeping your germs from me."

I wrap an arm around her and guide her back down, so her head rests on my chest. She's stiff, bracing most of her weight off me before she finally gives in.

"This is just a temporary truce," she says as she nuzzles into me.

My brain might know this is temporary, but my heart is punching to get out of my chest. It's belonged to her since the first time I met her.

Chapter
ELEVEN

Gavin

S HE FALLS ASLEEP AGAIN FOR A LITTLE WHILE, USING ME as a pillow, but then the coughing attacks start coming more frequently.

"Let me take your temp again," I say as I lean forward to grab the thermometer, careful not to jar her too much. I press it to her forehead and read the digital display. "Still one hundred and two."

She murmurs something intelligible.

My pulse quickens.

"Vi, we need to get your temperature down."

"Just want to sleep." She pulls away and then flops over onto the empty side of the couch.

My chest and side are sweaty from where she's been pressed up against me. I go back upstairs and find a washcloth, then run it under the cold water. When I get back downstairs with it, she's sitting up, and for a second, I think she's maybe feeling better but then her eyes widen with panic.

"Oh no." She stands quickly and wobbles. "I'm gonna be sick."

She rushes past me to the bathroom, slams the door, and a second later, I can hear her heaving into the toilet.

I pace outside. I want to give her privacy, but I'm also concerned. When the toilet flushes, I knock on the door. "Are you okay?"

"I'm fine. Go home, Gavin."

"I'm not going anywhere, Violet."

She doesn't respond.

"Can I come in?"

"I'm just resting a second. I'll be right out."

Resting?

"I'm coming in, Violet." Turning the handle, I open the door slowly to give her time to protest.

Violet's sitting on the floor next to the toilet, her back leaning against the wall, hugging her knees to her chest.

"You're shaking." I take two big steps to get to her.

"S-so c-cold." Her teeth chatter on each word.

I don't think. I scoop her up off the floor and hold her protectively. Tears fall down her cheeks and her body is slick with sweat.

"I got some on my shirt. I s-smell like vomit."

That gives me an idea. Instead of going back to the couch, I take her upstairs. I set her down on the vanity in the upstairs bathroom and start the water in the bathtub.

"My mom said a lukewarm bath helps break a fever."

"I just want to sleep." She wraps her arms around her waist.

"I know." I step back to her and push a lock of hair behind one ear. "Quick bath first, okay?"

Her dark eyes flash with resignation. "Fine, but I'm not getting naked in front of you."

"I figured. I'll be right outside if you need me."

"Wait," she calls before I close the door behind me.

"Yeah?"

"Will you grab me a clean T-shirt? My room is..."

"I'll find it," I say.

Violet's bedroom is all the way at the end of the hallway. I step over the threshold and flick on the light. As light floods the space, I smile.

I walk around, looking at the photos pinned to a cork board. Tons of her, Daisy, Jane, and Dahlia, and a few others with her parents. She has two framed Jane Austen quotes on the wall above a queen-size bed. Her nightstand is filled with half-empty water glasses and a big stack of books.

I could linger, taking in every detail for a lot longer, but I grab a clean T-shirt from the closet and walk back to the bathroom.

"I have your shirt."

The door opens. Violet stands on the other side with a towel wrapped around her small frame. "Thanks."

I swallow as my gaze drops to take in her bare shoulders and collarbone. "Yell if you need me?"

She nods and starts to shut me out again, but I stop it with a hand. "Don't lock it, okay? I won't come in unless you need me, but I don't want to have to kick down the door."

Her brows lift in question.

"Contrary to what you think, Vi, I care about you. If I thought you needed something, I'd do a lot more than kick down a door to get to you."

When she gets out of the bath, she goes to her room instead of back downstairs. I bring her more medicine and water as she's getting under the covers. It's late, after one in the morning. Out her bedroom window, I can see things next door are starting to wind down.

"You missed your party," she says as I sit on the edge of the bed.

"I didn't feel like partying tonight anyway."

She studies me over the rim of the glass as she sips. Once she sets it on the nightstand, she falls back onto her pillows. "And yet you were at a party and had a girl in your room."

"She came upstairs. I didn't turn her away."

She thinks that over for a second. "Since when are you not in the mood to party?"

I lift one shoulder in a small shrug. "I'm going to sleep downstairs in case you need anything."

She starts to shake her head in protest.

"I'm not leaving you like this by yourself. Even I'm not that big of a dick."

She snorts a laugh and then groans.

I pull up the comforter around her. "Get some sleep."

She reaches out to me before I stand, placing her hot, clammy palm on top of my forearm. "Jane has the biggest bed. She won't mind if you crash."

I nod. "How come you stayed back when your friends left for spring break?"

"I have a really important school project due next week." She sighs. "I still didn't come up with a design. I was supposed to do that tonight, so I could start working on it tomorrow. I'm running out of time."

"You'll figure it out, but first, you need to get better."

Her eyes close. "7-up, grilled cheese, and a day in bed."

"What?"

"Nothing. It's what my dad would do when I was sick as a kid. He was usually the one that would stay home with me because his job was more flexible. He's a terrible cook, but he'd make grilled cheese and we'd watch movies together all day."

"And 7-up?"

"To help settle my stomach. I don't know if it really works or if it's just what he said, but I always felt better."

"Sounds nice."

"What did your parents do for you when you were sick?"

I think back to my mom staying home with me. She mostly let me be and would check in on me. I have a few other memories of those days, talking to dad on the phone. It's one of the few times we talked while he was on the road traveling with the team. He liked to focus, drown out all the noise, while he played. I guess I never realized until now that included me and my mom.

Violet is still watching me for an answer, so I push down the hurt of that realization and say, "My mom made me take this awful medicine. I don't even know what it was—liquid Tylenol, Advil, maybe. It came in a red bottle and tasted so nasty. She'd make homemade bread and soup. And when I was feeling a little better, we'd put together puzzles."

"Puzzles, really?"

"I freaking love puzzles."

"I forgot what a nerd you are. You hide it so well."

"I'm not hiding it. I just don't really have time for it these days."

She yawns, covering it with the back of her hand.

"Get some sleep, Vi. I'll be in yelling distance."

Her eyes fall closed, but a hint of a smile tugs at the corners of her mouth. "Just the way I like you," she says. "Where I can yell at you, I mean."

"That's the way I like it too."

Chapter
TWELVE

Violet

I WAKE UP, THROAT DRY AND HEAD POUNDING, BUT MY stomach no longer feels woozy. Sitting up slowly, I groan as my head objects to the change of position. I must be delirious because I dreamt Gavin was here last night and took care of me.

I get out of bed and tiptoe down the hallway to Jane's room to see if Gavin is there. The door is open, lights off, bed made. It looks just like she left it. Yeah, definitely delirious. I'm never ordering Chinese takeout again.

After I stop in the bathroom to brush my teeth, I head downstairs. I'm pulling my hair up into a high ponytail when I spot him on the couch.

The TV is muted on ESPN and his arms are crossed at his waist. His chin is tucked low, resting against his chest, and his eyes are closed. He's in basketball shorts and a cut-off T-shirt, like maybe he just came from a workout or practice.

I didn't dream it. He was here and… he came back.

As quiet as I can, I descend the rest of the steps. Tiptoeing, I move at a snail's pace. The old floors in this house creak with every step, and I wince at each groan of the hardwood.

"Violet," Gavin's deep, sleep-filled voice calls behind me.

I take another step before I look at him. His lids are heavy, and his hair is a little messy, but he stares at me with a worried expression as he unfolds himself from the couch. Sometimes I still get struck by how handsome he is—even like this. Especially like this, if I'm honest. He's just rumpled Gavin and not the superstar jock everyone loves.

"Hi." I wave awkwardly. "You're here."

"Yeah." His voice breaks and he clears his throat. "How are you feeling?"

"Better. I think. I was going to try to eat something." I point my thumb in the direction of the kitchen.

He nods and follows me into the kitchen. On the table are grocery bags. The top of a 7-up bottle pokes out of one of the paper sacks.

"What is all this?"

He crooks an arm and rubs at the back of his neck, looking embarrassed. "I, uh, picked up a few things."

"For me?"

Chuckling, he moves into action, pulling items out. Bread, butter, cheese, soup, and a bunch of different medicines. After he empties the bags, he goes to the cabinet and gets a glass and fills it with water for me.

"You're very comfortable in my kitchen."

All the uneasiness in his demeanor shifts as he pulls out a skillet and then finds a knife. "It's not that big of a kitchen," he says. "Besides, people keep things in sort of the same spots."

I murmur my agreement and drink some of the water.

"What exactly is happening here?" I ask as he grabs a loaf of bread and tosses it in the air to his other hand, catching it with a wink. He is filled with energy and charm that makes my brain want to explode. Gavin is in my kitchen and... smiling? This is too weird.

"I'm making grilled cheese."

"Because?"

"Last night."

I stare at him blankly.

"7-up, grilled cheese, and movies."

I keep staring.

"You don't remember." He shakes his head. "Last night you said that when you were younger and home sick, your dad would make grilled cheese sandwiches and you guys would watch movies all day." He points to the 7-up. "I got that too in case your stomach was still upset."

"And the rest of it?" I pick up a bottle of Pepto.

"I grabbed a bunch of stuff. I wasn't really sure what you might need."

"I remember saying it. I'm just not sure why *you* are helping me."

He stops what he's doing and comes over to the table, bracing both hands on top of the chair. "I want to continue the truce."

I have a vague recollection of telling him that last night was a temporary truce. Or maybe he said it and I agreed? It seemed like a fine idea at the time. I'm not sure if it was because that's what I really wanted or if I just wanted someone with me when I was sick. Either way, I appreciate what he's done for me. Some people like to be alone when they're not feeling well, but I am not one of those people.

"Don't you have places to be?" I ask as I lie my head on the table. The cool wood feels nice against my cheek. I know the reason he stayed behind for spring break is because of basketball. I think they have the final tournament of the regular season next week. I try not to know these things, I really do, but this school looooves their basketball players.

"Not today." His brows tug together in concern. "You look pale. You should go lie down on the couch or get back in bed. I'll bring everything to you."

My instinct is to argue, but I think better of it. Instead, I trudge back up the stairs and get in bed. I'm shivering when I pull the blankets back over me. I'm so cold that my bones hurt and my teeth chatter.

Sometime later, the bed dips beside me with Gavin's weight. "Do you feel like eating anything?"

I shake my head.

"All right. Take this and I'll leave you alone." He holds out a small plastic cup of red medicine.

I sit up and take the cup. "Is this the awful medicine your mom used to make you take?"

A small grin pulls at the corner of his mouth and a small dimple appears. "It tastes awful, but it works."

I take it with a grimace. "It does taste awful."

Smiling, he takes the empty cup from me and continues to sit on the edge of my bed.

"Tell me more about your parents."

His brows lift.

"Entertain me, Leonard. I feel like crap and look worse. I need a distraction."

"My mom is the coolest. We're close. A lot closer than I am to my dad."

"Really?" Gavin's dad was a pro basketball player. I know things turned sideways between them after the rumors of his dad cheating on his mom surfaced, but I always imagined his childhood playing ball with his father, Gavin sitting in the stands cheering him on.

"He was gone a lot until he retired."

"How old were you when he stopped playing?"

"Thirteen."

"That young?"

"I was in junior high. I remember coming home after school and he'd be sitting outside by the pool, staring into space. It was hard on him, I think."

"Is that why you don't want to play in the NBA?"

"Aren't you full of questions today." He smiles.

It's something I always wondered. Gavin told me the night we met that he was going to be a sports journalist, and playing college on a nationally ranked team was his in. It made sense at the time, but since then I've learned just how good he is, and I can't wrap my brain around why he wouldn't want to keep playing.

"Well?"

"You should rest."

My head is fuzzy and I'm still so cold, but I don't feel like sleeping.

"Need or want anything else?" he asks.

"Can you grab my laptop off my desk? I want to put a movie on for background noise."

He does and I sit all the way up to open it. My fingers shake over the touch pad.

"Give me this," he says with a chuckle. He moves to sit on the bed next to me and I happily hand it over so I can pull the covers back up to my chin.

"What movie?" he asks as he gets situated with the device on his lap.

"*Persuasion* is up next."

"Right. The list. What is on the list exactly?"

"All of my favorite Jane Austen movies and miniseries."

His brows lift. "All of them? Are there a lot?"

"I pulled my top five."

"Okay. And why Jane Austen?" He waves a hand to the framed quotes on the wall above our heads. "Aside from your obsession, of course."

"It isn't an obsession. It inspires me." A coughing fit stops me from saying more.

Gavin finds the movie and hits play. I expect him to hand the laptop back and leave, but he repositions the screen, so we can both see and crosses his arms over his chest, watching intently as the opening credits play.

"You are going to watch *Persuasion* with me?" I ask, my voice hoarse. "Why?"

"I've never seen this one."

"And you've just been dying for the opportunity?"

His shoulder bumps mine. "Truce, remember?"

Right. I nod.

"Good." His gaze goes back to the screen.

Seconds tick by and I'm still watching him. He turns his head and smiles, catching me. "What?"

"Nothing." I pull the comforter tighter around me and force my stare on the screen.

Why does this truce suddenly feel like the worst idea ever?

Chapter
THIRTEEN

Violet

B Y SOME MIRACLE, I AM ABLE TO MOSTLY FORGET ABOUT
Gavin lying next to me and focus on the movie. It isn't one
of my favorites—the movie, I mean. In fact, I rarely rewatch
it, but I love the story of *Persuasion*. And some of the lines. Swoon.

They're separated for years and never stop loving each other.
Maybe it isn't realistic for the modern world, given all the tech-
nology that would make it the longest ghosting of all time, not to
mention people seem incapable of waiting more than a week or two
before jumping to the next relationship, but Captain Wentworth's
dedication makes him my favorite Austen hero.

When it's over, Gavin taps the spacebar and looks over at me.

"What did you think?" I ask.

"I don't understand some of the characters. Like what was
the deal with Louisa?"

I knew it. I knew he wouldn't like it. It just confirms that Gavin and I are two people with completely different ideas about love. "But Wentworth?" A grin lights up his face. "That was some epic hero shit right there."

A laugh spills from my lips. "Epic hero shit?"

"That letter. *You pierce my soul.*" He lets out a low whistle. "I bow down to Jane Austen. I get why it's your favorite now."

"Who said it was my favorite?"

He points up to the framed quotes—both from Persuasion. "As you said, it's some epic hero shit."

He smiles at me. "What's next?"

"More? Really?"

"I am hooketh."

"What?" I laugh, and then start coughing again.

Gavin hands me my glass of water from the nightstand. "Hooked. Hooketh? Whatever. You get the idea."

"*Pride and Prejudice,* the one with Keira Knightley, and after that *Pride and Prejudice,* the miniseries."

"What's the difference?"

"So many things. Colin Firth is Darcy in the miniseries. He's so good, and I just love it. It's six hours so you really get the full story. Daisy prefers the Keira Knightley one though because of the Darcy hand flex, and the walk across the field to get to her at the end. Which I will admit is pretty fantastic."

Gavin has a stunned, overwhelmed look on his face. "Six hours?!"

"No one is forcing you to watch them with me, Leonard."

"I'm invested now. Plus, I need to know what a hand flex is. Sounds kinky."

I push the covers back and sit up straighter. His gaze drops to my legs. The chills are gone, and I think my fever has broken too, but warmth spreads through my cheeks at how intimate this feels.

"Do you feel like eating yet?" Gavin asks, averting his eyes and swinging his legs over the side of the bed.

"No." I shake my head.

"All right." He goes to the door, and then stops and wags a finger at me. "Don't start without me."

While Gavin is downstairs getting food, I go to the bathroom to wash my face and brush my tangled hair. There's no use in trying to look good, but I'll settle for not looking like death. When I get back to my room, Gavin is already seated on the bed with a plate on his lap.

"Do not get crumbs in my bed," I say as he takes a big bite of grilled cheese.

"I won't," he speaks, mouth still full.

The aroma of cheese and bread hits my nostrils and makes my stomach growl.

"Not hungry, huh? Or were you just afraid I couldn't cook?"

"More like you'd poison me and blame my death on the flu."

His lips lift at the corners as he continues to chew.

"It does smell better than I expected."

He hands me the extra grilled cheese on his plate.

"Are you sure?"

"I can always make more."

"I just want half." I start to tear it into two diagonally.

His brows lift, and his eyes widen. "What are you doing?"

"I'm cutting it in half."

"Who cuts a sandwich like that?"

"Grilled cheese has to be cut diagonally. It's a rule."

"I don't think it's a rule," he says, laughing at the mangled half I hand back to him.

"Well, it should be. It's how my dad always made it."

The sandwich tastes delicious, but as soon as I've finished eating it, my stomach protests.

"Uh oh." Gavin's expression goes grave. "I swear I didn't poison it."

I take off for the bathroom at a run. I barely make it. Sweat beads on my forehead and heat courses through my body again.

Before I realize he's with me, Gavin is tucking the strands of hair that have fallen from my messy ponytail behind my ears.

There's barely anything in my stomach, but even after I've emptied the contents, I continue to heave and tears stream down my face.

I'm delirious by the time I finally slump over against the wall. Gavin wets a washcloth and presses it to my forehead.

"I can't believe you just watched me throw up. Again."

"Doesn't bother me. I have a strong stomach. Ready to get back in bed?"

I nod and don't bother protesting when he lifts me to my feet. He wraps an arm around my waist, and I let him walk me back to bed. I'd like to say it's some sort of payback making him take care of me like this, but I'm too sick to hate him right now.

He pulls the comforter over me and sits on the edge, facing me. The look in his eyes makes my pulse quicken.

"Try and sleep."

Impossibly, I do, and when I wake up again, the sun is setting.

"Hi," I croak.

"How are you feeling?" He pulls out an ear bud and hits pause on the movie.

"You watched it without me."

"I had to see the hand flex."

"And?"

He does it with his hand and smiles. "So good."

Gavin closes the laptop and sets it on the end of the bed. "You should drink something and it's time for more medicine."

He gives me the awful red medicine first and then holds out a glass. "It's 7-up."

I sit up and sip it slowly. "I can't believe I spent all day in bed, and you stayed to watch Jane Austen movies."

"I had a good time. Also, why do you have four copies of *Persuasion*?" He picks up the top one from the stack on my nightstand.

"I told you I like the story."

"So get one copy."

"They all have different covers."

The look he gives me tells me he doesn't understand. "But the story inside is the same?"

"Yes, but the covers are all so beautiful."

He sets the book in his lap. There are several bookmarks stuck in various points in the first fifty pages. He flips to each one. "Are these like your favorite pages or something?"

"No." I take the book from him and open to the first page. "I've probably read this page a hundred times, which correlates to about how many times I have attempted to read this book." I go to the last bookmark. "This is the farthest I've ever gotten."

"You've never read it all the way through?"

"Nope." I sigh.

"But you said…"

"I know what I said, okay?" I snap. "It *is* my favorite story. I know what happens and I've read chunks of it."

"But you've never read the entire book?" He still seems confused. "And you bought four copies of it anyway?"

"Haven't you ever wanted to do something or be someone slightly different than you are?" I shake my head. It's foggy, and the only explanation for me sharing so much personal insight. "Like in the best version of me, I work out five days a week and eat vegetables daily."

He snorts. "Okay. And how does reading this book play into that?"

"I love watching historical romance, especially Austen. The dialogue and the costumes, it's perfection. I have seen every version of *Pride & Prejudice* about a million times, and this story, *Persuasion*, in particular, just speaks to my soul, but every time I sit down to read it, my eyes glaze over."

"Lots of people don't like to read."

"You don't get it," I whine and turn onto my side. "I'm an Austen phony."

The bed dips as he shifts his weight, and when I open my eyes, he's sitting closer to me with his back resting against the headboard.

"Sorry," I say. "I think my fever is back."

"No, I think I understand, actually." He still has the book in his hands. His long fingers splay out over the cover and it's seriously sexy in ways my brain can't comprehend right now.

He opens the book and clears his throat. And then he starts reading.

"You aren't really going to read this entire book to me, are you?"

"I don't think I'll finish it tonight, no, but maybe we can beat your last record."

"Gavin—" I start, voice breaking. I'm not even sure what I was going to say, but Gavin stops me.

"I'm having a hand flex moment here, Vi."

A small laugh escapes, and a lump forms in my throat. I close my eyes. I feel like crying, which is so not me. Two days of being sick and Gavin being here and acting so nice, plus all the Austen, I'm a sappy, emotional mess.

I don't know how long he reads. At first, all I can concentrate on is his voice. Deep and smooth. He'd make a great sports broadcaster. It takes him a few paragraphs to get into it, but once he finds the flow, I escape into the story.

I'm so enthralled that the ringing of my phone on the nightstand makes me jump. Gavin stops and reaches for it. "It's Daisy."

"I texted her earlier and told her I was on the brink of death. I should let her know I'm going to live."

He hands it over. "Okay. I'll make us some more food. Anything sound good?"

"You don't need to do that. I'm okay. Really. I feel better than I have all day. Go home. You've done enough." I need him to go. This truce was a mistake.

I press accept on the call before he can protest then get up and walk over to the window as I answer.

"Hey."

"Hi." Daisy's voice is soft. "How are you feeling?"

"A little better."

While she apologizes for not being here, Gavin's footsteps cross the room and then the door clicks shut, announcing his departure.

I let out a slow breath. "It's fine. There's nothing you could have done. How was meeting Jordan's parents?"

My head is still a little fuzzy, but for the next few minutes, Daisy fills me in on her boyfriend's family and all the things they've done in the two days since they left. The Valley U hockey team had their final game of the season, and she watched it with his parents.

"Anyway," she says. "We were just heading out to dinner. Are you sure you don't want us to come back?"

"No, of course not. I'm sure I'll be better tomorrow and then I need to work on my design." My design, groan. I still have nothing.

"Promise to call if you change your mind?"

"I promise."

When we hang up, I crawl back into bed. The copy of *Persuasion* rests on my pillow. I open it to where Gavin left off and placed a cough drop wrapper as a bookmark. Page fifty-five. A new record.

I smooth the wrapper out with a finger. A light knock on the door is followed by Gavin's voice. "Violet?"

"Yeah." I get up and pull the door open. "I thought you left."

"I did, or I started to."

"Okay." I turn back to look at the bed and nightstand. "Did you forget something?"

"Just this." His right hand reaches out and caresses my hip, then he seems to think better of it and pulls it back. He rubs at his palm with his other hand. "I like you, Violet. I've always liked you."

I open my mouth to speak, but I'm at a loss for words.

"Can I come back tomorrow? We can watch six hours of Darcy and Elizabeth, if you want, or I'll read some more *Persuasion*. I want to spend more time with you."

My heart is racing in my chest. "I really appreciate everything you did last night and today. Especially considering what's happened between us in the past, but I don't think it's a good idea."

"Why not? Call it a permanent truce. Look how well we got along today."

"It was one day."

"Then we'll take it one day at a time."

"I can't. I'm sorry."

"Why not?"

I cock my head to the side. He knows why.

"I fucked up. I know I did and I'm not making any excuses. I'm sorry. *So* fucking sorry. I'd given up any chance of us working past what I did, but these past twenty-four hours, I felt a connection with you again. You can't tell me you don't feel this." He motions between us.

"Last night, I walked in on you making out with some other girl. Which is fine. You can hook up with whomever you want to, but I'm not the kind of person who can pretend that we're just two friends hanging out over spring break. You've seen me naked. You broke my heart. It's complicated..." I trail off, aware I'm rambling. I take a deep breath. "Besides, I have to work on my design and... I just can't."

"All right." His voice is soft and low. "Yeah, okay." He shuffles his feet. "If you change your mind or if you need anything, you know where to find me. Anything you need. Any time. I'm there."

"Thanks." I rub the hem of my shorts between my thumb and pointer finger. Somehow this feels like the end all over again.

He takes two steps backward, gives me a sad smile, and then disappears down the hallway.

Chapter
FOURTEEN

Gavin

WE LEFT TUESDAY NIGHT FOR VEGAS. THE tournament spanned three days and was a single-round elimination. One final test before the national tourney begins, and we dominate it, taking home the conference championship.

Immediately after the game, I'm pulled for an on-camera interview.

"Congratulations," the reporter, Bob, says. He's an old-timer, been in the business a long time, covering both men's and women's collegiate basketball games. "This is the second conference championship for the Leonard family with your mom and the Huskies winning their conference title last week. How does it feel?"

"It feels great," I say, still catching my breath. "Our team worked hard, and it paid off."

"Are your parents here tonight?"

"They're watching at home." I paste on a brighter smile and wave at the camera. I know at least one of them is actually seeing this.

Bob leans closer to shout over the crowd. "Twenty-one points today and four assists. You looked strong out there. Your performance tonight was reminiscent of your dad's final game before he went pro, where he also had twenty-one points and four assists."

He pauses, like he expects some reaction from me, but I'm not sure what—happiness at being compared to my dad, or maybe respect for the man who Bob thinks is responsible for my talent as a player. When I don't respond, Bob continues, "What do you think your dad will say when you talk to him?"

I always expect these types of questions, but they don't seem to get any easier to answer. The truth is my dad says very little about ball. Ever since I told him I wasn't interested in playing professionally, he stopped pretending to care. Which is fine by me, but the loving dad who supports his son, no matter what, is better optics. But I know what my mom will say, so I give him that. "He'd say congrats but don't get too comfortable because the real work is just about to start."

"Thanks for your time, Gavin. Good luck to you."

In the locker room, we celebrate—yelling and cutting up. It's true, the real work is just getting started, but we'll take tonight to enjoy. Coach Reynolds walks in, flashing a rare smile, and holds up a hand to get us to quiet down. "Nice job this week. You should be proud. You played smart, moved the ball, and kept turnovers low. That's what it's going to take every game from here on out." We're vibrating with energy. One step closer. He motions with his head. "Get in here."

We huddle up, hands in the middle.

"We're having dinner together as a team, then you have a night off."

Some of the guys start to whoop their excitement.

"Curfew is at eleven."

Those same guys groan.

Coach levels them with a serious stare. "I don't want to have to track anyone down. The bus leaves for the airport at seven o'clock tomorrow morning. You can have all the time off you want after we win the national championship." He nods his head to me, signaling he's done talking.

"One, two, three," I say, and together, we all lift our hands. "Run 'em."

Food is catered to a banquet room in the hotel. We get off the bus and a lot of guys head straight there, but I go up to my room first to call my mom. As expected, she watched the game and is full of happiness and praise.

"Did you see the interview after the game?"

"Yes, I saw it. Have you talked to him?"

I know exactly who she means. "He sent a text."

"You need to talk to him, Gavin. It isn't good to keep all this anger inside."

"Not tonight. I don't want him to ruin this."

She sighs but doesn't press. A few minutes later, we hang up, and I head down to meet up with the team.

I scroll the headlines about the game on my phone. Every single one mentions *him*. It straight pisses me off that he gets the credit. A few also mention my mom, but only as a coach, not as a great baller. She was a D1 athlete herself, and the real reason I have any skill on the court. She is the *only* reason I amounted to anything.

My mom spent hours running me to practices, rebounding balls, talking plays and strategy while Dad was gone. I never resented him for it until I got older and realized that him being an absent parent was a choice, not something he could blame on his career. Plenty of parents travel for work. He could have called or come home more. He could have fucking tried harder.

As I'm coming off the elevator, a guy, maybe mid-thirties,

recognizes me. "You're Anthony Leonard's son. Holy shit, you look just like him. Is he here, too?"

I shake my head. "Nah, man, sorry."

He sidesteps to get in my path, and he walks backward in front of me. "Is it true that he's dating that 90's supermodel? What's her name? Christy? Nah. Denise?"

"You'd have to ask him," I say as politely as I can muster. My jaw feels like it might break, I'm grinding down so hard on my molars.

"Can I get your autograph? My buddies are never going to believe that I ran into Anthony Leonard's son."

I stop and nod my agreement. The woman with him fishes out a pen and a piece of paper, which I scribble my signature on then hand back.

"Are you heading to the NBA too?"

Everyone close to me knows I'm not, but again—optics. I give him my rehearsed answer. "We'll see."

I start walking again and he doesn't follow, only yells after me, "Nice to meet you."

I feel like a dick, but it's not as easy to fake my love and admiration for my dad one-on-one like that. I don't want to shatter that guy's perception of him. Maybe I should, but I know what it feels like to have it shattered into a million jagged pieces.

It's funny that all the bad press hasn't stopped his hardcore fans from worshipping him. Shit, maybe it's even made it worse. They want every salacious detail. I guess it's a lot sexier to think your hero is banging celebrities and living the A-list life, than home being dad of the year with his wife and son.

By the time I make it into the banquet room, where they're serving food, I'm the last through the line and there aren't a lot of seats left. Coach and his wife, Blair, are at a table by themselves, so I head there.

"Okay if I sit here?" I ask.

"Of course." Coach has his arm draped over the back of Blair's chair. He eyes my plate with a chuckle. "Hungry?"

"Starving," I admit. I don't speak again for a solid five minutes while I devour half the food in front of me.

Seeing Coach with his wife makes me grin. He's a quieter guy, serious, always analyzing and working, but when she's around, he has this carefree, happy expression that totally transforms him into a big ol' teddy bear. The guys and I all know the best time to ask for anything is when Blair is nearby.

Noah drops into the seat next to me and looks at my plate. "Are you going to eat both those rolls?"

"Maybe. Why?"

"They're out."

I toss him one, which he immediately shoves in his mouth, then I slide my phone out of my pocket and pull up mine and Violet's text exchange. Mostly it's just me texting her. Since I saw her last, I've sent several to see how she's feeling, but all I've gotten back was one that said: *Better. Thanks.*

I fire off another: *Still feeling okay?*

She doesn't immediately respond, and I panic-send another: *We are heading back early tomorrow.*

The messages turn to read, but I don't get anything back. I'm not sure what I'm expecting from her. No, that's a lie. I'm hoping she'll be ecstatic that I'm back next door and want to hang out. A long shot? Hell yeah, but a guy can dream.

"Everything okay?" Coach asks.

I look up to find him staring at me with his brows pulled together.

"Yeah. Everything is great. I was just checking my texts."

"He's probably checking up on Violet again." Noah smirks, mouth closed, as he continues to chew.

I tuck my phone away.

"Is Violet your girlfriend?" Blair asks. She has dark hair that

Coach twists around his fingers absently while they wait for my answer.

"No. She's just a friend."

"A friend?" Noah barks a laugh. "She hates him."

My face heats. "She doesn't hate me."

"Well, she doesn't like you," he mutters.

"Uh oh." Blair has an infectious smile. She sneaks a glance at her husband and then asks, "What'd you do?"

"How do you know I did something?"

"Because I dated a twenty-one-year-old basketball player just like you once."

Coach scoffs. "Please. I was way better than him."

She rolls her eyes but laughs.

"I screwed up," I admit.

Blair gives me a sympathetic smile as she dips her shoulder to lean against coach. My chest tightens as I watch them. They have this ease between them, playful and loving. They say hindsight is 20/20, and I think that must be true because when I see them together, it makes two things in my life crystal clear.

Number one, my parents never had that. Or at least not as far back as I can remember.

Number two, I want that.

And I can only picture it with one person.

Chapter
FIFTEEN

Violet

AFTER I'VE RECOVERED FROM THE FLU THAT NEARLY killed me, I focus on nothing but my design for Penelope for the rest of the week.

I must listen to her album a hundred times as I sketch and drape fabric until I finally come up with an idea. By Saturday, I've constructed my design and am obsessing over the length. I like the movement of a long dress—the silhouette and the way it billows behind you as you walk. Most performers stick with short and skin-tight while on stage because it's easier to dance. I design with that knowledge, but it doesn't feel like enough, so I add a detachable train that snaps around the waist and flows out behind the dress.

That evening, while I'm staring at the dress, trying to decide if I've gone too far, Jane and Dahlia return from their beach vacation.

"Hey," I say, getting up from the middle of the floor in the living room to hug them. I have to step over several piles of fabric scraps and wadded-up pieces of paper.

"Hiiii." Jane's voice trails on as she glances around the room at the mess.

"It's a lot, I know. I didn't realize how bad it was until I saw your faces when you opened the door. I'll clean it up."

"It's fine." Dahlia laughs. "Are you feeling better?"

"Yeah, much better."

"For a girl that was sick all week, it looks like you've been busy. Is that the dress?"

"Sort of." I trip on my way to the bust. "Maybe I should clean up first. Tell me about your trip."

They do while I tidy the mess in the living room. When the floor is walkable again, I talk them through the dress I created for Penelope.

"Violet, it's gorgeous." Dahlia runs her hand along the skirt.

"It's not too much?"

"A little risky, but I think this one is going to pay off for you."

"What do you think, Jane?" While she isn't a designer, she has a great eye for fashion.

"It's gorg. Can I try it on?"

"Yes!" I'm dying to see it on a real person and Jane is a great model. She's about the same height as Penelope and everything looks good on her tall, model-like frame.

Jane holds her hands above her head, and I carefully bring it down over her tank top.

After I get it adjusted with a couple of pins around her waist and shoulders, we both look to Dahlia for her reaction.

Her mouth is open, eyes wide, and a pit forms in my stomach.

"The train is too much, right? I was afraid of that. Maybe I can adjust the skirt length. I like the volume." I make a move to lean down, so I can pin the fabric, but Dahlia reaches out and grips me by the elbow.

"Don't. It's perfect."

"Are you sure?"

Her dumbstruck look pulls into a wide smile. She repeats, "It's perfect."

"I wanna see." Jane shuffles into the bathroom a few feet away. She stands on her tiptoes and turns side to side.

"My boobs look great." She grins down at her cleavage. "God, I'm so jealous."

"Jealous of what?"

She treks back out to the living room and sits on the edge of the couch next to Dahlia, and I take a seat on the other side of her.

"Penelope. She's going to look killer in this, like she always does. Life isn't fair."

"She does always look fabulous," Dahlia agrees. "But that's because she has access to custom designs, hair stylists, and makeup artists, and probably anyone and anything else she wants."

"Where is this coming from?" I ask. "It isn't like you to be jealous. Not even of a celebrity."

It's true. Jane has the type of self-confidence that I thought was reserved for guys with porn-sized penises. She isn't conceited, but she knows her talents and her best assets, and she makes no apologies about either. I really admire that about her.

"I'm just being silly. I think I might be hangry."

"Well, there's very little food in the house. I basically lived off takeout this whole week." And grilled cheese. Gavin's face flashes through my mind and gives my heart a little tug.

"Let's go to the dining hall," Dahlia suggests. "I've been craving those little pizza bagel bites all week."

Jane laughs. "I took her to all the best restaurants I know, and what does she want?"

Dahlia and I join in, laughing with her. "Pizza bagel bites."

My stomach growls. "That does sound good."

Jane gets changed and the three of us walk to campus. It's a ghost town. We only see maybe one or two people on our way. The dining hall is located in Ray dorm, and it's a little more lively here, with people arriving back from break, hauling big laundry baskets and overnight bags into the dorms.

Only about half of the usual food stations are open tonight, but thankfully, one of those is our coveted pizza bagel bites.

We fill our plates full of them and make our way to our usual table. Only before we get there, Gavin steps in front of me.

I stop abruptly. Dahlia screeches behind me as she narrowly avoids running into my back.

"What the—?" Jane asks, and then she must see Gavin because she doesn't finish her outburst.

"Violet. Hey."

"Hi," I manage to squeak out. Hating Gavin was as easy as breathing, but this weird non-hating, appreciative, almost friendly vibe between us the last time we hung out is downright awkward.

"How are you feeling?"

"Good. Fully recovered."

His gaze flicks over my shoulder to my friends. "Did you finish your list of Austen movies?"

"I did." I nod. "Congrats on the thing. The game or, uh, tournament." Freaking eh, I can't string together a sentence. "Congratulations on winning the tournament."

I finally look into his eyes, which is definitely a mistake.

They soften as his mouth pulls into a killer smile. "Thanks, Vi."

I push down the frantic energy bubbling up inside me and step around him.

"What the heck was that?" Dahlia whisper-screeches behind me.

I set my tray on the table and take a chair, all while avoiding eye contact with my friends. "Nothing. Just being polite."

"Since when?"

I stick my tongue out at her, but she and Jane keep staring at me.

"Seriously, since when?" the latter asks, looking around the cafeteria. "He's still looking at you, and not with the usual intense stare he usually sends your way."

"It's nothing." My face heats.

"I know that look. Something happened." Jane leans forward on both elbows and Dahlia mimics her. They know me too well and they're not going to let this go.

"Friday night when I first got sick, I thought I had food poisoning. The delivery guy was pissed that he had to park so far away because of the party next door. Anyway, I went over and yelled at him."

"You didn't?!" Dahlia's green eyes grow bigger.

I wince at the memory. "I did. I couldn't find him downstairs or outside, so I went up to his room and walked in on him with a girl."

Jane fights to hold back her laughter.

"That isn't even the worst part. After I walked in and saw his make-out partner's boobs, I tried to get out of there, but I was all feverish and slightly delusional. Anyway, I ran into his door, he caught up with me, I yelled at him, then puked on his chest."

"Oh. My. Stars." Jane punctuates each word and then lets her laughter free.

"It was horrifying, but I was too sick to care. I think he carried me home. And he stayed to make sure I was okay since everyone was gone. Anyway, it was no big deal, the end."

I take a bite of my food, but my friends do not let me off that easily.

"He stayed, as in… for a few minutes?"

"All night," I mumble around my food. "Or most of it anyway."

"I am swooning," Jane says, holding her hand over her heart. "Did he sleep in your bed?"

My body grows impossibly hotter.

"He did?!" Dahlia gasps.

"No, of course not." I have no idea where he slept. Maybe downstairs? My face is on fire.

They both look downright disappointed. I hadn't planned to tell them the rest, but for some reason, I find myself wanting to make sure they know how much he did for me.

"But we spent all of Saturday together. He brought a ton of medicine, made me food, and we watched old movies."

"I thought hell would freeze over before the two of you played nice." Jane finally leans back. Her gaze goes back to where she was watching Gavin. I peek over my shoulder to see him and Noah heading out. He meets my stare, and then I'm the one who looks away first.

"What does this mean? Are you two friends now? Are you going to give him another shot?"

"It doesn't mean anything."

I can tell they're dissatisfied with my answer. And if I'm being completely honest, I'm a little dissatisfied with it too.

Chapter
SIXTEEN

Gavin

SATURDAY NIGHT, I'M SHOOTING HOOPS AT OUR HOUSE. One of the many perks of living here—our own court. A few of the guys came over to hang, along with the usual friends and girlfriends that are always down for a last-minute party, but I didn't feel like socializing, so I came up here to get away and think.

The door opens and Noah steps onto the court. "Thought you might be in here. Tommy called some people. The party is growing out back."

I shoot another ball and rebound it before I reply, "Not interested tonight."

"I thought as much, but there's someone here to see you."

I pause, ball in my hands ready to shoot, and look at him. "Someone is here to see me?"

"Yep." The grin he gives me sets me on edge. "She's waiting downstairs."

He leaves without saying more. A chick is here to see me? It isn't like that's out of the norm, exactly, but I usually have a heads up they're coming. Maybe Sariah? I told her I'd call her later last weekend as I was ushering her out of my room, so I could take care of Vi, which I didn't do, but it wouldn't be totally out of character for her to show up on her own. That's sort of the basis of our entire relationship. She's uncomplicated and doesn't seem to care that I'm not interested in more than an occasional hookup.

My phone buzzes as I rack the ball and head out. I pull it from my pocket, expecting it to be Sariah calling to tell me she's here, but instead, it's my mom.

"Hey," I say, after hitting accept and putting it on speaker, so I don't have to hold it up to my ear.

"Hey, Gavin. I'm glad you picked up."

I slow my steps. "Why? What's up?"

"I just got off the phone with your dad."

"And?" A knot settles in my stomach.

"He said he tried to call you a few times yesterday."

"I was busy." Also, I didn't want to talk to him.

She hums her displeasure. "Well, you're going to have to find some free time because he's going to be there next week."

"What? Here?"

Silence hangs between us and I can picture her face as she grapples for words.

"Why is he coming here?"

With a sigh, she says, "He's coming for the banquet. The director of athletics called and invited him."

The man hasn't showed up for a single game since I've been at his alma mater, but the head honcho of Valley athletics calls him and suddenly, he's happy to show up for some bullshit banquet?

"No, I don't want him here. It'll be a shitshow."

"What do you want me to say? They asked him and he felt like he couldn't say no."

"Of course, he couldn't. Someone *important* asked him."

"You should use this time to talk to him."

"Not going to happen. I'm bringing someone."

"Like a date?"

"Yeah, I'm bringing a date, so I'm not going to have time for a heart-to-heart or whatever he has planned."

I finally start walking again, fueled by years of frustration.

"I didn't know you were seeing someone. Who is she?"

My gaze snags on the girl standing on the bottom step watching me. Not Sariah.

"Violet?"

"Violet?" My mom asks. "Oooh. Is she the girl with the fever?"

"Mom, I have to go."

"Call your father, Gavin."

"I will." Maybe. "Love you, Mom."

I end the call as I come to a stop in front of Violet.

"Sorry for just showing up," she says.

"It's fine. Is everything okay?" My immediate thoughts are she's feeling crappy and needs someone to help her, but she looks good. Great, even. And I know Dahlia and Jane are back because I saw them with her at the dining hall.

"Yes. No fever all day and I managed to eat twice." She throws a little woot in on the end and that's when I realize she's nervous. But why?

"Do you want to come upstairs?"

"No," she says quickly, and then takes a breath. "No thanks. I only came over to thank you again."

"It was no problem."

"Yeah, see that's the thing. It was a lot. Even for one of my friends, and you and I aren't exactly friends." She smiles sheepishly. "I feel like I owe you."

Ah, I see. She's here out of obligation and misconstrued guilt, which pisses me off for some reason. Maybe because I want to be her friend. Nah, fuck that. Not her friend. I want to be her everything. "Don't worry about it."

I turn to go back upstairs. I can't do this right now. She follows, jogging behind me and reaching for my elbow. "Wait. I'm sorry. That came out wrong. It's just, I interrupted your make-out sesh with another girl, puked on you, and then you took care of me for twenty-four hours. It was a lot. I definitely owe you. There has to be something I can do to make us even."

Frantic energy courses under my skin. She walks beside me as I head to my room. I toss my phone on the desk with a thud. I'm so frustrated. With my dad and with myself. Why did I have to get so drunk that night with Bailey? I was pissed at him again for some reason I don't even remember, but that's no excuse.

"I could clean your room." She scans the space. "Although it looks pretty tidy. Do you have a maid?"

I huff a laugh.

"I could do your laundry or I could..." She snaps her fingers. "I could make you something to wear for the banquet. Sorry, it was hard not to overhear. A new shirt or pants, maybe a suit? Your date will be wowed."

"I don't have a date. I lied."

"You lied to your mom?" She sounds outright appalled.

"Yeah, I don't feel great about it."

Her voice softens. "Things are still touchy with your dad?"

"Worse than ever," I admit. "He's coming to the banquet, acting like he's father of the year. It's all bullshit."

"And you told your mom you had a date, so you had a buffer?"

"I didn't think. It was the first thing that came to mind."

She steps closer and chews on her bottom lip. "I'll go with you."

I'm quiet as I process her words, so she repeats them more confidently. "I'll go with you. I'm a great buffer."

"He won't really leave me alone just because I bring a girl with me." Though he might play a little nicer.

"Then I'll be so charming and distracting that he won't know what hit him." Her dark eyes are bright with excitement, like she thinks this is the best idea she's ever had. She's charming as hell, but my dad is still a dick.

"You don't know what he's like." I should just say yes and shut my mouth. Spending more time with Violet, in whatever capacity, is a dream come true, but I don't want to put her in the middle of the drama with my dad. She doesn't have any idea what she's agreeing to. I never know what I'm in for with him and, yeah, if I'm being honest, I don't really want the girl I'm into seeing all the messy, dysfunctional pieces of my life.

"Aren't these banquets like fancy and catered?"

"Y-yeah and filled with jocks."

"I'll be fine for a couple of hours."

I don't know what to say. She can't seriously want to do this.

"Look, things are weird between us, but I don't want them to be. It was sort of nice not hating you." She closes one eye and gives her head a shake. "That didn't come out right. What I'm try-ing to say is, I want to repay you for being so great to me while I was sick. I feel like it gave me a little closure somehow. Let me do this for you."

"Okay."

"Yeah?" She steps back with a smile on her face. It's been a long time since she's smiled at me like that. "Text me the details?"

I nod to keep myself from saying something dumb like 'you don't need to do this.'

"Great. See you then, I guess." It's only as she starts to leave that I see the weight of what she's agreed to sinking in. She shuf-fles awkwardly and hesitates, but she doesn't go back on her word.

And after a year of wishing for a second chance, I finally have a date with Violet.

Chapter
SEVENTEEN

Violet

WHEN I COME DOWN THE STAIRS TUESDAY NIGHT dressed for the banquet, my friends are all sitting in the living room. Their conversation stops and all eyes are on me.

"You look beautiful, Vi." Daisy stands from where she sits on Jordan's lap and comes over and hugs me.

"Thanks. Can you help with the clasp?" I hold the gold chain around my wrist with trembling hands.

"I got it," she says in a soft, reassuring voice.

My heart is in my throat, and I haven't been able to get a full breath all day. It's silly and I know my body's reaction is overkill for the non-date, favor plus-one situation, but I can't seem to control my anxiety. I think maybe it's from lack of sleep. I've been stressing over my design for Penelope, which is due this week. I love the dress I made, but I'm not one hundred percent on it yet. Oh, and I've been studying for a history test on Thursday. I also decided this was the week I needed to finally reorganize my closet.

Basically, I've done my best to put the whole banquet out of my mind until now, which has not been easy. Suddenly, everywhere I turn, things remind me of Gavin. My house used to be a safe space, free of memories of him, and now it's become enemy number one. I swear I still randomly catch a whiff of him in my room.

"He is going to die when he sees you," Jane says from the couch.

"Wait. Was that the plan?" Jordan asks, eyes widening and forehead wrinkling in concern. "Do I need to warn him?"

"No, of course not," Daisy answers for me, then adds, "It isn't, right?"

"No. I am not trying to kill anyone." I release a nervous laugh and shove my phone in my purse. "I'm returning the favor for helping me last weekend. That's it."

My friends don't look convinced, but thankfully, the doorbell rings, ending our conversation.

I open the door, totally unprepared for the sight in front of me. Gavin is dressed in navy slacks and a lighter blue shirt. His tie is yet another shade of blue, this one brighter. It's the first time I've ever seen him dressed in anything but athletic clothes or jeans. I stare blankly at him, neither of us saying a word.

"Hey, man, looking sharp," Jordan calls from the couch, snapping me out of it.

"Hi," Gavin says to him, then his gaze comes back to me. He does a long sweep over my blue dress all the way to the silver heels laced up my calves.

I glance down quickly and hold back a curse. My dress is nearly a perfect match to the color of his tie. It's like we're going to freaking prom and purposely coordinated our outfits.

"What are you doing here? I thought we were meeting at the banquet."

"It's nice out tonight. I figured we might as well walk over together." He shoves both hands in his pants pockets.

All the anxiety and nerves I've been battling all week come to a head. Designing a dress for a celebrity seems like a simple endeavor compared to spending the rest of the evening with Gavin on a date. Yeah, it's a date. I don't know how I thought I could play it off any other way, but seeing us together in our swatches of blue, him picking me up, we're most definitely on a date. I should have just owed him one: redeemable for free parking outside our house without me yelling at him, or something much simpler and less anxiety producing.

"Sure. Yeah. Fine," I say in a casual tone that is all fake bravado. I don't look at my friends. The only one who seems to understand or worry is Daisy. Don't get me wrong, Dahlia and Jane would kill him if he hurt me again, but they both seem so hopeful right now, and I don't want hope. *Can't* have hope. Not if I have a prayer of getting through tonight.

The banquet is held at Ray Field House, which is conveniently located across the street from our houses. Gavin and I walk side by side down the sidewalk and then across the road.

Inside, we are ushered to a large banquet room. I think it's actually two rooms with a divider open to make it one big space. There's a bar in one corner and the rest of the room is set up with circular tables. Servers in black and white are bringing pitchers of water to the tables. Candles are lit in the center of each one. It's all way nicer than I would have predicted for the basketball team.

"Do we have assigned seats or..." I let my question trail off.

"We can sit wherever. You pick."

"Outside, perhaps," I mumble under my breath.

"Sure," he says without missing a beat. He's scanning the room and fiddling with the cuff of his left shirt sleeve.

"We should just skip the whole thing, get drunk, take off all our clothes."

"Mhmm." His mouth is locked in a tight line.

REBECCA JENSHAK

I was so caught up in my own nerves that I didn't realize Gavin is anxious too. Except his anxiety has nothing to do with me.

I follow his line of sight across the room. Anthony Leonard is a handsome man, and the resemblance is undeniable. Tall, broad shoulders, thick, dark hair, and a square jaw. I've seen pictures of the older Leonard when he was at Valley U, and it's like looking at his son.

I step closer to Gavin. *A favor for a favor.* The reminder why I'm here and the knowledge that he has more on the line than me tonight puts me at ease and pushes me into action. I slide my hand around his bicep, fresh anxiety swirling in my stomach.

"Ready?"

He glances at my fingers resting on his arm. His throat works with a swallow, and he nods. "Yeah. Let's do this."

For the first thirty minutes or so, we move around the room and chat with players and members of the coaching staff. Gavin introduces me to everyone, and I do my best to keep them all straight. A lot of the guys I know, of course, either from living next door or from classes, a few even from back when Gavin and I hung out last year.

Since then, I've avoided not only Gavin, but his teammates and friends—anyone that had any connection to him. It was too hard. Gavin and I were a blip in time, but it was such a great blip. Until we weren't. I think maybe the hardest part of how things ended between us is that it felt so out of character, so wrong. How could he be this great guy who made me feel beautiful and important, and then cheat on me with my roommate?

I was dreading this part of the night more than anything else—making nice with his friends, but it isn't as awkward as I expected, and I'm actually having a decent time. It scares me how easy it is to be with him again. Hating him was simpler.

A man steps in front of the microphone at the front of the room to thank us for coming and to let us know it's time for dinner. We're seated at a table with Noah and Tommy, neither of who brought dates. The last I saw Mr. Leonard, he was across the room, talking with some guy in a suit and tie who looked important, so I lost track of him until he pulls out a chair next to his son.

I hold my breath as he flashes a smile around the table. It's so much like Gavin's, but not at all either. Mr. Leonard's smile has no real warmth behind it. I imagine it comes from years of donning it for the media. I don't want to have any sympathy for him, but I imagine it must be hard to have cameras pushed in your face everywhere you go. Regardless, I like that Gavin's smile, rare as it may be aimed at me, never feels anything but authentic.

Gavin bounces his leg under the table. Otherwise, he looks perfectly calm. I only notice because his knee brushes mine with every bounce, sending a whole host of new butterflies swarming in my stomach.

Servers begin to bring out plates, and the hum of conversation starts back up throughout the room. Mr. Leonard has a presence that is impossible to ignore and none of us speak until he does.

"Good to see you, son." He's looking at Gavin, but when he doesn't respond or even look up, Mr. Leonard shifts his attention to Tommy and Noah. "You boys are having a hell of a year. Noah, that shot you made against UCLA last week was incredible."

Noah thanks him and then he and Tommy fall into conversation with Gavin's dad, but I don't hear any of it because all I can focus on is the man next to me. His shoulders start to shake and then laughter spills from his lips.

"It's good to see me?" he mutters the question to himself. His laughter grows in volume and then he cuts it off with a snort. "Really, Dad? It's good to see me? That's the best you got after almost two years of not being in the same room as me?"

Noah and Tommy look down at their plates, pretending to give them privacy. Two years? I knew things had been rough, but I can't imagine not seeing either of my parents for that long.

Mr. Leonard doesn't respond. He probably doesn't have a comeback fitting for the accusation. Instead, he puts on that fake smile again and looks to me. "Who is this beautiful young lady? I didn't know you had a girlfriend, Gavin."

I expect Gavin to correct him, to tell him I'm not his girlfriend, maybe introduce me, but he just twists his mouth into a scowl and shakes his head.

"I'm Violet." I start to offer my hand, but Gavin leans forward blocking my path.

"How would you expect to know anything about my life? We haven't even talked in months. You only call when Mom guilts you into it or so you can pretend to be father of the year in interviews. You don't give a shit about my life so don't waltz in here and put on some act for my teammates."

His dad lowers his voice. "This isn't the time or the place."

"Then when is?"

"Keep your voice down. You're making a scene," his dad warns. The server approaches our table and sets plates in front of me then Gavin.

"Thanks," Gavin says politely, then pushes back from the table and stands. "I think I'm gonna get some air."

He takes off toward the banquet room doors. I give Mr. Leonard a tight-lipped smile, excuse myself, and follow his son.

Gavin's long legs make him impossible to catch. He finally stops outside.

I'm not quiet about my approach, but Gavin doesn't turn around to look at me. He stares off into the horizon. The sun is setting, but the warm air still lingers in the air. He raises both hands and places them behind his head, then let's out a guttural growl as he fists his hair.

"I'm sorry," I say, and take two steps to reach him. I'm so far out of my depth here. I have no idea what to say or do. "I can't imagine what it's like seeing him after all this time or having a dad that's in the headlines constantly. The only time my dad ever makes the news is for the Nerdy Derby. He participates in it every year and won first place last year."

Gavin lets his hands drop to his sides. His dark eyes soften as he asks, "Nerdy Derby?"

"Yeah, it's like souped-up handmade vehicles."

"I thought those kinds of things were for kids."

"Oh, they are. Second place was a seven-year-old."

He finally chuckles, and I can tell the release takes some of the weight off his chest.

"Don't let him ruin tonight for you. Isn't this supposed to be a fun night?" His friends certainly seem to be having a good time.

"I'm not hoping for fun tonight. Just survival."

Honestly, same. Except the more time I spend with Gavin, the harder it is to remember that this is a truce, and not us picking up where we left off.

"We could move tables," I suggest.

"No." He shakes his head. "Maybe it's juvenile, but I don't want him to have the satisfaction of feeling like he ran me off."

"I get that," I say.

"And as much as he pisses me off, I don't want to wake up tomorrow to some bullshit headline about us."

"Your dad thinks I'm your girlfriend." I lift one brow and then laugh. It feels weird to say the word. Even when we were together last year, we never put a label on it.

"Yeah, sorry," he says with a sheepish grin. "I should have corrected him, but the less he knows about my life the better."

"It's all right," I say. The air is thick with the tension surrounding him. "Are you going to be okay?"

"I'm fine."

He's lying.

"Try again."

He smiles; a real smile that makes me hate his dad's fake one even more. "I'm pissed right now, but I will be fine."

"Better." I tip my head toward the door. Another hour or two and we'll both be free. "Shall we?"

He nods and falls into step next to me. "Too late to take you up on your offer of getting drunk and naked?"

My mouth falls open as I suck in a surprised breath. "You heard me?"

"It took a couple of minutes for it to register, or I would have immediately agreed." He holds the door open for me, and something in his playful smile and dark brown eyes holds me captive as he says, "I always hear you, Violet."

Chapter
EIGHTEEN

Gavin

I'M ABLE TO KEEP MY SHIT TOGETHER DURING DINNER. Stuffing my mouth with food definitely helps.

After our plates are cleared, Violet excuses herself from the table and takes off toward the door. She's probably just going to the restroom, but I panic that maybe she's leaving. Without her at my side, I feel a lot less capable of doing the right thing.

And I miss spending time with her. Even though I know she's here purely to repay me for taking care of her, I can't help but wonder if there's a chance she could forgive me and get past the really shitty thing I did to her—sleeping with her roommate.

Seeing my dad, the reminder of how I did to Violet the same thing he did to my mom, makes acid rise in my throat. Maybe alcohol will help.

Noah catches me on my way to the bar.

"All good?" he asks.

I'm not even close to all good, but saying so won't help anyone. "I'm sorry for making dinner awkward."

"Don't sweat it." He shrugs his shoulders and falls into step beside me.

"Tommy hasn't said a word in almost an hour."

"Yeah, well, how would you feel if you discovered your idol is a shit person?"

I'd feel like my whole life was a lie.

"He isn't a shit person." The words tumble out easily, but I'm not sure they're true.

A lot of my teammates idolize my dad. His old Valley U jersey hangs in our fucking gym, so I get it. My instinct is always to defend him against other people. It's a weird spot to be in, wishing people knew what your dad was really like but, at the same time, wanting to protect him.

And the thing is, I don't really think he's all that awful, unless you're counting on him to show up and be part of your family. He's really good at popping in, putting on a smile, and making people feel at ease. I've seen him do it so many times through the years. Fans come up to him, shaking with excitement, sometimes crying, and he asks them a few questions about themselves, taking the focus off him, and makes sure they feel like they had a genuine connection.

Is it bullshit? I don't know. I don't even think he knows.

But that sort of drive-by attention wasn't enough as a kid and it isn't enough now. I'd almost rather him completely leave me alone than drop in after months of no contact and pretend like everything is cool.

And yeah, I get it. He has made an attempt lately, but it's too little, way too fucking late.

"I'll talk to Tommy."

"And say what? That you're holding on to some old-fashioned teenage resentment toward your father?"

Seems legit enough. "Something like that."

"Do me a favor. No, do Tommy a favor. If you're going to talk to him, tell him the truth. Tommy deserves that. And more than that, he wants it. You're his friend, his teammate. His loyalty is to you."

Noah leaves me to think over his words. I get a drink and linger around the perimeter of the room. I see her the second she steps back inside. Violet scans the room. My chest tightens when her gaze finally lands on me, and the corners of her mouth pull up into a nervous smile.

She crosses the room with long, confident steps. Violet is a freaking ten any day of the week, but tonight, in that blue dress with her hair wavy and those shoes… damn those shoes, she steals the air from my lungs.

"Everything okay?"

"Yeah." A small smile lifts the corners of her mouth. "Dahlia called while I was out there. She wanted to make sure we hadn't killed each other."

A laugh slips from my lips. "Hadn't even crossed my mind."

"Mine neither, surprisingly."

I lean in. "The night is young."

It's hard to pull back out of her space. Being in her bubble feels a hell of a lot better than being anywhere else. Her tongue darts out to wet her lips as our gaze stays locked on the other. She looks away first and eyes the drink in my hand.

"Want something?" I ask, moving back and angling my body to the bartender.

"Ummm."

She's still thinking when my dad's voice interrupts. "Gavin, son, can I have a minute?"

Violet looks between us. I love the reluctance on her face, like maybe she doesn't want to leave me. Ultimately, she does, though. Putting a step between us, she says, "I'll be at the table."

"She's pretty," he says after Violet's gone. "How long have you two been together?"

REBECCA JENSHAK

"Does it matter?"

"Just trying to catch up on everything going on in your life. I know it's been too long. I've been trying to call."

Silence hangs between us.

"The team has never looked better. Valley U is a lot of people's favorite to go all the way this year."

I still say nothing.

"Have you given any more thought to your future?"

At his question, my temper flares. "You know my plans. They haven't changed."

He pulls a business card from his pocket. "I hate to see you wasting your talent behind a desk. At least consider your options. You're a great player. Way better than I was at your age. You could have a long, successful career in the NBA. Don't throw away your future because you're pissed at me."

He pushes the card at me until I take it and shove it in my pocket without looking at it.

"This has nothing to do with you."

"Got it." His mouth pulls into a straight line. "How's school and everything else?"

My frustration has reached its max level. I don't want to do this. "Everything is great, Dad. Is that what you came here to hear? I'm great. Now you can go back to your luxe life and your many girlfriends. Mom and I are doing just fine without you."

I walk off before he can respond, adrenaline pumping through me. Violet looks up as I approach. Taking her hand, I tip my head toward the exit. "Want to get out of here?"

"Sure." She hesitates, but then grabs her purse and stands.

I don't let go of her hand, even when we reach the hallway. Her fingers curl around mine just slightly. It's something.

"Up for a little mischief?" I ask her as we weave down the hall toward the locker rooms.

"As long as it doesn't land me in jail or the dean's office, then okay."

110

"Probably not." I open the door.

"Probably not?"

I tip my head and she finally goes in ahead of me.

"Wow," she says as the lights flicker on. Violet walks slowly into the space, letting her gaze roam over every detail of the locker room. "This is nice."

"This way." I move toward the lounge area. Couches and chairs are set up in front of a TV with every gaming system imaginable.

I plop down on the closest couch and pick up a controller.

"This is your idea of mischief?" She sits tentatively beside me. "I thought we were going to fill lockers with shaving cream or hide all the practice jerseys."

I hand her a controller. "Girls aren't allowed in here."

She laughs as I power on the Nintendo Switch and navigate to Donkey Kong original.

"Know this one?"

"I'm sure I can figure it out." A determined glint flashes in her eyes.

For the first five minutes, neither of us speaks. We play the old-school game together, taking turns. The longer we play, the less I feel like breaking something and the less hesitant Violet seems. She shifts closer and relaxes into the couch. I undo my tie.

We make it to stage two before Violet says, "I guess I wasn't such a great buffer tonight."

"There is no buffer strong enough when he's in the same room."

"Still. That is why I'm here."

I glance over at her and smirk. "And here I thought it was because you wanted to spend time with me."

She laughs softly and then holds my gaze. "Why is your dad here tonight?"

"The athletic director invited him." I lift one shoulder and let it fall.

"And he wanted to see you."

I don't say anything, so she pauses the game. "He did. You

know that's why he's really here, right? As screwed-up as things might be between you two, he came here because of you."

"Maybe that's true, but he could have seen me any time, and he chose to do it in front of all my coaches and teammates. Tonight wasn't about me. It was about him looking like a good father to the people whose opinion he cares about."

She looks at me with pity and sadness, neither of which I want from her. Standing, I move to the small kitchen area and jump up on the counter.

"What are you doing?" She follows me, laughing.

I toss two bags of Takis to her, then hop down and open the fridge. "We have Gatorade, water, or soda."

"Snacks, video games, and naked men. This place is almost perfect." She reaches in and grabs a Diet Dr. Pepper.

I snag a Gatorade, and we go back to the couch. "There are no naked men in here. Wait, was that another attempt to get me to strip down?"

"Another attempt?" She smiles as she opens her bag of chips.

"Earlier. You asked if I wanted to get naked."

"I wanted to see if you were paying attention." She flicks a hand in the air. "This is a locker room. I'm assuming people get naked in here sometimes, yeah?"

"Yep." I pop the p. "People like me."

"Hence *almost* perfect."

"Hence?" I'm smiling and feeling better than I have all day. "You're a trip."

She tosses a chip in her mouth and chews. "I know your relationship with your dad is tough, but how are things with your mom?"

I pull one knee up onto the couch and tilt my body toward Violet. "Mom is great. Her team made it into the national tournament for the first time in the school's history."

"That's amazing! Are the men's and women's tournaments

played at the same place? Will you be able to see her while you're there?"

I shake my head. "Nah. If I'm lucky, I'll be able to catch a few games on TV. Same for her."

"And your dad? Will he be there?"

I shrug off the question. I imagine he will be, at least for the championship game, whether I'm in it or not.

"He's a lot. I wasn't expecting to be so intimidated by him."

"Don't be. He's just a regular, flawed dude, trust me."

"You two look a lot alike."

"You mean my dad is hot?" My lips pull into a wide smile.

"I did *not* say that."

We smile at each other. It feels so good being here with her. Having her smile at me again. "I missed this."

Violet visibly withdraws at my words like it's reminded her that I'm not a guy she wants to spend time with, smiling and laughing. She sits straighter and the shield that is so often between us returns. "It's getting late. We should probably get back."

We toss the trash and turn off the TV before walking back to the banquet hall. When we are steps away, I pause and face her. "Thank you."

"For what?"

"Being here."

A flicker of that ease between us from earlier returns. "You're welcome."

I don't look around for my dad when we enter the room, but I do notice he isn't at our table, so that's where I lead Violet.

I pull out her chair and she takes a seat.

"Where have you guys been?" Tommy asks. "You missed dessert."

"What he means to say is that he ate yours." Noah punches Tommy on the arm.

"I didn't want it to go to waste."

I rest my arm on the back of Violet's chair. A week ago, she would've batted my hand away or maybe moved to a table clear across the room. But tonight, she doesn't flinch.

Coach Reynolds speaks into the microphone. "Hey, everyone. Before we leave tonight, I wanted to say thank you to everyone for coming. It has been a great season. I'm so proud of the hard work and dedication shown by this group of guys."

Applause starts somewhere across the room then spreads. Coach waits for it to die down before continuing. "Can I get Gavin up here?"

My legs feel heavy as I push back from the table and start for the front of the room. I finally spot my dad standing at the bar next to the athletic director. Coach extends a hand for me to shake when I reach him, then he claps that same hand on my shoulder. "Behind every great team is a player that looks out for his team, leads by example, and is a mentor to the younger guys. Gavin Leonard has been that for this team. He makes my job easy." Coach laughs and the room joins in. "Well, he's made my job *easier*, anyway. The team voted and named Gavin our MVP."

Coach plucks a small trophy from the podium and hands it to me, then pulls me into a hug. "Congratulations."

"Thanks, Coach." I lift the trophy as I acknowledge the guys clapping for me. I don't look at my dad. Instead, my gaze snags on Violet. She's wearing an amused smile as she brings her hands together.

When I get back to the table, her smile gets bigger and slightly taunting. "Congrats on being top jock."

"Top Jock? Is that like king of the dipshits?"

"You said it."

"Thanks." I laugh as I set the trophy on the table and take my seat. Coach has more awards to give out, so I move my chair closer to her and whisper, "How much do you wish I'd taken you up on your offer to get drunk and naked now?"

"This is fine. How many awards can there possibly be?"

I point to the table next to the podium with a dozen or so trophies.

She groans.

Laughing, I ask, "Want something to drink?"

"Definitely."

"Be right back."

"I'll come with you."

Quietly, we make our way to the bar. My dad is nearby but stuck in conversation. We almost get away without him coming over, but just as the server hands us our drinks, he steps up behind me.

"Congratulations. That's a strong statement from your coach and teammates. I'm proud of you."

"Thanks." The word falls from my lips with only half as much disdain as I feel.

"I'm going to head out soon."

I nod and swallow around the lump forming in my throat. It doesn't make sense to be upset about him leaving when I didn't want him here in the first place, but I feel it anyway.

"Unless you want to grab a drink after." His gaze slides to Violet. "Both of you, of course."

"We can't," I say quickly. "We have plans."

He slides both hands in his pockets and stays quiet, like he's giving me time to reconsider.

Violet steps closer to me so that her arm rests against mine.

"We have tickets for…" She looks to me and her eyes widen as she tries to come up with something. Violet is a terrible liar. "An art show."

"You're into art?" my dad asks me.

"Depends on the artist. Violet is a designer. A really great designer."

"What do you design?" he asks her.

She blushes. "Dresses, mostly."

"Did you make the one you're wearing?"

She smooths a hand over her waist and nods.

"You made that?" I ask.

"Yeah." She laughs lightly.

"It's beautiful," my dad says. "I'm glad I got to meet you, Violet."

She looks to me before responding. "You too, Mr. Leonard."

Dad takes a step closer to me. "Good luck at the tournament, and don't forget to call Artie. At least hear him out before you decide."

"Thanks for coming," I force the words out.

When he walks off, I let out a long breath.

"Are you okay?" Violet asks, stepping in front of me. I miss the heat of her arm against mine. "I'm sorry. I started talking without a plan. I don't do well on the fly."

"I'm good." I glimpse around the room to see more people heading out. Coach is flying through the trophies. I guess he's as eager to get out of here as I am. "Looks like things are wrapping up here. Ready to go?"

"Yeah. Let me grab my purse."

At the table, she gets her stuff, and I tell the guys we're leaving. The sun has set, and Violet rubs her hands over her arms as we step into the cool night.

"Did you really make that dress?"

"Yeah. It wasn't really that hard. The design is simple. Just your basic slip dress."

"Well, the execution is amazing, and you look great. I don't think I told you that earlier, but you do."

"Thanks." She ducks her head to avoid eye contact, and we take slow steps down the sidewalk to our houses. Tonight has been a lot, but I don't want it to end.

"Did you finish your design for Penelope?"

"I told you about that?"

"You let all sorts of secrets spill last weekend."

"I bet I did. I was delirious. And yes. The design is done."

"Now what?"

"My professor will give us feedback tomorrow and then we start finalizing everything. A rep for Penelope Hart is coming to look at them in a couple of weeks."

I can see how much the opportunity means to her in the anxious way she stares straight ahead and twists her fingers in front of her.

"I bet she picks yours."

"Based on what? You haven't even seen it."

"I don't need to. I know you."

The wind blows her hair around her face.

"Who is Artie?" she asks as she smooths the wild strands behind one ear.

I pluck the card from my pocket and hand it to her.

"Arthur Walten, Sports Agent. Walten Sports Management Group." She looks up in question after she finishes reading.

"My dad's agent."

"Are you entering the draft?"

"No. Much to my dad's disappointment."

"But Arthur, or Artie, wants to represent you? So you could play, but you don't want to. Why?" She studies me.

I step closer and rest a hand on her hip. She drops her gaze to where we're connected.

"It isn't what I want."

"What do you want?" She looks up at me through dark lashes.

Instead of answering, I lean down and brush my lips over hers. For the briefest of moments, she kisses me back. Hope and adrenaline surge through me and then crash when she steps back and brings a hand to her mouth.

"I'm sorry," I say quickly. *Fuck.*

"It's okay." She lets out a shaky breath. "But I should go. Thank you for tonight."

And with that, she speed walks away from me.

Fuck, fuck, fuck.

I count to five while I think through both scenarios—going

117

after her or leaving it be. I know where leaving it be gets me, no-where, so I take off after her. "Violet, wait."

She whirls around, stepping away from her front door. "Why did you do it?"

"Kiss you?"

"No." Her eyes fill with tears, but her body vibrates with anger. Hope at the progress I thought we'd made is quickly stolen from me. "Why did you cheat on me last year? I've been over it a million times, looking for clues that it was all in my head and we didn't really have this great connection that I thought we did. But then tonight, I felt it and..." She pauses, takes a breath, and speaks quieter. "Why did you do it?"

"I don't know," I say honestly. "I wish I did. I spent a lot of time trying to remember exactly what happened."

I don't remember hanging out with Bailey that night, let alone going home with her. I was crazy about Violet. I went out that night to some stupid date auction, counting the hours until I could leave and go see her. What the hell happened in the four hours between being there and showing up at Violet's room with her freaking roommate?

"Maybe I just had too much to drink, maybe she tricked me somehow, but the truth is that it doesn't even matter why it happened, because even if I knew, I can't take it back or make you forgive me."

I'm not sure I even deserve her forgiveness. No, that's not true. I *know* I don't deserve it. It's why I haven't pushed harder. What if she forgave me and then I just fucked it up again?

She nods slowly, resigned disappointment etched over her features.

"It wasn't in your head, though. I've never met anyone like you or had such a strong pull toward someone." I rub a hand over my chest. "Those weeks we were talking are filled with some of my best memories. Whatever you want to believe about me, know that it wasn't in your head."

Movement in the front window of Violet's house catches my attention. Dahlia, Jane, and Daisy are all peering out through the curtain at us.

Violet swivels around, and they scatter.

"I better go," she says.

"Okay."

I'm frozen watching her leave.

"Hey, Vi?"

It's two long seconds before she looks over her shoulder. "Yeah?"

"I am truly sorry for what I did to you. You didn't deserve that. No one does, but especially you. You're incredible." I shove my hands in my pockets. "I regret it every second of every day."

Her chin tips in the smallest nod.

"And, uh, thanks for going with me tonight. It sucked a lot less with you there."

"You're welcome, Gavin." This time, she's the one that hesitates. "I'll see you later."

Chapter
NINETEEN

Violet

PROFESSOR RICHARDS STARES DOWN AT MY DESIGN AND then at the dress. Her mouth is pursed and one perfectly manicured finger rests below her bottom lip. Her expression gives nothing away, and if she doesn't speak soon, I'm going to combust.

"I love the concept," she says finally. "It's risky and bold. Two things you always do well, but I worry that it doesn't say Penelope Hart to me. It says Violet Johnson. If she were walking the red carpet or posing for a photograph then that would be okay, but on stage, her clothes need to sell *her*."

"That makes sense," I say as dread pools in my stomach.

We chat for a few minutes on different options to make the design more functional, basically toning down all the things I love about it.

"Great job," she says before she leaves. "I can't wait to see the final piece."

Dahlia comes over when Professor Richards leaves.

I flip to a blank page in my sketchbook, and her face pales. "You're starting over?"

"Yep."

"But your dress is gorgeous."

"It's too *me*."

She scoffs and puts one hand on her hip. "Well, *you* are fantastic and so is that dress."

I pick up my pencil and then tap it on the table. "She has a point. The dress shouldn't distract from Penelope and her lyrics."

"It won't." She rests both hands on the dress protectively. "The girl knows how to rock a designer dress. It isn't going to swallow her. If Jane can pull it off, so can Penelope."

That's true. Still, I worry as I look around the room and see the other pieces. This is such a big opportunity, and I want it more than I've ever wanted anything.

"Don't be afraid to be you. You're the coolest designer I know."

"Thanks, Dahlia." I smile at my friend. "What'd she say about yours?"

"Basically, the opposite advice she gave you. Less comfort and more va-va-voom."

"Together, we could rule the world," I say, and take a seat.

"Something tells me you're going to do just that without any help from me." Dahlia heads back to her table and I stare at my dress.

Do I stay true to my original vision or start over? When class is over, I still haven't decided.

Since Dahlia is going to the library after class, I walk home alone. I'm deep in thought, head warring with indecision, when Gavin calls my name from the front porch of his house.

He lifts a hand in a wave and jogs toward me.

I have spent every minute since I saw him last, since he

freaking kissed me, trying to forget the hum of electricity it sent through me. I haven't told a soul about what happened. I'm still trying to make sense of it. How can I still want him even after he crushed my heart?

As he reaches me, he flashes a charming smile with a hint of nerves.

"I'm glad I caught you before I left." The sleeves of his T-shirt fit snug around his biceps and the athletic pants hug his thighs.

"Late practice?" My voice wavers with anxiety at making idle conversation with him. We're in this weird place between hating each other and being friendly.

"Film review."

I nod slowly and wrap my hands around the straps of my backpack.

"I'm sorry again about last night." He pauses and then adds, "For kissing you."

"It was a weird night. A lot of emotions and pretending to be together." I wave it off. "Already forgotten."

No chance in hell I'm ever forgetting it.

Gavin clears his throat as a muscle in his cheek jumps. "Good. Because I've been thinking about us all day. I can't take back what happened in the past, and I know you might not be able to forgive me, but I really like being around you. Maybe we could... hang out again or something?"

He sounds so hopeful it pulls at the part of me, the very large part, that wants nothing more than to forgive and forget. If only it were that easy.

"I had a lot of fun last night, Vi, which is saying something considering my father was in the same mile radius."

I did too, at least in moments, but I can't bring myself to admit it to him.

"Anyway, in the spirit of wanting to be friends, I was hoping you might be free tonight?"

What? The question must be written on my face because he keeps going.

"We're short a bowler tonight. Actually two, but Daisy already agreed to take one of those spots. Any chance you want to be our fourth?"

I'm thrown and unable to form words. "I..."

He smiles. "Trying to think of an excuse?"

"What?"

"You're not a very good liar. You trail off and get this wide-eyed look." His eyes widen until I don't think they can get any bigger.

"I do not look like that."

"You do." He chuckles and rubs his hands together in front of him. "If you don't think you can spend any more time with me, without wanting to tear all my clothes off, then I'll completely understand." His words take me by surprise, but then he grins playfully, and it finally breaks the weird tension between us.

If we're not fighting, then we're too nice and polite, tiptoeing around each other. I don't know what to do with that kind of relationship with Gavin, but cocky and taunting? I know how to handle that.

I fake gag. "You wish."

"Prove it then." He walks backward. "Seven o'clock. Don't be late."

At five 'til seven, Daisy and I walk into the bowling alley, followed by Dahlia and Jane. In other words, I brought reinforcements.

Gavin and Jenkins are waiting for us. Jordan and Liam, the other members of their weekly bowling league, had a hockey team dinner tonight to celebrate the end of the season.

Gavin flashes me a smile that makes my stomach flip, then tosses me a team shirt that smells faintly of him.

I pull it on and go to find a ball. Jane falls in next to me and reaches down to pick up a fourteen-pound bowling ball. "How about this one?"

Gavin steps up beside me and takes a blue ball off the rack.

"Fourteen pounds?" He nods to a lighter one in bright pink. That cocky smirk that makes my pulse quicken is etched on his face. "Maybe stick to something you can get all the way down the lane."

I know he's goading me, but it works.

"Don't mansplain bowling to me. I'm perfectly capable of choosing my own ball." I swipe the one Jane is holding. Holy crap, it's heavy.

Gavin watches me struggle to hold it with amusement. "Perfect. See you over there."

I hand it back to Jane as soon as he walks off, and unlike me, she doesn't seem to be having any issue with it.

"Something seems different between you two." She looks past me to Gavin. "What happened with you two last night? You didn't say much when you got home."

She focuses her attention back on me and narrows her gaze. I don't like this level of scrutiny from my friends. I always cave and spill everything. I don't know why I'm so hesitant to tell them we kissed, but I want to hang on to it a little longer.

"Nothing." My voice is entirely too high-pitched. "I..."

She gasps. "It did. You just did that bug-eyed thing."

"Seriously? I don't do that."

"You totally do." She steps closer and whisper-screeches, "What happened between you and Gavin?"

When I walked in the door last night, my roommates were waiting to hear how it went. They saw us arguing but missed the kiss before that. They assumed we'd spent the entire time fighting. Fighting would have been less complicated.

"Nothing," I try one more time, careful to keep my tone even.

She waits, brows raised like she knows I'm not telling her everything.

"He kissed me."

"What?!" she yells so loudly we get a few stares aimed in our direction.

"It lasted for a second. It was barely a kiss. It didn't mean anything." I take the ball back from her. Seriously, how is she holding it so easily?

"Okay. Wow." She blows out a breath. "We need to loop in Daisy and Dahlia."

"We're about to start, and if we tell them, they're going to spend the entire night gawking between me and Gavin like you're doing now."

She tears her eyes off Gavin and gives me an apologetic smile. "I will tell them when we get home. Okay?"

Jane blows out a breath. "Wow. I was sure hell would freeze over before anything ever happened between you two again."

I nod my agreement. "Nothing is happening between us."

"If you say so."

Once we're all ready, we begin. Jenkins starts us off with a strike, and then Daisy walks up to take her turn with concentration radiating off her.

"Care to make things interesting?" Gavin asks as he takes the seat next to me.

I arch a brow. "You play every week. Are you trying to hustle me? Because I already know that you can beat me."

"I *am* pretty amazing." He flashes a wide smile. "No hustle. I'll play left-handed to even the playing field."

"Why do you want to prove you can beat me so badly?"

"Just trying to make it more exciting." He rubs his palms together. "I thought you'd be eager to show me up."

"Fine, but you have to throw left-handed and turn in a circle five times."

"O-kay." He chuckles as he says the word.

"And whistle while you throw."

"Anything else?"

I shake my head. "What do I win when I beat you?"

"What do you want?"

"You first."

"If I win, you have to buy me a drink when we're done."

"Oh," I say. I expected something... more.

Daisy calls for me to take my turn.

"That works for me," I say as I stand. "Loser buys the other a drink."

Chapter
TWENTY

Gavin

J ENKINS PLACES HIS HANDS ON MY SHOULDERS AND THEN spins me around while Violet and her friends count. When they get to five, my buddy releases me. I stutter-step while I regain my balance, whistle "Jingle Bells," and then send my ball smoothly down the lane.

Playing left-handed is a disadvantage, but only a slight one. When all the pins fall, I turn back and flash Violet a victorious smile. Arms crossed, mouth open in shock, she takes slow measured steps toward me. When she reaches me, she drops her arms and holds out a hand.

"Congratulations."

I slide my palm into hers and hold her fingers captive. "Nice game."

"You too." She pulls her hand free. "I guess I owe you a drink, but unfortunately for you, I can't buy alcohol."

She smirks like she thinks she's pulled one over on me. I don't care if it's a glass of tap water, I just want to spend more time with her.

"I'm not drinking tonight anyway. We leave for Utah tomorrow for the first round of the tournament."

"Oh." She shifts her weight from one leg to the other. "I can't stay long. I rode with the girls, and Daisy has a test tomorrow. Let me just make sure they're cool waiting for a few minutes."

"I can give you a ride home."

Her expression is impossible to read while she considers my offer. "Give me one sec."

Jenkins and I each brought our own vehicles, so I let him know I'm hanging back, and wait for Violet to say bye to her friends.

When she walks back over to me, she looks nervous, and I second-guess this idea. The bowling alley doesn't have a full bar; instead, there's a window next to the shoe rental, where you can get pitchers of beer, soda, water, and a few different types of food.

"Can I get a Pepsi?" I ask when we reach the window. I turn to Violet. "Do you want anything?"

"Diet Pepsi. Thanks." She reaches for her purse, but I hold up a hand.

"I've got it." I place some cash on the counter. "It wasn't really a fair bet."

When we have our drinks, I point to a couple of free seats behind the lanes.

"Why wasn't it a fair bet?" she asks once we're sitting.

"I'm ambidextrous."

"You *were* hustling me!"

I grin.

"Oh crap. I think I knew that. Did you tell me that before?"

"Sounds like something I might have tossed out in hopes of impressing you."

"That's a weird way to pick up girls."

"Sometimes you have to get creative. You never know what might make a person give you a chance."

She laughs off my answer.

"You've never been attracted to someone because of something like that?"

"I don't think so." She looks up like she's thinking. "You?"

"Oh yeah. The list is long. I once had a thing for a girl in high school because she always smelled so good. It was like the perfect amount of perfume. Not too strong, just this light, clean, subtle scent when she walked by."

"Oh, I've totally looked twice at a guy who smells good."

"See?"

"What else?" she asks with a smile that transforms her face and sends a rush through me.

I turn in my chair and let my knees brush the side of her leg. "Tommy dated this girl freshman year that could do these crazy gymnast flips and turns. I wasn't attracted to her at all until I saw her do a few."

"That one makes sense. You're an athletic guy, so you appreciate it in others. Jocks attract jocks." She rolls her eyes. She really has a thing against jocks. Or maybe just me.

"Maybe. Have you ever dated another designer?"

"No. Never. I really haven't dated since…" She lets the words trail off. "And I didn't know any before I got here."

I swallow and nod. I walked myself right into that one. Violet and I met and started talking the first week she got to Valley. She was outgoing and excited about college and making new friends. A lot of people show up at college and want to play it cool, but not Vi. I really dug how honest and genuine she was. It's still one of my favorite things about her.

"Speaking of design, what did your professor say about your dress for Penelope?" I ask, after taking another drink of soda.

"She liked it. Said it was my best work yet and applauded me for taking risks."

129

"That's great. Why don't you sound happier?"

Her shoulders slump forward. "She wants me to make some changes, tone down some of the elements."

"And you don't want to?"

"I'm torn. I don't know what to do."

"Do you have any pictures of the dress?"

"You want to see a dress I designed?"

"Absolutely."

Hesitantly, she pulls her phone out, and I shift closer. She flips through several of a black dress before stopping on one of Jane wearing it. The skirt comes up high in the front, but the back has some sort of flowy train that hits the floor. The sleeves are sheer and off the shoulder.

"I don't know a lot about dresses, but this is seriously hot."

Light laughter spills out of her as she takes the phone back and stares down at her creation. "Jane makes everything look hot."

"It isn't Jane."

"You don't think Jane is hot?"

"Sure, she is, but I wasn't looking at her."

She flips to another with the same dress on a headless mannequin. "Professor Richards thinks I should lose the train, maybe the sleeves too."

Her mouth twists as she keeps studying it.

"What do you think?"

"I love the dress. I'm proud of it. But I'm struggling to keep my vision separate from the customer's needs. If she can't perform in this dress, then I've failed to do my job, and simply created a really beautiful dress to shove in the back of my closet with all of my other costumes."

"There are a lot of layers on that thing," I say, and shoot her a sheepish grin.

"I know, but I love the way it cascades behind her. I can see it on stage as she walks." Her lashes flutter closed as she smiles.

I swallow thickly. When she reopens her eyes, she catches me staring. "It's silly, I know. I need to let go and focus on making it work in the real world. I lose sight of that sometimes. Wearing dresses, costumes, that was always fun for me. I'm perfectly willing to suffer for fashion occasionally, but not everyone feels that way."

"I bet Penelope does."

Vi's lips pull into a slight smile. "I'm not sure."

We sit in silence for a few minutes. I finish my soda and Violet continues to flip through photos of her dress.

"Are you anxious to get back and work on your dress?" I ask.

"Sorry." She locks her screen. "I'm being rude. I get lost in it sometimes."

"Nah, it's fine. You want to obsess over your work. I get that." We stand. "I have a few hours of obsessing left to do tonight too."

"Game film?"

"Yeah, Oregon's defense is tough."

We get in my car and start back to the houses.

"How long are you gone for the tournament?"

"Depends. Hopefully until Saturday. If we lose the first game, then Thursday."

"You won't lose. Oregon has a decent defense, but they're struggling on offense since they lost… someone."

"Manning." A laugh bursts out of me. "How do you know that?"

"I read the news," she says with a coy smile.

"Even sports news?"

"Sometimes," she admits.

The rest of the ride back is quiet but not uncomfortable. I feel like we've moved forward a tiny bit, but I still want more.

I pull up to the curb between our houses, neither of us making a move to get out.

"Do you—" I start at the same time she says, "Thank—"

We both stop and smile.

"You go first," she says.

I run my hand along the leather of the steering wheel. "It was dumb."

"I'll be the judge of that." She shifts in the seat to better face me. "Tell me."

My pulse quickens. "I was wondering, do you think we could ever really be friends again?"

She's quiet and her gaze falls to her lap.

"Told you it was dumb." I drop my chin as I let disappointment settle over me. I had to know. At least now, I feel like she doesn't hate me. Hate might have been easier to live with, though. A little of Violet isn't enough. I want to get lost in her, obsessed.

"Kiss me."

My head snaps up. "What?"

"Kiss me again."

My mouth opens to ask a whole bunch of questions, but I turn off my brain. When a hot girl asks you to kiss her, you fucking kiss her and you kiss her good.

She meets me halfway, leaning over the console between us. Our lips meet in a soft caress of uncertainty and intrigue, but it's quickly replaced by an overwhelming desire for more.

My hand slides around the back of her neck, drawing her closer, and she comes with no hesitation. Her fingers push into my thigh.

"Violet," I murmur her name.

She responds by opening wider. Our tongues tangle and my heart fucking hammers.

I'm not sure which of us pulls back first, but we're both out of breath.

Woah.

She unbuckles and opens the door. I'm still struggling to get brain function back when she says, "No, Gavin. I don't think you and I can ever be friends."

Chapter
TWENTY-ONE

Violet

"TELL IT AGAIN FROM THE BEGINNING," JANE SAYS, bringing the bottle of wine with her from the kitchen to the living room.

"No. Start with him kissing you last night," Daisy interjects.

Dahlia inches closer to me on the couch. She's quiet, but just as eager as Jane and Daisy to hear the story again.

I oblige them, a giddy feeling buzzing inside me as I talk.

"I can't believe it," Daisy says.

Me either.

"I thought if you two ever hooked up again, it'd be hot hate sex, which you'd regret and then inevitably repeat."

I snort a laugh.

"I had a whole intervention planned," my cousin states.

"Don't count that out just yet." I hold out my glass and Jane pours more wine into it.

"What does it mean?" Dahlia asks.

"Are you going to start kissing more often?" Jane's eyes are filled with excitement.

"I don't know." I take a long drink, the chilled wine doing nothing to dampen the heat still rushing through me from that kiss. God, that kiss. "He asked if we could hang out when he gets back from his games this weekend, but maybe it isn't a good idea. He seems remorseful, but can I really trust him?"

"What does your gut tell you?" Dahlia bumps my shoulder with hers.

"That it's risky and it might blow up in my face again."

"But you still want to try." There's no question in Jane's statement. She knows I do.

"Am I crazy?"

"No, you're human."

I blow out a breath. "He won't be around that much for the next month, if they do as well in the tournament as everyone is predicting."

"Maybe that's good," Daisy says. "It'll give you time to ease into things and decide what you want."

My friends all nod. They're right, of course. Going slow would be the smartest path forward. But then why do I want to do something dumb like walk over there and demand he kiss me again?

As soon as class is over Thursday, Dahlia and I turn our living room into our design workshop. Daisy is with Jordan at his dorm, and Jane sits on the couch, reading and occasionally glancing up to check our progress.

We order takeout and turn the music up. I used to love going to parties, but nights at home, hanging out with my best friends, listening to loud music, and eating junk food is the best.

I'm in the zone, sewing and singing along with the lyrics when Jane comes up beside me.

"You scared me," I yell over the music.

"Sorry. Thought you might want to see this." She holds up her phone to show me the final score of the Valley game.

"They won."

"Yep." She scrolls down to a picture of Gavin in uniform. "And your boyfriend had a record game. Twenty-six points."

A spark of pride lights inside me. "He's not my boyfriend."

"Why not?" She takes her phone back. "I know you. You like him. There's no going slow with you two. You look at each other and practically combust. Plus, he's a good kisser and looks good sweaty."

"How do you know he's a good kisser?" I don't mean for it to come out in an accusatory tone, but Jane's brows lift, and her lips part then pull into a wide smile.

"Because you kissed him... twice in two days."

"I did not initiate the first one."

"Why did you ask him to kiss you?" She turns down the music and plops onto the couch. Dahlia looks up from her work and they both wait for my answer.

"The first time he kissed me, I was shocked. I could barely process how I felt about it because he caught me completely off guard. So, I thought if he kissed me again and I didn't feel anything, we could forget about the past and be friends."

"And?"

My face flushes. "I wish I hadn't felt anything. That would make things so much simpler."

"Simple is boring," Jane says.

"Hey!" Dahlia objects.

"You aren't simple or boring," Jane tells her. "You are a freaking goddess. Anyone with eyes can see that."

"I meant my design. Is it still too simple?"

"No," Jane insists. "Penelope loves that color and she's a sucker for a jumper."

"She is?" Dahlia asks.

"Yeah." Jane waves a hand dismissively. "She's photographed in them all the time."

"Then this one needs to stand out even more and right now it's blah." Dahlia steps back and stares at the jumper.

"It isn't blah," I insist.

I abandon my own work, so Jane and I can focus on helping Dahlia until she feels certain of her design again. Seeing someone else question their natural inclination pushes me back to my original concept. Sometimes I think traditional education is a total mindfuck for artsy people. We all have our own natural design aesthetic, but we spend four years being filled with information and ideas that muddy that vision.

Not all of that is bad, of course, but I have to believe that the thing that makes Dahlia's work special, the thing that makes *my* work special, is that it provides a different perspective.

Simple isn't boring. Imitation is boring.

Around midnight, we call it a night. I have class at nine tomorrow, so I head up to bed. My thoughts are still on my dress when a text from Gavin lights up my screen.

We won. Looks like you get to enjoy the quiet next door for another night.

In my room, I flip on the light and look over at The White House. It's almost eerie, sitting there so dark and silent.

I don't respond to his text until I'm ready for bed and under the covers.

Congrats! Maybe the girls and I will throw a party at your place tomorrow night. I assume the liquor is stocked. Can you tell your keg guy to drop a couple by?

My keg guy? Who has a keg guy?

I'm assuming YOU do.

I'll let Petey know we need our usual order. Anything else? A stripper, perhaps?

Sure, why not. Is there a stash of dollar bills ready in your room? Maybe under the mattress?

I'm already smiling when his next text pops up on the screen.

Close. Sock drawer with my lube.

Ah, of course! That's where I keep mine too.

Your lube?

My dollar bills.

What have you been up to? Besides missing me like crazy.

Class, working on my dress. Nothing.

The dots appear and then stop. A few minutes go by without a response, and I watch the screen, hoping for more. I actually have missed him. I know it's silly, but for as long as I've lived next door, Gavin has been a constant presence. Often an annoying presence, but a presence nonetheless.

Sorry. I fell asleep. Long day.

When do you play next?

Saturday. We have the early game, so we should be back sometime that evening. Hang out when I get back?

He says it so casually, like hanging out is something we do on the regular. Maybe we do now.

Sure.

Great. I'll text tomorrow.

Good luck.

Valley wins again on Saturday, and to no one's surprise, the guys at The White House decide to throw another party.

"Are you sure you want to come over?" Gavin asks. "We could go to The Hideout or something."

I look out my window to see him staring back at me. For the past fifteen minutes, since he got home, we've been chatting on the phone and simultaneously catching glimpses of each other from our respective windows.

"No. It's fine. Daisy and Jordan will be there, so if you ditch me at least I'll know someone."

"Good to know your expectations are high." His rough chuckle rumbles through me. "What about Dahlia and Jane?"

"They're going to a concert."

He looks over his shoulder as Noah steps into his room. I can't make out his roommate's words, but a second later, Gavin says, "I have to go help out downstairs. What time are you coming over?"

My stomach is suddenly a ball of nerves. "I guess I'll just walk over with Jordan and Daisy. I think they're planning on going around ten."

"All right." He looks at me through the window. I can see him smiling from here. "See you in an hour."

We hang up and he waves before leaving his room. I turn back to my bed and the dozens of dresses I pulled out of my closet. I have no idea what to wear.

It's been more than a year since I went to a big party like the ones at The White House. It's not my scene anymore; it barely ever was.

Even before things got ugly with my old dorm roommate Bailey, I struggled with the really big campus parties.

I enjoy a good party as much as the next person, don't get me wrong, but the thing about hanging out and drinking with the most popular and desired people on campus is everyone sort of loses their minds.

People say and do things they wouldn't normally when they get in a group that large. Then the morning after, they're filled with regret and shame, and that always made me uneasy. Especially after Gavin, because I felt like maybe it had all been out of character for him and I was only seeing his true character when he slept with my roommate.

Bailey used to say that she became someone else when she stepped through the doors of a party. And as absurd as it sounded at the time, I think it happens to all of us on some level. The alcohol and the music, the peer pressure to look and act a certain way, it's heightened, but in this quiet way, where you don't even realize it until you're waking up the next morning hungover after promising yourself you were going home early to study.

I'm not immune to it. I've done things I wouldn't normally do with a little liquid courage and my friends' encouragement, but it's different when you're surrounded by people you trust.

I don't trust Gavin, at least not fully. And I don't know what version of him I'm going to get tonight.

Ugh. This was a terrible idea. Daisy and Jordan will be off being adorable and in love, and Gavin and I are barely past hating each other.

A knock at my door pulls me from my downward spiral. I sit on the mattress. "Come in."

Daisy peers in and smiles when she finds me sitting next to the pile of dresses.

"I'm a lost cause. Go on without me."

"I thought you might be in here suffocating under your outfit options."

"You know me too well."

"I do." My cousin moves a few articles of clothing out of the way to sit next to me. "Which is why I think it's silly you're stressing about how you look. You could wear what you have on and still be the hottest, coolest girl at the party."

I glance down at my old high school winter formal T-shirt. The design is faded and the material thin from a thousand washes.

"You're full of shit."

"Nope. Totally serious." She laughs and scoots closer to me. "Stop stressing about what you're going to wear and tell me why you're really freaking out."

"Do I have to say it?" I wave an arm toward The White House. "What if this is a mistake?"

"Do you think it is?"

I pick at the hem of a purple dress at the top of the pile on my bed. "You know when you're about to do something stupid but you're too excited about it to stop? That's how I feel right now."

She says nothing, but her mouth pulls into a sad smile.

"What do you think I should do?"

Daisy is the smartest person I know, and I trust her opinion and that she always wants the best for me. She'll know what I should do.

"Honestly, I have no idea."

I groan.

"*But* I think that you need to do this. You need to know if there's still something there or not so that you can move on one way or another."

"I tried to move on." A million times over the last year. I dedicated myself to school and having fun with my friends, but… "He's too far under my skin."

"I get that," she says softly. "You don't have to make any big decisions right now. Tonight, let's just have fun. And if at any point you want to leave, just say the word and I'm with you."

I let out a breath. She's probably right. I'm making too big a deal out of hanging out with Gavin. It's just a party. I can leave any time I want. "Thank you."

She stands. "All good or do I need to grab the wine and we'll do a little fashion show?"

"I'm good." I relax as I realize she might be happily in love and planning on spending all night making out with her boyfriend, but she will be there in a flash if I need her. "I'll meet you downstairs."

She stands and walks to the door.

"Hey," I call after her, "thank you."

"For what?"

"Always having my back."

She smiles. "Always."

Chapter
TWENTY-TWO

Gavin

I'VE BEEN PACING THE KITCHEN FOR THIRTY MINUTES, where I have a clear view of everyone coming in through the front door.

"Gavin!" someone yells from outside.

I tear my gaze from the party entrance for only a second to find the source. Tommy and a group of girls stare back at me, grinning. Tommy holds up a bottle of Jager and one of the girls motions for me to join them.

I shake my head, and when I glance back at the front door, she's finally in it, stepping over the threshold behind Jordan and Daisy.

My heart leaps at the sight of her. Jean shorts and a yellow top with sleeves that fall off her shoulders. As she walks, she gathers her dark hair and pulls it to one side.

Five long strides get me close enough that Jordan sees me.

"Gavin, hey," my buddy says with a chin jut.

Violet looks up when she hears my name.

Staring at her, I nod to Jordan and Daisy. "Hey, guys."

Jordan slaps me on the shoulder. "Congrats on the games."

"Thanks."

I put myself another step closer to Violet. "You look stunning."

She lets out a nervous chuckle. "Oh boy, are you already drunk?"

"Sotally tober," I say, pulling a real smile from her. "Come on, let's see if we can rectify that."

The four of us head back to the kitchen as Noah's coming in from outside.

"Do you want something to drink?" I ask Violet.

"Have any hard seltzer?"

"Do we have any hard seltzer." Noah cuts in with a sarcastic huff. He opens the fridge. It's a work of art, really. Truly and White Claw cans fill three shelves and part of the door. If you build it, they will come. If you keep the seltzer cold, the girls will stay.

"Wow," she says, stepping forward. She grabs one and thanks him.

"Anyone else?" He takes two for himself, stacking them in one hand.

Once everyone has drinks, we go outside. Some of the hockey guys are already here and Jordan and Daisy leave us to go say hello.

Noah cracks his first drink open and takes a long swallow. "Pong, anyone?"

Violet's gaze darts around the yard. She fidgets with the tab on the can, pushing it side to side.

"Vi?"

"Maybe later."

Noah leaves with a salute and I'm finally alone with Violet.

I'm still so stunned she's here, standing by my side. She catches me gawking at her and an uneasy smile tugs at the corner of her lips. "You're creeping me out, Leonard."

"Sorry," I say. "I can't believe you're really here."

"Yeah, me neither. I never thought I would show my face at one of these parties again."

"We had some good times at these parties."

"Did we?"

"Yeah. Remember the night we had all those Jell-O shots and then decided to walk to Taco Bell. Only the dining room was closed and we hassled the poor drive-through kid, trying to get him to take our order."

Her lips part in a smile. "Then he finally caved and neither of us had any money."

We share a laugh and Violet angles her body, closing us into our own little circle. I like it—being in a circle with just Violet. She glances around the party. "What now?"

"Are you still a shark at washers?"

Her lips twist into a competitive smirk. "Would a shark admit to that?"

"Fair enough." I chuckle. "Guess we'll just have to find out."

On our walk across the yard, where the game is setup, we run into Daisy and Jordan again. We split up into teams, boys against girls.

Violet stands next to me, holding the washer in one hand, and focused solely on the box twenty feet away. Her dark hair hangs forward, blocking part of her face from view.

If I keep staring at her like this, she's going to yell at me for being creepy again, but I just can't help it. She's so fucking gorgeous, and she's here with me. I don't want to blink and miss a second of it.

The party is big tonight and has that energy of a special night that only few parties, like the first and last of the year, tend to have.

Violet seems to be having an all-right time, but her guard is up, and I find myself wanting to reach out and touch her but then stop myself. We're in this weird limbo, somewhere between friends and more, and as much as I would like to leap over that line straight to MORE, I can tell she is not ready for that.

We've kissed twice now since she started hating me, but the way she's holding herself from me seems like she isn't so sure she wants to do it again.

"I need another drink," Daisy says, her cheeks flushed from the alcohol.

Jordan wraps an arm around her waist. "Let's get you another drink then."

I nod to Violet. "Ready for another one?"

She lifts her can. "Not yet."

By unspoken agreement, we walk across the party. It's slow going, weaving through groups of people. I take Violet's hand, so we don't get separated, her slim fingers gripping mine.

Tommy is standing near the pool with a group of our teammates.

"Leonard!" Tommy lifts both arms over his head and stumbles. Jenkins steadies him. "Easy there, buddy."

Tommy shrugs out of Jenkin's hold and says, "Someone was just looking for you, Leonard."

I pull Violet to my side, and it feels like Coach drew up a play for this very moment as all my teammates' eyes sweep down to my and Violet's joined hands and then their brows rise.

"Who was looking for me?" I ask, breaking the silence.

Tommy transforms from a drunk, stumbling mess to someone far too sober. He glances at Violet again and sidesteps to put more distance between us. Slowly, my brain cycles through his odd behavior until I realize, too late, what he's trying to tell me.

"There you are." The feminine voice squeals over the music and conversation, and then Sariah tackles me from my right.

I have to pull my left hand free from Violet's to catch my balance.

"I've been looking for you all night." She pulls back, beaming at me. "You were supposed to call me."

I step closer to Violet. "Hey, Sariah. Sorry about that. Do you know Violet?"

It goes from mildly uncomfortable to the pit of hell when Bailey falls in beside Sariah. Violet stiffens.

"Oh my gosh." Bailey's mouth drops open. "Violet?! Is that you?"

Vi lifts two fingers around her can. I'm honestly surprised it isn't the middle finger she flashes her.

"I thought you transferred. I haven't seen you in, in like, forever."

"Forever wouldn't be long enough," I think I hear Vi mutter.

Bailey is oblivious to any weirdness between them as she turns her head to share a laugh with Sariah. "This is my old roommate from freshman year."

"Oh, right." Sariah nods and looks Violet over.

Bailey continues to smile. "This is just like old times. You, me, Gavin."

I can feel Violet's rage, but she stays quiet.

"We should hang sometime and catch up." Bailey pulls out her phone. "Air drop me your number."

I brace myself for the verbal lashing that I'm sure is coming, but Violet just nods. "Yeah, that'd be, like, so awesome."

Bailey doesn't catch the sarcasm, but I do. Part of me wishes she'd yell at her. I don't blame what happened between us on Bailey. Whatever went down that night, I made the choices that ultimately had me ending up in her bed, but the fact that she can stand here, acting like everything is just peachy, is unnerving.

Violet lifts her can and fakes a smile. "I think I am ready for another drink."

Without another word, she disappears into the crowd.

The smallest hint of a smirk pulls at the corner of Bailey's mouth. I don't understand chicks. Was that whole thing a show to make Violet uncomfortable? Fuck. A protective rage fills me.

I take off after her. She hasn't gotten far, thanks to the mass of people here tonight.

"Violet," I call.

When I reach out and grab her arm, she glances back and then tries to tug out of my hold.

"Leave me alone, Gavin."

"Would you hold up a second."

A big group blocks her path, giving her nowhere to go. I take advantage of the moment and step in front of her.

"This was a bad idea. I shouldn't have come."

"Fuck them."

"You already did," she snaps. The fight in her dies a little as the people around us look our way. An embarrassed flush tints her cheeks.

"I'm sorry. I wasn't prepared to run into them. What can I do? Do you want to go somewhere else?"

"I should have known they'd be here." She won't meet my gaze as she speaks. "This is not my scene anymore. I don't belong here. I'll see you later."

She turns sideways in order to fit in the small space between the group of people and the pool. Only someone steps back as she gets in their path, and the little bump sends Violet teetering on the edge. She throws her hands up to her sides to catch her balance but can't quite get it and her eyes widen in panic.

"Vi!" I reach out for her. She grips my wrist, and the next thing I know, we're both hitting the water.

When I come up, I search for Violet. She's a few feet away. Her back is to me and her shoulders shake.

"Are you okay?" My T-shirt and jeans stick to my body. We're in the shallow end, so I easily cut through the water to get to her.

When she looks up, water hangs on her lashes. Her whole body shakes with... laughter?

"You okay?"

"No, I'm not okay." She laughs harder. "I'm soaked."

147

"Don't worry. It's not the first time people have jumped, or been thrown in, fully clothed."

We stare at each other until I take her hand and we walk out of the pool. I pull off my T-shirt and ring it out.

"Must be nice," she says as she tugs at the wet material sticking to her stomach.

"Come on. I have some towels inside."

We head into the house and then upstairs. I grab two towels from the bathroom and take her to my room.

"Thanks." She squeezes the water out of her hair and then dabs her clothes. She pulls her cell phone from her pocket. "Well, that sucks."

"Oh, shit. Want me to put it in some rice?"

"No. I'll do it. I'm going to head to my place and change."

I step in front of her and block the door. "Don't go. If you go home, you won't come back."

"I am not wearing wet clothes all night."

I lean over to my dresser and snag a pair of shorts. "Problem solved."

"You're more than a foot taller than me." She places the shorts at her hips. They fall all the way down past her knees.

"They have a drawstring. I'm confident you'll make it work." I get her a shirt, too. "I can toss your stuff in the dryer if you want."

"What about the rest of me?" She waves a hand in front of her face. "I should go. This whole thing was a bad idea."

"You look gorgeous." I get myself some dry clothes. "I'll change down the hall. Open the door when you're done."

"Okay." Her gaze drops to my bare chest.

I don't move because, hello, a hot girl is checking me out. Her eyes slowly lift back up to my face. I can't help it, I smile.

"You know what?" She flings the shorts and T-shirt over her shoulder and sashays past me. "I'll go to the bathroom. You can stay in here and keep flexing."

She disappears out the door. I quickly change, then run

downstairs to get a bag of rice for her phone. Violet returns a few minutes later.

The shorts are rolled several times, so they hit her mid-thigh and the T-shirt is tied up in the back. She has her wet clothes in hand.

"Want me to put those in the dryer?"

"No. It's fine." She sets them on top of the towel and glances down at her outfit. "Okay. I'm ready. This night can't possibly get any worse at this point."

I keep a mini fridge in my room, and I open it and pull out two beers. "Let's have a drink in here first. It's so loud out there."

We sit on the bed. I lean back on an elbow and kick my feet up and Violet sits cross-legged across from me.

"I'm sorry about Bailey and Sariah."

"I knew I was going to run into her someday. Do you hang out with her a lot?" Her stare drops to the beer in her hands.

"Bailey?"

She nods.

"Definitely not." In fact, I've avoided her. Bailey is an awful reminder of what I'm capable of. "I run into her occasionally at parties, but nothing has ever happened between us." I lower my voice. "Nothing else."

"Right." She brings the can up to her mouth and takes a small drink.

"And I didn't know she was friends with Sariah."

"You don't know the friends of the girl you've been hooking up with?"

"It wasn't anything serious."

"Neither were we." She shakes her head. "I can't figure you out."

"What do you want to know?"

"I want to know which version of you is the real one. Are you the asshole who slept with my roommate and then continues to hook up with random girls, without getting to know them, or the sweet guy who carried me ten blocks when my sandal broke and stayed up all night, wanting to know every detail of my life? I can't reconcile the different versions. Are you the worst mistake I ever made or..." Her lip quivers.

"I think I'm a little bit of both guys." I swallow around a lump the size of my many mistakes.

"So where does that leave us?"

Chapter
TWENTY-THREE

Violet

G AVIN SITS UP, ELIMINATING THE DISTANCE BETWEEN us. One long finger wraps around the end of a wet strand of my hair.

His voice is low and thick with emotion. "I know we can't start over, but can we try and move forward?"

I wet my lips and nod. That's why I'm here tonight, right? Because despite all that's happened, I still want him.

His gaze drops to my mouth. He tugs my hair and leans closer. I can't breathe in the seconds it takes for his lips to reach mine.

It isn't our first kiss, but it feels bigger than all the others. It feels thought-out and intentional instead of reactionary.

The kisses before this were doused in frustration and desperation. This one starts softer. His lips rest on mine, and he makes a little humming sound that vibrates and tickles.

That finger around my hair comes to my chin, and he holds

me in place as he finally slants his mouth over mine and kisses me with everything he has.

And what he has… there are no words except to say that Gavin is the MVP of kissing.

He sits up, taking me with him. Those fabulous hands are everywhere—sliding up my sides, tangling in my hair, caressing my face. Somehow it still isn't enough. Using his shoulders for balance, I scoot closer until I'm practically in his lap. Immediately, his hands wrap around my waist, pulling me against him.

The only time we seem to make any sense is when we're fighting or kissing. I forgot how much I wildly prefer the kissing.

He fists my wet hair and pulls my head back, giving himself access to my neck and lavishing it with kisses. A moan slips from my mouth. It feels so good. His long fingers dance along the hem of my shirt.

I press my lips against his and circle my arms around his neck. "You're wearing too many clothes."

I pull back, meet his molten gaze, and lift my arms above my head.

The material lifts slowly, his eyes locked on mine the entire time. Only when the T-shirt is tossed aside, does his stare drop, and a shiver rolls up my spine from the intensity in his dark eyes.

"You're beautiful." His hands circle my waist, and he glides his thumb along my ribs.

My heart feels like it's going to leap out of my chest.

"Less talking. More kissing."

His mouth quirks up at the corner. "Yes, ma'am."

Gavin hooks an arm around my back, like he's worried about me running away, as he captures my mouth again in a brutal kiss that makes my toes curl.

Minutes pass with us making out like neither of us can believe this is really happening. His lips drop to my shoulder, and he places an open-mouth kiss that he follows with a playful bite. I push at his chest, so he falls flat on his back onto the mattress.

He stares up at me with a smirk, but when I shift my weight, so my center presses into his hard length, he groans.

Heat pools low in my stomach. I glide my hands over his abs and up to his pecs, then down along his sides. "When did you get this?"

I trace along the edges of the tattoo on the inside of his forearm, near his elbow. I thought it was writing before, but up close, I realize they're numbers.

"Last summer."

"Are they coordinates?"

"Mhmm." His hands go to my knees and slide up, under the basketball shorts until the tips of his fingers brush along my panties.

"Where?" I ask, voice quivering as he teases me through the damp satin material.

"Half court."

I stare at him, waiting for more of an explanation.

"It's the center of the basketball court at Valley."

"You had that tattooed on your body? Why?"

He chuckles. The movement jostles us and that tiny bit of friction silences us both, lost in overwhelming sensation.

Gavin moves his hands higher, so he's gripping my hips under the shorts, and he holds me in place as he rocks up into me. If he's trying to avoid the question, he's doing a fabulous job of it.

My eyes close as a shudder wracks my body. Gavin flips us, so I'm now lying on my back as he hovers over me. He places a finger on my chest and draws a straight line, over my bra and down the middle of my stomach.

"I can't believe you're here. I must be dreaming."

I pinch his side.

"Ouch. What was that for?"

"Proving you aren't dreaming."

Laughing, he leans down and bites my nipple through my bra. I thread my fingers through his thick hair. I don't want to stop, but the last time we were here, tearing each other's clothes off, I thought things were a lot more serious than they were. I can't make that mistake again.

"Gavin." My voice is so quiet and raspy, I have to repeat it. "Gavin."

"Yeah?" He brings his mouth back up to mine.

"I know this isn't our first time, but I need to take this slow."

"Okay." His eyes blaze into mine. And he brushes his lips softly against mine. "Can I slowly kiss you again?"

I press my mouth to his and then sit up. He sits back on his heels.

"Yes, kissing is good. I'm just not ready to have sex with you again."

"That's it? Anything else off-limits?" He lifts both brows in question and searches my face. It softens something inside me at how eager he seems to know my limits.

"That's it."

A slow smile creeps across his face and his eyes darken. "Oh, baby, that still leaves so many possibilities."

We kiss until my lips hurt. Slow and sensual, then fast and desperate, cycling through like it's a dozen make-out sessions in one. We kiss until I've forgotten everything but being with him right now. Despite his words, Gavin doesn't try to push it any further than that. And I'm thankful even though my body begs for more.

It's incessant buzzing from Gavin's phone that eventually breaks us apart.

He picks it up off the nightstand. "It's Jordan. Daisy is looking for you."

"What time is it?"

"After one."

"Are you serious?" I sit up and run my fingers through my hair. It's mostly dried, but a tangly mess. "We've been making out for hours."

"Not nearly long enough." He kisses me gently. "Do you have to go?"

"Yeah. I really should."

"All right." He rests his hand on my hip. "We have practice tomorrow, but can you hang after?"

"Yeah. I'd like that."

He stands and helps me to my feet. I put on his T-shirt again and then corral my messy hair into a ponytail.

"Moment of truth." He reaches for the Ziploc bag and opens it, then pulls out my cell.

I power it on and sigh in relief when it comes to life. "Oh, thank goodness."

A dozen texts from Daisy pop up on the screen. The latest one from just a few minutes ago. I send her a quick reply, so she knows I'm alive, then grab my wet clothes and sandals.

Gavin pulls on a T-shirt and shoes, and we walk out of his room together. The party is still going, but there are a lot less people when we get downstairs.

"I'm sorry about tonight," he says, taking my hand. "I should have taken you on a real date."

What he's not saying is, he's sorry I ran into Bailey and the girl I walked in on him with a couple of weeks ago.

"I knew I'd have to face her eventually."

"You really haven't seen her since you moved out of the dorms?"

"Once at The Hideout, but she was too busy trying to get the attention of some football player that she didn't notice me." Classic Bailey, always out for the hottest or most popular guy in the room.

"She was awful to you. I know I was too, but—"

I place my hand over his mouth. "Moving forward, remember?"

"Right." He walks me all the way to my front door.

"I look like I'm doing the walk of shame." I motion down to his shirt and shorts that I'm wearing.

He leans in, brushes a loose strand of my hair that's fallen from my ponytail into my face, places a swift kiss on my lips, and then whispers, "I look forward to that."

The house is quiet when I get inside. I go straight upstairs. My roommates are all in bed. I'm so keyed up from tonight, I can't even think about sleeping. I take a quick shower to wash off the chlorine, and then get ready for bed. A text is waiting for me from Gavin, *My bed smells like you.*

As I read it, I walk to my window and look out. Gavin's room is dark, but I send him a reply anyway. *Considering I just washed off the chlorine smell, I think you're a liar. It smells like pool water.*

Come back over and I'll prove it.

It looks like you're sleeping.

A second later, the light flicks on and Gavin appears in the window, and then my phone rings in my hand.

Laughing, I answer, "Hi."

"I'm not sleeping," he says.

"I see that."

"I'm too amped up. Too horny."

I snort. "Looks like there are still some people out back. You could probably find someone to take care of that."

"You don't really think I'm that much of an asshole, do you?"

I think for a second. Do I? I shake my head. "No, I don't."

"Good." He disappears from sight but keeps talking. "Because I'm not screwing this up again."

He grunts and then a sound like something scraping along the floor makes me wince, so I hold the phone out.

"What are you doing over there?"

The awful sound happens again and then the bed scoots into view. Gavin pops up a second later, grinning as he checks the position, pushes it some more, and then he lies on the bed and picks up the phone. "There."

"You did not just move your bed, so you can stare creepily into my room while I sleep."

"Oh, I so did. It's pretty awesome. Want me to come over and move yours?"

"I am not moving my bed, but if I were, I'm perfectly capable of pushing heavy things all on my own."

"Suit yourself." He crosses one leg over the other and crooks an elbow behind his head.

I roll my eyes. "One second."

I swear I can see his smug smile all the way from here. I toss the phone on my bed and then use every ounce of my strength to push the heavy wooden bed frame away from the wall. This bed belonged to my grandparents, and they sure knew how to make indestructible (and immovable) furniture back then. I move the pillows to the end, so that I can lie on my side and see into Gavin's window.

"Happy now?"

"Mhmm."

We're both quiet for a few seconds. The only sound is the faint beat of the music still going from the party next door.

It's all so surreal. Part of me wants to fight this thing between us, fight him. That is my natural reaction to all things Gavin-related. But then I bring my fingers to my swollen lips and smile. I can practically still taste him on my tongue and feel his mouth on my body. That felt so much better than any fight.

Chapter
TWENTY-FOUR

Gavin

I WAKE UP WITH THE SUN IN MY EYES AND MY PHONE RESTING on my chest. I have one of those moments where I can't remember where I am or how I got here. Memories slowly filter in of talking to Violet until… well, shit, I don't even know.

I pick up my phone, smiling when I see we're still connected. We fell asleep talking on the phone.

I sit up and look out the window. The only reason I know she's still in bed is the dark hair peeking out of the pile of pillows and white comforter.

My phone is dangerously close to dying. I screenshot the time-stamp of our call, shaking my head as I do. Six hours? Damn. I hang up and tap out a text to Violet, telling her good morning and sending her the photo of our epic all-night conversation. I plug in my phone and then head for the shower.

I need to get in a workout and check in with the trainer about an old wrist injury that's been flaring up, then we have film review, practice, and I need to do some homework.

We leave Thursday for our next game and, fingers crossed, won't be seeing a lot of time in Valley until the tournament is over.

Noah, Tommy, and Jenkins are already downstairs in the kitchen. Tommy sits at a stool with his head resting on the counter. I'd forgotten how drunk he was last night.

"Morning, buddy." I clap him on the shoulder.

"Ughh." He lifts his head an inch.

Jenkins tosses me a muffin.

"Ooooh. These fresh out of the oven?"

"Taylor made them this morning before she left."

His girlfriend is going to culinary school in town, and she's the only reason we eat anything that doesn't come out of a paper bag.

"I'm heading to the gym," Jenkins says.

"See you in a bit." I move to the pantry to grab the protein powder.

"Is Violet upstairs?" Noah asks, leaning against the counter.

"No, she went home last night."

Tommy's head snaps up and he rubs the spot between his eyes with his thumb. "Violet was here?"

Noah and I exchange a look before I say, "Yeah, man. You talked to her."

"I did six shots of Patron the second we got back last night. I don't remember a lot after that." He slides off the stool and walks over to the faucet. Instead of grabbing a glass, he places his mouth under the stream of water.

"Good thing you aren't practicing today," Noah says as we watch Tommy gulp down water straight from the tap.

He stands tall and wipes his mouth with the back of his hand. "If I were practicing, I wouldn't have done any shots last night."

I quirk a brow.

"Okay, fine," he relents. "But I definitely would have done less."

After washing down the muffin with a protein drink, Noah

and I head across the street to the fieldhouse. We get in a quick lower body workout, then I head to Will, one of our trainers, to have my wrist checked. I sprained it at the beginning of the season during a game when I got knocked to the floor during a shot and awkwardly landed on it. It's basically healed, but I still have to check in once or twice a week to do the physical therapy exercises and have the trainer examine it.

I dress for practice and plop down in the lounge area where Vi and I hung out just a week ago. Smiling, I turn on the TV. I love this time of year. My life is always ball, but for one glorious month of the year, the entire world seems to share my obsession.

There's report after report covering matchups and tournament predictions. My smile doesn't falter until my father's face pops up on the screen.

The news reporter grins as he says, "Is Anthony Leonard up to the same old tricks?"

My stomach is in knots as he continues.

"Only six months after his divorce was finalized amidst rumors of numerous affairs during his twenty-year marriage, Anthony Leonard, the five-time All-Star finds himself in another cheating scandal. His girlfriend of two months, Rylie, blasted her now-ex on Twitter. The former model and brand ambassador posted a picture of herself standing next to a dumpster with the caption, *Just dumped two-hundred pounds of garbage. Once a cheater, always a cheater.*" The man winces. "Ouch."

My fingers clench around the remote. I don't know how to make sense of the disappointment that I feel. Why the hell do I care if he cheated on some woman I've never met?

Instead of mulling over that bullshit, I head out to the floor to shoot around. Jenkins, Noah, and a few other guys are already here. Even Tommy is dressed and rebounding balls.

Coach Reynolds sits on the sideline with an iPad in his lap.

"Hey, Coach." I grab a ball from the rack and fall into the

chair next to him. I love the way the worn leather feels against my palm. It grounds me. It's my lifeline when everything else sucks.

He glances at my taped wrist. "Giving you any trouble?"

"Nah. Will wants me to keep it taped as a precaution."

"Good call. You don't want to go out on a stupid injury. Trust me."

I nod my agreement. Coach Reynolds' college basketball career ended in the final months of his senior year due to an injury. I can't imagine a worse way to go out.

"What do you have planned for us today?" I glance at the screen of the tablet in his hand. He's watching film of our last game.

"Just a light scrimmage. I imagine you boys partied pretty hard last night." His mouth curves as he waits for me to deny it.

I give him a rueful smile.

"I don't need anyone puking on the court today. We'll run through our inbound plays, and a few defensive drills. Defense is going to be key in our next matchup."

I chuckle. "I think the only one in danger of puking today is Tommy."

Standing, I dribble the ball from hand to hand. Coach follows.

"I got a call last night from a network reporter that's covering the games next weekend."

My body flips into high alert, but I answer calmly, "Oh yeah?"

"They want to do a father and son interview with you and your dad."

I blink several times at Coach, trying to make sense of his words. But that means… "He's going to be there?"

Coach shrugs.

I assumed my dad would be at the championship, but that's still weeks away.

I shake my head. "I just want to focus on basketball this weekend."

"You're sure? I can set my own demands if the time or place makes a difference."

"It doesn't."

Coach stops in front of me, blocking my path to the basket. "This is a good opportunity for people to see you. You are a damn good player. I hope like hell we continue on this year, but all any player can plan for is the next game. Between the game and a spotlight interview just before, you're going to have their undivided attention. Trust me, that is a rare thing. Some extremely talented players go their whole career without the right people seeing them at the right time. This is your moment."

It isn't my moment. Anthony is in damage control, once again trying to look like the perfect father. Fuck that. This is his moment and I want no part of it.

"I'm not entering the draft."

"I know your plans don't include the NBA right now, but—"

"Not ever. If they want to interview someone, pick one of the seniors. Noah or Maxwell."

He's quiet for a beat, giving me a chance to change my mind. I won't.

"Okay. I'll let them know."

I walk over to the guys. Noah shoots a basket and then glances at me. His stare lingers when he sees my face. I must look as pissed off as I feel.

"What happened to you? When I left you at the training room, you still had a Violet-induced perma-grin."

"Nothing." The ball leaves my fingertips and sails toward the basket, hitting the rim and going right.

Noah jogs to grab it and holds my ball hostage until I speak.

"Some reporter wants to do an interview with me and my dad before the next game."

"Makes sense."

I scowl.

"Okay, I know you have beef with your dad, but you have to see that you're the most interesting story at the tournament this year. Between your dad being an NBA player and your mom a badass coach, also at the tournament, plus your handsome mug and mediocre talent."

I flip him off, and he chuckles.

"Hell, any reporter that isn't asking for a piece of that story should be fired."

"I can't sit next to him with a camera aimed at my face and pretend like we're some father/son dynamic duo. It's bullshit."

"What are you going to do?"

"Nothing. I told Coach I didn't want to do it."

I'm thankful when Noah drops it, and we silently shoot around, giving my brain the time it needs to shut out everything but basketball.

When it's time for practice, Coach walks out onto the middle of the court and blows the whistle. He tells us to take a seat, and we comply, spreading out around him on the wooden floor.

"All right, boys." He holds a whiteboard at his hip. "I hope you all had fun last night."

A few people look to Tommy.

Coach grins. "I get it. I do, but starting now, until our season is over, I need your focus here." He points to the court.

We all nod.

"Okay, then. Let's get back to work."

Practice is light, as Coach promised, and the time focusing only on ball helps me forget about my dad, which significantly improves my mood.

Noah and I head back home together, and he looks over at Violet's house. "She really didn't stay over last night?"

I shake my head. "Nah."

"How'd you blow that? The last I saw her, she was soaking wet and heading up to your room to change." He waggles his brows.

I bark a laugh. "I love how you say that like a girl falling into the pool after a confrontation with the last person I slept with is an all-star setup for hooking up."

"Was she pissed about Sariah?"

"I think she was just not expecting to be confronted with all of it last night. I know I wasn't." In hindsight, it was dumb of us to think we could hang out at the biggest party of the year and not run into Sariah or Bailey, but I really hadn't given either of them a thought. I was just excited about hanging out with her.

"Where'd you leave things?"

"I'm not sure, actually."

We reach the front door, and he holds it open for me, cocking a brow in question. "Were you wasted?"

"No. We, uh, fell asleep talking on the phone."

He stares at me a beat and then chuckles under his breath. "That's some real romantic shit, Leonard."

"What about you? I thought you were going to ask out Jane."

"I tried." He rubs at the back of his neck. "I don't think she's interested."

"Did you say the words, 'will you go out with me?'"

"She knew what I was trying to ask."

"If you say so."

"I do. Besides, there is no time for anything but homework and ball right now."

"That's true."

Noah heads toward the kitchen and I start for the stairs.

"Hey," he calls, "do you want to go to The Hideout or something later?"

"Can't. I have plans."

I catch just a glimpse of his smile before I jog out of view. In my room, I laugh at the scene in front of me: my bed pushed in front of the window. Out of habit, I glance over at Violet's window, but I don't see her. My phone is still plugged in on my nightstand, and when I check it, I have a dozen texts. My stomach clenches at a new one from my dad, but the unsettling feeling only lasts for a second because at the very top is one from the girl next door.

Chapter
TWENTY-FIVE

Violet

"YOU KNOW, WHEN YOU SAID YOU WANTED TO TAKE me on a date, I did not imagine it would include wearing a bikini."

"All the best dates require swimwear." Gavin treads water in front of me, his wet hair shining under the twinkle lights. The sun has set, and the air has cooled off. I came over as soon as he got back from practice, and he had a whole poolside party thing happening for the two of us, complete with a cooler filled with water, soda, and seltzer, and music pumping through the outdoor speakers.

It's such a great outdoor space. When it's crammed with people, it's hard to really appreciate it, but we've played washers in the yard (I won) and volleyball in the pool (we didn't keep score because he was killing me) and floated on big inflatable animal rafts (Gavin somehow still looks hot sitting on top of a unicorn).

Sometime ago, we moved to the deep end, keeping everything but our heads below the surface to keep warm. I skim my hand across the water and then send a splash in his direction. Gavin closes his eyes for a second, his smile already pulling up both corners of his lips. Water drops slide down his chiseled jaw and I want to reach out and capture them.

"I guess we'll have to go out again until I figure out something that feels like a real date to you," he says as his hand under the water finds the curve of my hip. His fingertips slip along my skin, as he draws me closer.

It's been the best date, but I don't tell him that. Some part of me still needs to keep the full weight of my feelings for him to myself. Ninety-nine percent of the time it feels so easy being with him and I want to let down my guard completely, but then I have these moments of panic that I'm about to willingly fling myself off the ledge of a cliff and he won't be there to catch me.

"Are you hungry?" His fingers stop exploring but stay glued to my side.

"A little," I admit.

We get out of the pool and Gavin grabs our towels and tosses me one. I wrap the fluffy blue material around my body and squeeze some of the water from my hair.

Gavin runs his towel over his head and then tosses it on a lounge chair. His body is insane. Red trunks sit low on his trim hips and mold to his thighs. He has a smattering of dark hair on his chest that trails down his stomach.

"I'll be right back. I'm going to put the pizza in the oven," he says. My gaze is still on his abs, which freaking glisten, when he looks at me, so I quickly look to the ground.

"Okay."

I feel his smile more than I see it before he turns and heads inside. Walking back over to the pool, I sit on the edge and dangle my feet. I'm staring over at my house across the fence when he comes back out and takes a seat next to me.

"Twenty-five minutes."

"Hmm?" I ask, giving him my attention.

"The pizza will be ready in twenty-five minutes." He reaches over and wipes his thumb under my left eye.

"Do I look like a raccoon?"

"A little, but you're a very cute raccoon. Nothing like those scary ones up in the mountains that barge in on unsuspecting girls who leave the tent open."

Heat seeps into my cheeks and I bring both hands up to scrub away any mascara.

"It could have been a bear or a mountain lion."

"Good thing I was there." The playful taunt in his voice does funny things to my heart rate.

"Yo," Jenkins calls from the back door, "can we come out of our rooms yet, Dad?"

"Can't you see I'm still on a date?" Gavin takes my hand and holds them up.

"Yeah, yeah. We'll behave." Jenkins pushes the door farther open, and he steps out, followed by Noah and Tommy.

Gavin drops our hands but doesn't let go.

"You banned them from coming outside?" I ask, smiling as I think about how that conversation must have gone.

"I wanted a few hours with you to myself." He squeezes my fingers. I really like how gently he does it, and the way my body reacts to such a simple touch. "And I didn't want it to turn into a scene like last night."

"You mean a scene like running into every girl you've hooked up with in the past year?"

He blanches.

"I'm kidding."

The guys, except Tommy, get in the pool. They stay at the other end, giving us a little space and privacy.

I slide my hand free, and then stand and let the towel fall to my feet.

Gavin's gaze lifts slowly, and when his eyes meet mine, they're filled with warmth. I've never had body issues. Sure, I wish my butt was toner and my stomach flatter, but I've accepted it the same way you accept that some people are smarter or have better hair. I am who I am, and I've worked hard to like that person.

But the way he looks at me sparks a confidence inside me that makes me feel like the most beautiful person on the planet. I wonder if that's how he makes all the girls he hooks up with feel.

I jump in the water and let my body descend toward the bottom of the pool, enjoying the way I feel so weightless and free. When I come back up, Gavin is still sitting and watching me.

"Are you coming in?" I ask, swimming to the side of the pool and wading in front of him.

"Maybe." He doesn't move.

I float on my back and kick water in his direction, splashing him until he moves.

He's quick. So quick that he's diving in before I realize it and pulling me under the water; I fight against him even as I smile.

We come up together, my arms wrapped around his neck.

"You two want to play volleyball?" Noah asks from the other end of the pool.

Gavin looks to me.

"Which one is better, Noah or Jenkins?" I keep my voice low as I speak.

"Noah, why?"

"No reason." I push off his shoulders, give him a haughty look, and swim away from him. "I'm on Noah's team."

Gavin and I sit at stools in his kitchen, still in our bathing suits, as we devour an entire pizza. His thigh rests against mine and we smile happily at each other, mouths full.

Tommy comes in and goes to the fridge, grinning at us like he's in on some private joke.

"You two are cute."

"Fuck off," Gavin says with a smile and shakes his head.

"I'm serious. You're giving pops and his new girlfriend a run for their money."

I swear the temperature around Gavin drops ten degrees.

"What did you say?"

"Your dad and that soap star. I can't remember her name, but she is smoking hot."

"Right." A muscle in his jaw ticks.

"Shit," Tommy says, "I forgot things were weird between you two. I didn't mean to—"

"It's cool," Gavin says in a tone that isn't all that convincing.

Tommy tips his chin. "Are you guys coming back outside?"

Gavin seems lost in his thoughts and doesn't answer. I shrug and Tommy slips back outside with an apologetic grimace.

When he's gone, Gavin stands and takes his plate to the sink. I can feel the shift in him, but I don't completely understand it.

I bring around my plate and he takes it with a smile that reminds me so much of the fake one his dad flashes, and it makes my insides hurt.

"Are you okay?"

"Yeah." To his credit, the question seems to bring him back a little from wherever he went. "What do you want to do next?"

"Your date, Leonard."

A small laugh fills the space between us. "Movie?"

"Sure, but I'm going to change first."

"Same."

We head up to his room. I changed in the bathroom when I came over, but I'm feeling giddy and a little daring. Gavin is getting dry clothes from his dresser, not paying me any attention when I pull the string from my bikini top and bring the wet material up over my head.

Adrenaline courses through me at the possibility of being caught. I put on my purple bra. It's warm against my cold, pebbled nipples.

Gavin turns, like he's going to say something, and then stills. I pull on my tank top next and then hook my fingers into the bikini bottoms. He tracks every movement, and then, as if he's just realized what he's doing, spins and mutters, "Sorry. I think I went into a trance there for a second."

"It's fine," I say, quickly. "Nothing you haven't seen before."

One side of his mouth quirks up. "And want to see again."

We change, both of us stealing glances, but not outright gawking.

When we're both dressed, he asks, "How do you feel about *Rocky?*"

"The movie?"

"Yes, and before you answer, I feel like I should warn you that this question is a deal breaker."

I bite back a laugh. "I've never seen it."

"What?" His hair is still a little wet and messy, and he looks so boyish that I can't help but smile at him. "I am about to blow your mind."

I sit in front of the TV while Gavin brings out blankets and then gets some snacks and drinks.

Finally, he takes the seat next to me. "Ready?"

He hits play and I curl up in my chair with one of the blankets. Gavin reaches over and rests a hand on my thigh, without taking his eyes off the screen. The lights in the room are off, but the giant TV gives me enough glow to see his reaction when the opening scene starts.

It's true that I've never watched *Rocky*, but I've seen enough clips in my lifetime that I know the basic premise. I'm glad I'm seeing it for the first time with him. He squeezes my leg every time he gets excited over a scene, and during the training montage, he bobs his head to "Eye of the Tiger."

By the end of the movie, our legs are tangled underneath the same blanket, and I've moved so that I'm leaning back against his chest, the smell of popcorn and sunscreen wrapping around us in a happy cocoon.

"What did you think?" he asks as he navigates away from the movie to regular TV. I'm not the least bit surprised when he leaves it on ESPN. Sportscasters sit around a U-shaped desk talking sporty-things. I'm too busy trying to keep a straight face as I say, "Eh. I guess it was okay."

He doesn't speak for several moments, and I can't hold it in for one more second. The laughter bursts out of me, and Gavin mutters, "Oh, that's it."

Both of his muscular arms come around my waist to hold me in place, and he tickles me until the only sounds coming out of me are gasps for air.

"Kidding. I was kidding. I liked it."

"Liked?" His fingers dance along my ribs.

"Loved." My body floats with happiness. "I meant to say loved."

Gavin's assault stops, but when I turn, his gaze is on the TV instead of me.

"What—" I start as I look from him to the monster screen, but I have my answer when Anthony Leonard's face fills half the screen.

"Thanks for having me," Gavin's dad says with that practiced smile.

While the reporter asks him a question, I scoot back in my seat. Gavin's jaw works back and forth while his dad talks basketball and gives predictions on some games—the NBA playoffs, I think.

Gavin watches in silence. I don't hear any of it, really, because blood pounds in my ears as Gavin becomes a pillar of anger next to me. When the interview's over, he picks up the remote and mutes the TV. He blinks and looks over at me like he's just remembering I'm here.

"I'm sorry."

"It's okay." I'm not even sure why he's apologizing. I doubt he knows either. "Why were you so upset earlier when Tommy mentioned your dad and his new girlfriend?"

He doesn't answer immediately, and I worry that I've just turned this date from awkward to tragic.

"You don't have to answer. It's none of my business."

"I used to think there was a limit to how much disappointment I could harbor when it came to my dad. I thought that I'd get to a point where it didn't feel like a punch to the gut every time he fucked up."

I don't know what to say, so I slide my hand into his. He laces our fingers together.

"We don't need to talk about this. I'm good. It's been a long day, and that's the second time I've seen his apology tour. Do you want to watch *Rocky II*? I promise it's as good as the first." A little of the happy glint returns to his eyes. Honestly, I'd rather talk about his dad. Not because I want to force him into telling me, but because I don't want to pretend everything is great, when I can tell it isn't.

"I should probably get home. I have a biology quiz tomorrow and I want to read through my notes one more time."

"Okay." He stands and pulls me to my feet with our joined hands. "I still owe you a real date."

"Promises, promises," I say with a taunt, and step into his body. Warmth seeps off him. "I'm sorry about your dad. If you want to talk about it or whatever, I'm here."

Instead of taking me up on that, he kisses me.

Chapter
TWENTY-SIX

Violet

I'M IN THE KITCHEN THE NEXT NIGHT, GRABBING ANOTHER Diet Dr. Pepper when Gavin calls.

"Don't you know it's rude to call without texting first with a heads-up?" I answer with a smile. A smile that's been on my face pretty much nonstop for the past two days.

I can hear the smile reciprocated in his voice. "My hands are full. Come answer your door."

"My door?" I turn, so I can look through the kitchen and living room to the front door of the house, and even though I can't see through the solid wood door, my heart does a funny little skip in my chest anyway.

Taking the can of soda with me, I cross through the living room to the front door. Jordan and Daisy are on one end of the couch, Dahlia on the other, and Jane is stretched out in the armchair. They're all focused on the TV since we're on our sixth hour of binge-watching *Euphoria*.

No one looks up as I go to the door and pull it open.

Gavin stands on the other side. He has a case of hard seltzer under one arm, a bottle of wine in his hand, and in the other, a box wrapped in colorful, striped paper, where his phone is resting.

"Did we make plans?" I run a hand over my messy ponytail. It's been a chill evening, sitting around with the roommates and watching TV since we all got home from classes. Gavin texted earlier and said the team had mandatory study hour after practice, so I hadn't expected to hear from him again, or see him standing at my front door.

"No, but I come bearing gifts."

I step back and let him in. Someone must have paused the TV because all eyes are on us as I close the door.

"Leonard!" Jordan calls from his spot.

"Hey." Gavin looks around the room. "Sorry to interrupt."

"Is that for us?" Jane asks, pointing to the seltzer.

"Yeah." He angles his body. "We had a bunch of booze left over from the last party and we're sober for the foreseeable future. Thought you might put it to better use than us."

She gets up and takes the alcohol from him. "Thank god. I need a drink. This show is tense. Is this what high school was like for you guys?"

"Definitely not," Dahlia says.

"It's not even my birthday." Jordan juts his chin toward the rectangle package in Gavin's hands.

"Not for you." Gavin shifts the package from one hand to the other and then extends it to me.

"What is this for?"

"Insurance, so you'd open the door."

"Oh, uh, thank you." I run my fingers slowly over the paper.

"What is it?" Jane yells from the kitchen.

Everyone is looking at me, waiting.

I tuck it under my arm. "Who else wants a drink?"

It's quiet for a beat, but then Daisy takes pity and rescues me. "I'll take one."

"Me too." Jordan nods his head.

I smile. "Dahlia?"

"Sure. I think I need alcohol to get through this show too."

I disappear into the kitchen, set the present on the counter, and swap my soda for a seltzer.

Jane smirks as I take a drink.

"Don't say anything," I say.

I stare at the present. Am I dying to know what's inside? Yes. Do I want to open it in front of everyone? Definitely not.

"He knows how to make an entrance. I'll give him that." She hands me two more seltzers and grabs two for herself, before taking them into the living room.

Gavin is sitting on the couch between Daisy and Dahlia. The latter stands. "Let's put on some music or something and finish the show tomorrow."

With wide eyes, she looks to me, indicating I can take her seat. I hand her a can on my way to sit next to Gavin.

"Are you sure you don't want one?" I ask him.

"No thanks."

Jordan pulls Daisy closer to him and peers around her to talk to Gavin. "When do you guys leave for the next game?"

Gavin shifts his big frame and puts one arm around the back of the couch behind me. It's all so easy and casual, but my heart hammers in my chest anyway. We've blown past taking it slow, at least emotionally. I like him. I like him so much.

"Thursday night. Game on Friday." Gavin bobs his head with excited anticipation as he speaks.

"I'm jealous," Jordan says. "I already miss it."

Jane grabs her phone and puts on a playlist that instantly changes the atmosphere to a more casual and fun vibe.

While Gavin chats with Jordan, Jane pulls me into

conversation. I couldn't even tell you what we talk about. Hanging out with Gavin, just the two of us, or even at a party, is one thing, but here in my house, in my living room with my friends is...well, not strange exactly, but it's definitely different.

"How far did you guys get in *Euphoria?*" Gavin asks when he and Jordan are done talking sports. "Did you see the part where—"

"Don't spoil it," Dahlia blurts out, and then her cheeks turn pink. "We're only on episode six."

Gavin chuckles. "Sorry. That show had me in a chokehold for two days. I don't mind re-watching it if you guys stopped it on my account."

"I'm maxed out on drama," Jane says.

Dahlia and Daisy nod their agreement.

Jane pops up from her seat. "We should play some cards or something."

We settle on Monopoly and the six of us sit around the coffee table.

After all the properties are purchased, our collective interest in the game wanes and we make a drinking game out of it. Every time someone rolls a double or goes to jail or lands on free parking, or even passes go, they drink. And if you land on someone's property, they get to decide on how much you drink. Everyone except Gavin, since he's sober.

His thigh is pressed against mine and he keeps one arm behind me, his fingers absently playing with the ends of my hair. I think I could die a happy death while Gavin plays with my hair. It's just about the sexiest thing ever.

"I give up," Daisy says when she lands on Park Place and Jane makes her take five drinks.

"Same." Dahlia pushes away from the table. "I have an early practice tomorrow and I do not want to throw up on the course."

One by one, my friends quit the game.

"Leonard's crushing us all anyway," Jordan says.

Gavin sinks back into the couch with a proud smile. "It pays to be sober sometimes."

"Do you want me to put Euphoria back on?" I suggest.

"No. Let's try on dresses!" Jane is already standing and going to the coat closet, where we've started keeping our favorites.

Before I can protest, she and Dahlia are pulling out the gowns.

I don't remember how it started, but since the four of us moved in together at the beginning of the school year, we often end the night by playing dress up. We put them on while we sit around and talk about boys or rewatch *Pride and Prejudice* for the hundredth time, or more frequently, talk about boys while rewatching *Pride and Prejudice*.

The first time we did it, it was one or two dresses that we took turns wearing, but since then it's turned into a whole thing. I love making dresses for my friends, seeing them light up in their favorite color or style. Now we need an entire closet to store my creations.

Each of us has our favorite, the dress that gives us that magical feeling, but occasionally we mix it up.

"Do you want the black or white one tonight?" Jane asks, holding up both.

"I'm not sure," I say. "I'll grab it when I'm ready."

"Okay." She drapes both over the arm of a chair.

Jane pulls on an emerald sleeveless dress over her clothes. Dahlia and Daisy disappear into the bathroom and come back in theirs—a light pink princess dress that is so not Dahlia's usual style, but that is stunning with her bright blue eyes. Dresses aren't usually her thing, but she humors us by joining in on the fun. Daisy is in a sexy, red dress that is bold and racy in all the ways she is on the inside, despite her shy exterior.

"You made all these?" Gavin asks as the girls stand in our living room. Jane turned the music back on and they're dancing, twirling and moving in their gowns.

"You sound so surprised."

One side of his mouth pulls up. "Nah, I mean I know this is what you do, but this is pretty awesome. Which one is your favorite?"

"I can't answer that. It's like choosing between my favorite copy of *Persuasion*."

"The one with the pink cover."

I look at him, unblinking. That is my favorite one, but how does he know that?

"It's always on top of the stack, and it's the one you've tried to read over and over."

I glance at the dresses on the arm of the chair. "The white one."

"Because?"

"I can't explain it. It's the feeling I get when I wear it."

"Can I see?"

"You want me to put it on?"

"Mhmm."

"What are you going to do for me?"

He full-on grins. "A favor for a favor, huh?"

I nod, pulse racing.

He thinks for a second. "I'll read to you later."

A thrill shoots through me. I try to play it cool, like I'm not dying for that to happen, but Gavin's voice is just…sigh.

"Hmm. I'm not sure."

He leans in and frames my face with gentle fingers. His lips ghost over mine, and he recites a few lines from the book. *For the love of Captain Wentworth.*

"Deal," I whisper quickly.

His deep chuckle vibrates against my lips, and then he presses a harder kiss to them. When we pull apart, everyone is watching us. It isn't a secret that Gavin and I have been making out, but I guess it's the first time they've witnessed it.

"Someone hand me the white dress," I say, breaking the silence and standing.

Later, after everyone has abandoned us to go to bed, Gavin and I head up to my room.

"Can I take this off now?" I ask, running a hand along the waist of my dress.

"Oh, please do." His brows lift.

I sit on my bed and toss a pillow at him.

He catches it and comes to sit in front of me. Setting the pillow down, he hands me the present. "You didn't open it."

I take it in my lap. "I didn't want to have an audience, in case it was something weird."

He barks a laugh. "Like what?"

"I don't know." Heat hits my cheeks.

"Open it."

I tear away the paper and my breath catches. When I look up, his lips curve up in the biggest smile.

"Where did you find this?" I ask, running a hand over the cover. It's an old version of *Persuasion* with a cover I've never seen before.

"I can't give away all my secrets."

I open it and flip through the pages. It smells old and musty and absolutely divine. "Thank you. I love it."

"You're welcome." He takes it from me and sets it on top of the other copies. "I wanted to thank you for last night. I didn't mean to get all weird about my dad."

"You were fine. I told you, you can talk to me."

"Right now, I can think of a lot better things to do than talk." His mouth drops to my collarbone and he places a gentle kiss.

"I thought you were going to read to me?"

"I will, but first I need to kiss you." He pulls me onto his lap. "You were right about the dress. It gives me a feeling too."

I laugh as I wrap my arms around his neck. "I don't think it's the same feeling."

He hooks his arms around my waist. "Go out with me tomorrow night."

"I've spent the last three nights with you."

"Yeah, but I still owe you a real date. Dinner, conversation, more kissing..." He brushes his lips along my neck and skims his hands over my back. I inch farther onto his lap until I can feel him hard below me.

He groans quietly. "Is that a yes?"

"It's not a no." I place my hands on his shoulders.

Lifting his head, he chuckles. "Has anyone ever told you that you're very beautiful and sometimes very frustrating?"

"Only you."

He takes my mouth. All the tenderness is gone. We struggle to get closer, to kiss deeper.

"How do I get you out of this thing?" He pulls the tiny straps down over my shoulders and leaves kisses across the top of my cleavage.

I reach around and unzip it for him. The white fabric falls around my waist. I ditched my bra when I changed earlier.

"Fuck, you're beautiful."

His words are sweet, but it's the look in his eyes that makes me bolder. I lunge for him, kissing him and tugging his T-shirt up over his head. We scramble to get each other naked, only breaking the kiss when absolutely necessary.

I slide his boxers down and his dick springs free. His chest rises and falls quickly with his breathing. I wrap a tentative hand around him.

"Oh, fuck, Vi," he says gruffly. His head falls back, and his Adam's apple bobs with a swallow. He's the hottest thing I've ever seen.

He lets me explore him a few seconds longer, and then he stands and puts distance between us. "Woah, woah. Wait."

"What's wrong?"

"You wanted to take it slow, and I just about ripped that dress off you, and now you're looking at me like..." He waggles a finger. "Like that."

A laugh bubbles up in my chest. "I'm okay. Promise." I reach for him, and he takes another step back.

When my gaze drops to his dick, he covers it with both hands. "I'm keeping you from doing something you might regret later."

"I promise you, I'm not going to regret this. Just no sex, remember?"

"Toss me my boxers."

"Are you serious?"

He doesn't move, so I relent and toss them at his face. Gavin steps into his underwear and then puts his hands on his hip. Only, his dick is still hard and tenting his boxers, so it's comical.

"You're a real killjoy, Leonard."

"Plenty of time for that, baby."

My heart flutters at the endearment.

His stare follows me as I walk naked from the bed to the closet.

I put on my pajamas and come back out. Gavin's pulled on his jeans but left them unbuttoned. He has my favorite *Persuasion* in one hand and he's leaning against the headboard of my bed. I retract all my earlier statements: Gavin like this is the hottest thing I've ever seen.

Chapter
TWENTY-SEVEN

Gavin

"I'M SO SORRY. I LOST TRACK OF TIME AT THE DESIGN lab. Give me ten minutes?" Violet pleads when she opens the door for me the next night. Her hair is in a high ponytail and she's wearing a baggy T-shirt that hides all but a sliver of the jean shorts underneath.

I'm picking her up and taking her out on a real date that requires no swimwear (though let's be honest, swimwear makes any date better).

"You look great."

"I'm a mess. Ten minutes top. I'll be quick. Daisy and Jordan are in the kitchen." With that, she races up the stairs.

Slowly, I walk through the living room toward the kitchen at the back of the house. My buddy and Daisy have their laptops open and an array of books and papers spread out on the table.

Jordan looks up as I enter. He has a pencil in his hand and slides it behind one ear. "Hey. What are you doing here?"

"He and Violet are going out on a date," Daisy answers for me. She gives me a look that speaks volumes of her distrust.

"Oh yeah?" Jordan's lips twist into a smirk. "Where are you taking her?"

"There's an art and food festival downtown."

"Niiice." He bobs his head with approval, and then kicks the leg of a chair to push it out for me. "Might as well sit."

"She said she'd be quick." I take a seat anyway.

"They always say that."

When I glance at Daisy, she's staring at me with a questioning expression.

"What?" I ask with a small laugh. "Should I have picked something else for the date?"

"No, I'm sure she'll love that."

"But?"

"What are your intentions with Violet?"

"My intentions?" I squeak out.

"You heard me."

Jordan starts to laugh, and then covers it with a cough and quickly looks at the table.

"I like her a lot."

"And did you like her a lot the last time?"

I swallow. Damn. Is it hot in here? Daisy is shy, and usually when she talks, her voice is unassuming and quiet, but right now, she's downright scary as she busts my balls.

"I never stopped liking her, but I understand what you're getting at. The last thing I want is to screw this up again."

"You really hurt her. I know she plays it off like nothing gets to her, but deep down, Vi is sensitive and idealistic. She deserves someone who won't trample on her romantic heart."

Words don't feel like enough, since it's my actions that have made me untrustworthy, so I nod.

183

"This is so cool. How did you know I love street festivals?" Vi beams at me when I park in a lot near the art and food fair lining the downtown street.

"Lucky guess."

We start at one end and slowly work our way to the other. Vi stops at nearly every single booth. She chats with the artists and admires their creations. Even when I can tell the art isn't for her, she finds something to appreciate in the finished product.

I appreciate the food. The smell of grease and sugar wafts around us, and I indulge by grabbing us pretzels and then corn dogs, tamales, and finally, a funnel cake.

I hold out the plate to offer her the final bite.

"No way. I'm so full." She holds a hand to her stomach. The wind blows her hair around her face. Not trying to contain it, Violet tips her head back and looks up at the sky. "This was the best night."

"It's not over yet."

We've gone up and down the street twice now, but I lead her to a small booth, where a man is drawing caricatures. I pay him, and he motions for us to sit in the chairs in front of his easel.

She pulls on the hem of her black dress—another one she made.

"How'd you get into fashion design?"

"Well…" She smiles as she begins to speak. "There were a lot of small indicators as I was growing up, I guess. I liked clothes but hated if someone had the same outfit as me. That led to me customizing my own stuff. My mom used to get so mad. I'd draw designs on my jeans and cut my shirts. Eventually, she got me a sewing machine and let me enroll in some local classes." She shrugs. "I love it. It's fun, but also really hard and frustrating."

"I get that. There's a certain satisfaction in doing difficult things."

Excitement lights up her brown eyes. "Right? Every time I get to that point in a design, I wonder why I do it, and then I finish and it's the best feeling."

I bump her knee with mine. "You're really good at it."

She tries to wave the compliment off.

"I'm serious, Vi. You're incredible. I don't know a lot about fashion, and even less about what goes into it, but you're really great at it, and it makes people happy. I could see it in your friends when they put on those dresses last night."

"Thank you."

The artist finishes and hands the paper to Violet.

"Let me see." I lean closer, and she angles it to give me a better view.

Violet looks gorgeous, even like this, but I laugh when I see myself. Caricature me is looking over at her and there are actual hearts in my eyes.

"That seems scarily accurate," I say as we stand. I thank the guy and we start for my SUV.

When we're almost there, Vi stops in front of me. "Thank you. This was perfect."

"You're welcome."

Her hair blows in her face again, and I brush it away and lean in to kiss her.

"Want to sleep over? Strictly sleep. I just don't want this night to end."

She nods as she says, "Me neither."

Chapter
TWENTY-EIGHT

Violet

"WHAT ARE YOU GOING TO WEAR?" JANE ASKS.
She and Dahlia are sitting on my bed while I stand in front of the mirror on the back of my closet door, combing out my wet hair. I took the world's fastest shower after Gavin dropped me off after our date and changed into more comfortable clothes.

"I don't know." I look down at my cut-off shorts. "This?"

Neither of them says anything.

"We aren't going back out. I'm just going over there to sleep." I pull on the hem of the frayed jean material. "Is this not okay?"

"You look great. You always look great," Dahlia says.

I look to Jane for confirmation.

"I mean, yeah, you look hot, but for a sleepover? How about a sexy slip or a bralette with some tiny cotton shorts?"

"You want me to walk over to The White House in a bra and booty shorts?"

"Oooh. Oooh." She bounces and waves her hands around. "Do you have one of his jerseys or a T-shirt with his name on the back?"

"No."

"Oh well." She shrugs and sits back down. "It was just an idea."

I go to the bed and sit between them, then fall onto my back. "Why am I so nervous?!"

"You are going to be fine." Dahlia shakes my leg. "He's crazy about you. We could all see it when he was here the other night. Couldn't we?"

Jane nods. "Yeah. It's true. I'd still go for sexier loungewear, though."

I'm more nervous now than I was all night. Twenty minutes later, I walk to The White House. Gavin meets me at the door.

"Hey, you made it." He steps back to let me in while running a hand through his wet hair.

Sweatpants hang low on his hips and the white T-shirt clings to his damp body.

"Vi?"

"Yeah? What?"

He chuckles. "Are you coming in?"

I glance down at my outfit. I'm going to kill Jane. I ended up in the same dress I wore earlier because I couldn't figure out how to do comfy/sexy in a way that didn't feel presumptuous or overeager.

"Should I go change? I was going to wear something more casual, but then I wasn't sure. This is too much. Nobody sleeps in a dress. I'll be right back."

I turn, but his fingers wrap around my wrist to keep me from fleeing. "Get your gorgeous ass in here. You can borrow some of my clothes later."

His grip loosens and falls to my hand. He laces his fingers through mine and leads me to the theater room.

Noah and Tommy sit in the front row, kicked back while staring at the screen.

When they see us, they both lift a hand to wave.

"Hey, Violet," Noah says.

"Hi."

Gavin and I take seats in the row behind them.

"Are you guys cool with this or want me to put something else on?" Tommy asks.

"I don't care what's on the TV," Gavin says, looking at me as he reclines his chair and crosses one ankle over the other.

"See this is the problem with a dress," I say as I try to mimic him, tucking my dress tightly around my legs, so I don't accidentally flash his friends.

"I got you." Gavin lifts the arm rest between us and brings my legs over onto his lap. I'm only flashing the wall now, and maybe him, but he does a good job of keeping his eyes on the big screen at the front of the room.

We don't make it two minutes before Gavin and I start whispering and kissing instead of paying attention. To be fair, it's hard to concentrate with Gavin's fingers stroking my legs.

"We're out of here," Noah says, sometime later.

I break away from Gavin's mouth, long enough to give Noah an embarrassed smile and wave.

"See you later." Gavin angles his body closer. His chest rests on top of my thighs and his thumb traces circles around a tiny scar on my knee. "How'd you get this?"

"Roller skating with Daisy. It was late summer, just before the school year started. I think we were going into sixth grade. We only saw each other a couple of times a year usually, but that summer her parents were traveling for work and she stayed with us for two weeks. I was showing off and crashed into a guardrail. I was lucky I didn't go over and end up in the creek below."

Gavin smiles.

"Daisy always made me want to do crazy things I wouldn't normally."

"Daisy?" He lifts both brows. "Really? She is not the kind of girl I would have expected to be a bad influence on you. More like the other way around."

"She wasn't. Not exactly. She was shy and quiet, just like she is now, but I could tell she looked up to me. She thought I was brave and exciting because I was more outgoing than her. I liked that she thought that about me, because the truth was, I wasn't really that interesting or popular when I was a kid." I shrugged. "I leaned into being that person she thought I was. Eventually, it made me realize I was capable of doing big and exciting things all on my own. I just needed a little push."

"That's kind of beautiful." He presses his lips to the tiny scar. "And you have a little reminder in case you forget."

"What about you? Any interesting scar stories?"

He shakes his head and holds up his hand. There's a faint line above the knuckle of his left ring finger. "This one is from a knife."

"A knife?!"

"Yeah. Me and my buddies were doing that thing where you spread your fingers out on the table and try to quickly stab the knife between each finger. I missed."

"Boys are so weird."

He chuckles. "No doubt."

We fall quiet and I run my finger along the numbers of his tattoo. "Are you nervous about the games this weekend?"

"No, not really. I think we have a good shot at going far this year, and I want to make the most of it, in case we don't get back next year, but I feel like we've put in the work. Now it's just time to find out how we measure up."

"I heard Tommy talking about all the media and scouts that will be there. Pretty intense."

"That's all just noise to me. I'm not interested in impressing anyone."

I don't understand Gavin's relationship with basketball. I know what it means to him, how much he loves it, but as long as I've known him, he hasn't entertained the idea of continuing to play. And from what everyone says, he could get drafted *today* if he wanted. His dad certainly seems to think so, and I assume he'd know.

I'd like to say his disinterest in the NBA has something to do with his dad, but I can't quite make sense of that either, since he followed in his father's footsteps coming to Valley U, his dad's alma mater. Gavin even wears number 31. His dad was 13, and they retired it. That can't be a coincidence.

"You don't think you'll change your mind when you're closer to graduation?"

"No," he says definitively. "This is it for me."

My chest is tight with the pain that radiates off him. I don't understand it, but I can feel it.

"Come on." Gavin stands and pulls me to my feet. "I've been looking forward to having you in my bed again since you left the last time."

"Can I ask you something?"

"Of course." Gavin lies on the bed with one arm crooked behind his head.

"What happened between you and your dad?"

His brows lift.

"I'm just trying to understand you. Were you ever close with him?"

"We were in our own way. He was gone a lot when I was young. It wasn't just the games. Those guys spend hours training and practicing, even in the off-season. But we had a lot of equipment at home, too, and a court downstairs. I'd sit on the sideline and play or do homework while he was in there. I looked up to him, even if we weren't super close." Gavin turns on his side and drags a finger along my calf.

"Did you ever want to follow in his footsteps?"

"Of course. There were moments I was up in the crowd and people were screaming his name that I thought, I want that. Or the time they won the NBA championship. You should have seen it. Grown men were sobbing." He has a faraway look on his face, like he's remembering it all. Then the smile on his face falls. "I know my dad is this famous guy that people love, but he was just Dad to me. I had a few friends, guys on the team had kids about my age, and my life didn't seem any different than theirs. I guess I thought everything was as it should be."

His hand moves up and his long fingers splay out on my thigh. "When the rumors started about him cheating on my mom, I didn't want to believe it. It wouldn't have been the first time the media had run with something that wasn't true. There used to be this thing I'd read about how my dad woke up every morning and ate a dozen raw eggs. It was in all kinds of articles."

"It wasn't true?" I ask, shuddering a little at the thought of eating raw eggs.

"No. Dad said he had no idea where they'd gotten it."

We laugh a little and then Gavin falls quiet again.

"He'd been retired for years. He stayed on with the team as an ambassador, which basically meant he made special appearances in the community, but as far as I could tell, things were good between him and my mom. I was getting ready to leave for college, so admittedly, I was caught up in my own stuff and didn't give it a lot of weight. I thought it was all just more bullshit, but then women started coming forward—too many to discount."

"I'm sorry. That must have been an awful way to find out."

"Yeah." He lets out a quiet chuckle. "The worst part was, I even asked him once. The day before I left for Valley U. Not outright, but I sort of danced around it. I think I said something like, 'Must be a slow week for real news.' And he gave me some line about the importance of family and honesty. A week later, he was on TV apologizing to the world."

My heart squeezes in my chest. "You didn't know the truth until then?"

He shakes his head, without meeting my gaze. "Nope. Jenkins and I were playing Xbox with Jordan and Liam. Remember our dorm rooms were right across the hall from each other?"

I nod. "How could I forget? We did some scandalous things in that room."

"Yeah, we did." He rolls onto his back and takes me with him.

"What did you do when you found out?" I stare down at his brown eyes. They swirl with an unresolved hurt that he tries so hard to mask with anger.

"I got really, *really* drunk."

I wrap myself around his big frame the best I can. "I'm so sorry."

I hold on for a few moments longer. He kisses me, slow at first, and then with more need like he's channeling all his pain and frustration. I can feel it. Taste it. I take all of it that he gives me. He nips at my bottom lip as he pulls back.

"Do you want to go in the gym and slam basketballs against the wall really, really hard?" I ask as I catch my breath.

Low laughter rumbles in his chest. "Is that what you do when you're pissed off?"

"Oh no. I'm much more likely to angry-sew an entire dress or write a mean letter that I'll never send." I remember seeing a pen on the nightstand and I reach for it, then hold it up in front of him. "Want to write a mean letter?"

"Dear Dad, you suck. Signed, your disappointment of a son," he says without making a move for the pen.

I click it three times, take one of his hands, and glide the pen across his skin. He watches me with a smirk, not trying to see what I'm writing until I stop.

He brings his hand up and reads my words silently, then says, "I think you're pretty awesome too."

I go for his forearm next, writing, *And super hot.*

"Right back at ya, baby."

He lets me mark up his body with sweet and silly words, all the while stroking my back and tangling his fingers in my hair. I scribble, *Property of Vi*, just above the waistband of his sweatpants.

"That one is at least true." His dark stare softens. "I'm all yours, Vi."

I wriggle down and place a kiss next to my mark. The muscles tighten under my lips. When I glance up, Gavin's eyes widen.

"Vi," he rasps, "don't you dare bring that pen near my di—"

The sentence is cut off when I slide my hand under his pants and wrap my fingers around him. He lets out a strangled sound that makes my heart gallop.

I stroke him lazily a few times before pushing his sweats down. He helps me and we toss them to the floor. He's so handsome. So big.

I bring the end of the pen to my mouth and bite it gently. His gaze goes molten. "Be gentle."

Lightly, I draw a tiny heart with my initials in it on the side of his dick and then toss the pen.

His breathing is shallow, and his fingers take up residence in my hair. "I survived."

"I don't want to hurt you," I say, and bring my lips to the head of his dick. That first, light touch sets off a string of curses from him.

I keep going, covering him completely with my mouth.

"Fuck, Violet."

He praises me with more throaty noises and gentle pulls of my hair along with saying my name over and over again.

When he's close, he pulls me up to his mouth and kisses me hard.

"Come here."

"I am here."

He hums against my lips. "Turn around."

"What?"

Instead of repeating himself, he picks me up and sets me on his chest so that I'm facing the wall. I only have two seconds to wonder what he's up to before he flips up the skirt of my dress, guides my hips back, and presses his mouth, over my panties, to my center.

I'm lost in the heat of him and the sensations that zap through me. I don't even realize he has the pen, until I feel the cool tip dragging over my skin. I guess fair is fair, but he's writing on my ass and I can't see what it says.

"What did you write?" I ask.

He dives back in without answering, sucking my clit through the material and then moving my damp panties out of the way, so there's nothing between us.

"Oooh." The word is a plea as much as an understanding.

His fingers spread me open. I feel like I should be embarrassed how on display I am like this, but I'm too desperate for more, more of him and his mouth.

Leaning down, I wrap my fingers around him and take him into my mouth. I try to draw it out, tease him, but as my orgasm builds, so does the tempo in which I glide over him.

He groans against my sensitive flesh and the sensation sends me over the edge. I suck hard as he comes, loving every shudder and sound that it draws out of him.

My body is like jelly as the adrenaline starts to wear off, but my heart feels like it's just waking up. He smacks my ass playfully, and I fall onto the mattress next to him in a sweaty, exhausted heap. I curl around him, so I can see his contented grin.

"You're so beautiful." He reaches for me and runs a thumb along my bottom lip. "Lips swollen and hair messy." He smacks my ass. "*Mine*. That's what I wrote."

Chapter
TWENTY-NINE

Gavin

"**G**OOD LUCK TONIGHT," I SAY TO MY MOM WHEN SHE calls Wednesday afternoon. Her team plays tonight, trying to capture an Elite Eight spot.

"Thanks. You guys leave tomorrow?"

Lying on my bed with my feet hanging off the edge, I toss the ball up into the air over and over again. "Yeah. Tomorrow afternoon. I can't believe it's almost here already. The week has flown by."

She laughs into the phone. "I figured you were counting the seconds tick by until the game."

"We're practicing every day, reviewing film, fine-tuning things. The time hasn't been wasted."

And I've been spending every free second with Violet. If we keep winning, it'll be more than a week until we're back in Valley.

A long freaking time not to see the girl I'm falling hard for all over again.

"I talked to your dad last night."

I pause with the ball resting in both hands. "Oh yeah? Did he have anything useful to say?"

I can't imagine why my mom still talks to him. At first, I understood that she was doing it to salvage some sort of relationship between us, but I've made it clear that I'm not interested in that and still she entertains his bullshit.

"He told me that you declined the TV interview."

"You sound surprised? There's no way I'm getting on national TV and pretending we're tight for the sake of his image."

"The interview wasn't his idea. They reached out to him."

"Whatever. Either way, not happening."

"You might be angry with him, but you're just as stubborn as he is." The words hit me square in the chest and make it hard to breathe.

"I'm nothing like him."

Silence hangs between us and then she sighs. "Do you know how I got my first college coaching job?"

"No," I say as I try to think back on any prior conversations. My mom worked in pharmaceutical sales until she got pregnant with me. She stayed home for a few years and then started coaching high school. I was eight or nine when she moved up to the college level. Dad was still playing then, so I spent a lot of evenings and weekends on campus with her.

"I was at a fundraiser with your dad. He rarely asked me to go to those kinds of things. They were often in the middle of the week, and we'd have to travel. I didn't like to leave you or to take off work for it, but he kept bringing it up, so I knew this one must have been important to him."

"We showed up and it was this small event. I think they were raising money for local youth or something. Nothing like the events I'd been to with him in the past."

My pulse thrums loudly in my ears.

"Anyway, your dad knew that the athletic director would be there and that they'd just lost their women's basketball coach."

"Okay. So he introduced you and you got the job. I'm sure it worked out in a way that made him look good somehow."

"He didn't want to go to that fundraiser. He did it because he knew it would be a great opportunity for me."

I'm skeptical, but I keep my mouth shut.

"Your dad doesn't do a good job of explaining his motives, but he wants the best for you."

"What's best for me is focusing on the games and not getting distracted talking to reporters about dad's glory days."

My door opens and Noah pauses when he sees I'm on the phone. I sit up and lift a finger to indicate I just need a minute.

"Okay, but if there's even the tiniest chance you're considering playing ball after college, then this could be a—"

"I gotta go, Mom."

She makes a sound that clearly shows her irritation, but she says, "All right. I need to get ready, too."

"Good luck tonight," I say, and stand. "And, Mom?"

"Yeah."

"You don't owe him your success. Maybe he made an introduction, but the rest was all you. Someone would have swooped you up eventually."

"I love you," she says.

"Love you too. Bye."

I toss the phone on the bed. "Ready?"

Noah doesn't pry until we get onto the court. "Did something else happen with your dad?"

"No. Same old shit."

He nods. "Listen, I wanted you to hear it from me. After you passed on the interview, the reporter, Bob or whatever his name is, asked to do a sit down with me."

"That's great."

He stares back at me. "Really? You're okay with it?"

"Of course, I am. Congrats, man. That's going to be huge."

"You don't think I'm a sellout?"

"Definitely not." Noah's a great player. He's shorter than the average college or pro player, and he's battled some injuries during his time at Valley. Those things, combined with the team not making it past the second round in the tournament the past couple of years, have kept him from really getting the credit or recognition he deserves. This could be huge for him.

He lets out a breath that makes me realize how worried he was about telling me.

"Seriously, super stoked for you."

"Thanks. I hope I don't puke on camera. I'm already so nervous."

"Well, now that would be entertaining."

He flips me off, then we continue to shoot around for a few more minutes.

"Is Violet coming over tonight?"

"Yeah, I think so." I hope so.

"That's every night this week you two have hung out. Have you made things official and taken her off the market?"

"I never understood that phrase in regard to relationships."

"You're dodging." He rebounds my ball.

"I'm not dodging. She's mine."

"She said that?"

"Not with words." I smile as I think of the tiny heart she drew on my dick. The rest of the ink scrubbed off, but I left that one.

"I don't know what that means." He quirks a brow.

"We haven't had the big talk about being exclusive, but I'm not worried."

Except now that he's brought it up, I kind of am.

"Why do you want to know so bad? Are you planning on making a move?" I narrow my gaze.

"No. Never."

"Violet not good enough for you or something?"

His deep laughter echoes in the high ceiling of the fieldhouse. "You sound insane right now."

"I think it's a fair question. She's beautiful, smart, and talented. You can seriously tell me you wouldn't want to be with her?"

"I can seriously tell you that."

"Why?"

"Because, dickhead, you're in love with her and I'd never do that to a buddy." He tosses me the ball a little harder than necessary. "And I'm pretty sure she's in love with you too."

"You think?"

"I do."

"She's pretty fucking great."

"Maybe you oughta think about locking that down then." He shakes his head and laughs. "With words."

I'm still thinking about our conversation after practice. The house is packed. As instructed, the guys have stayed alcohol-free, but they've traded booze for boobs. There are so many girls in the pool, it looks like an episode of *The Bachelor*.

Tommy comes inside, pushing his shades to the top of his head. "Leonard, my man, are you coming out?"

"I don't think so."

"The only people drinking are the girls. Scout's honor."

"You were never a Scout."

One side of his mouth lifts. "They want to see us off."

I look past him, out the window, where tops are starting to come off.

"I'm good. Have fun, man."

Violet is working late at the design lab to finish up her dress for Penelope Hart, so after a shower, I grab dinner and head to campus.

My phone rings as I'm pulling into the parking lot behind the art building. As soon as I see who it is, I hit ignore. I can't deal with my dad right now.

I find the lab and poke my head in. Violet waves me over to a table in the back corner. She and Dahlia are set up on opposite sides. A bunch of other people, classmates, I assume, are at other tables. It's quiet and the mood is thick with frantic energy.

"Hungry?" I ask as I walk toward her. "I brought you guys some food. Figured it might be a long night."

"Thank you. You're a real hero. We've been in here since noon." She takes the food and sets it at an empty table, but not before stealing a fry from the open bag and groaning.

I nod my head toward the black dress on the bust. "I finally get to see the infamous design in person."

"I don't know about infamous, but that's it, yeah."

I step closer to get a better look at it. The pictures didn't do it justice. I don't know a lot about fashion, but it's the kind of thing I'd expect to see on a red carpet or the cover of a magazine. "I can't believe you made these. It blows me away every time I see something you've created."

Vi blushes. "Thank you. This is Dahlia's."

Dahlia has moved over to the food, but Violet walks me to her friend's design. It's a blue jumper with big legs and a halter top. The two are so different, but both obviously well done, and I know a lot of time and effort went into them.

"You guys are incredible. This is great, Dahlia."

"Thanks." She covers her mouth with a hand to answer while chewing.

"What time do you think you'll be done? Any chance you can come over later? Or I can take you out for second dinner."

"I don't know. We need to finalize the designs and then photograph them. Penelope's rep will be here tomorrow to decide." She blows out a breath. "I'm a wreck. Can I text you when we're done?"

"Of course. I'll get out of your hair so you can get back to it, but, uh, can I talk to you real quick first?"

"Sure." She looks wary.

I take her hand and we walk out of the classroom to the hallway.

"Is everything okay?" she asks when I lean against the wall and wrap my arms around her waist.

"Yeah." I tug her closer and kiss her. "I have a question for you."

"All right."

"Fuck it. I'm just gonna ask because I don't know how else to do this."

She looks terrified. I don't blame her.

"Do you want to be exclusive? Like, not date other people. I'm not, for the record. Dating other people that is." Heat creeps up my neck.

It takes a second for my words to hit before she smiles. Then it grows and she starts to laugh.

I should have rehearsed. I've never asked anyone to be my girlfriend. In high school I went on a few dates, but nothing serious. Then when I got to Valley... Well, I guess getting a girlfriend stopped being important when I realized people expected me to follow in my dad's footsteps in all aspects. *Like father, like son.* Was there ever a more confining expression?

The closest I ever got to wanting to be exclusive with someone was Violet, sophomore year, but we never put a label on it. I'm not sure if that made how things ended better or worse. It hurt like a bitch either way.

"I'm sorry. You just surprised me." She keeps on giggling, burying her face in my chest.

"It's okay. I should go."

"Don't you want my answer?"

"Was laughter not an answer? Because it felt like an answer."

"I drew my name all over you last night, including your dick. Of course, I don't want to date other people."

I tighten my grip, pulling her even closer to me. "Really?"

"Really. I just wasn't expecting you to ask like that. I'm not dating anyone else, and I have no plans to while we're... whatever."

"Dating, *exclusively*, not whatever." I nip at her bottom lip.

"Come over later, girlfriend. No matter how late it is. I'll be up."

"Okay. I think we'll be done in a couple of hours. Let's go out first though. I want to hold your hand in public, where everyone can see that you're mine."

A possessive flame burns through me. "Same, baby."

We kiss again. An urgent tangling of tongues and clash of teeth. When a door shuts somewhere in the building, Vi pulls back. "I have to go. I'll see you later."

"Boyfriend."

"What?" she asks, taking another step away.

"I'll see you later, *boyfriend*," I say.

She holds my hand until the distance pulls them apart. "I'll see you later, *boyfriend*."

Like father nothing.

Chapter
THIRTY

Violet

"I DON'T THINK I'M GOING TO BE ABLE TO SLEEP TONIGHT. I'm so nervous." I turn the water glass around in my hands. We're sitting at the bar at The Hideout. His mom's team just won their game, and it was so fun to watch his face light up with pride.

"That sounds like a challenge." His palm covers my bare thigh and sends goosebumps racing over my skin.

My heart feels like it might burst. It has since I woke up this morning in his bed. We fell asleep talking again. Though I have to say, it was a nice change to wake up without my phone plastered to the side of my face. And Gavin's voice is even sexier first thing in the morning.

All day I've thought about him, counted the minutes until I might get to see him. He leaves tomorrow for Texas, and it's weird to think how much I'm going to miss him.

"You're going to be great. The dress is killer." He squeezes my leg.

I let his words fill me with confidence. "I believe in the dress and in my design, but this is such a huge opportunity."

He takes a drink of his soda. "That would be so cool to see something you made on a concert stage."

"On Penelope-freaking-Hart no less."

His mouth curves up. "My girlfriend designed a dress for Penelope Hart. Shit, my boys will be begging for you to introduce them."

My body vibrates with nerves. "She hasn't picked my dress yet."

"She will if she's smart."

A laugh escapes my lips. "I hope she's very, very smart."

His hand inches higher, and he leans over to brush his lips over mine.

"Think your house is cleared out yet?"

When I got back from the design lab, there were so many cars parked in front of our house for a party next door. It was a glimpse of old times. Except this time, I found myself a lot less aggravated by it all.

"Probably not," he says with a grimace. "I'm sorry."

"Jocks are the worst," I mutter with a smile. "Except Dahlia."

"Glad to know where I stand." He growls and kisses me harder. His fingers push past the hem of my dress and dance along the edge of my panties.

"Yo, Leonard!" someone calls to him.

He pulls back slowly and moves his hand only slightly lower before he turns.

I squeeze my legs shut, which just eggs him on.

"Hey. What's up, Walters?" Gavin lifts his chin in acknowledgement to a group of guys gathered around two tables pushed together; three pitchers of beer sit in the middle of the tables along with a dozen or more empty shot glasses.

"Come join us. Let me buy you a beer. Having a fucking stellar season, man," one of the guys says.

"It's fine," I say, when Gavin looks to me and I tip my head to encourage him to go say hi.

He stands and faces me, putting his back to the guys. "They won't save you, baby."

He takes my hand then leads me over to the table.

"We can't stay." Gavin pulls out a chair for me and takes the one next to me.

The table of guys all aim their gazes at me, and Gavin puts an arm around the back of my chair.

"Felix Walters meet Violet," he says.

"Hey, Violet." He has a nice smile, black hair, and eyes that are a stunning light blue. He proceeds to rattle off the names of all the other guys at the table.

"Hi." I lift a hand in a small wave. "Nice to meet you all."

I look at Felix, studying his face closer. There's something about him. "You look familiar, but I can't figure out why."

"Walters is QB of the football team," Gavin says. "You've probably seen his face plastered all over campus."

Felix smiles, looking a little embarrassed. "I hate those posters."

"That's it!" I sit forward. "Oh my gosh. The poster with your face staring out from behind your helmet."

Felix groans. The guy sitting to the right of him lifts his glass. "To Blue Steele!"

They all cheer as Felix continues to look embarrassed by it all.

"Do you two want something to drink?" he asks. "We can get a couple of glasses."

"No, thanks," Gavin says. "We really can't stay."

"All right. Well, it was good to see you. After you guys win the tournament, let's get together."

"Definitely." Gavin stands and takes my hand.

Felix returns my wave as we head away from them and out of the bar.

"He seems nice."

"Nice?"

"Yeah, you know, like not a jerk."

Gavin cocks a brow. "Since when do you like nice?"

"Oh my god, are you jealous?" I fight to hold back a laugh.

"What? No." His voice goes up an octave, and he doesn't meet my gaze, which tells me everything I need to know.

"You are." I grab the front of his T-shirt and pull him closer. "Admit it."

He turns his head, but his jaw ticks.

"It's okay, Leonard." I press up on my tiptoes to bring my lips closer. "You're right. I don't like nice."

He leans down, taking my legs out from underneath me, and lifts me into his arms. He kisses me while walking across the parking lot. I don't tell him that I think he is nice. Tonight, this date, the book he got me, talking on the phone all night, taking care of me when I was sick. He's shown me just how amazing he can be. But, right now, there isn't anything nice about the way his mouth crushes mine or the bruising hold he has on my legs. And I like that too.

When we get back to The White House, the block is still lined with cars.

"I'm sorry," he says as he leads me inside.

"It's okay. People are excited and they want to celebrate with you guys. Do you want to go hang out?"

"No, and you won't either when you take a look outside."

I cock my head to the side. "Come on, how bad can it be?"

Following the noise, I walk through the house to the kitchen. The patio and pool are lit up with twinkle lights strung around the yard. At first glance, it looks like a normal party, but then two girls catch my attention. They're totally naked, standing on the edge of the pool at the deep end. They raise their joined hands and squeal as they jump into the water. When they surface, two guys join them.

"Just an average Wednesday night," I mutter. My cheeks are on fire. "I feel like I'm watching soft-core porn."

"Yeah. Don't look too closely or it might not be as soft as you think." He chuckles and places a kiss on my shoulder. "Let's go upstairs."

"You really don't want to go out there?" I face him and search his expression.

"I really don't."

"I'm not sure if I believe you."

His head drops until he's whispering next to my lips. "Those people out there are missing out, not the other way around." He moves my hair away from my neck and places an open-mouth kiss behind my ear. "Trust me."

And the scariest thing is, I do.

Chapter
THIRTY-ONE

Violet

"**O**H MY GOSH. SHE'S HERE!" DAHLIA BURSTS through the front door and launches her backpack on the couch next to me.

"Who?" Jane and Daisy ask at the same time.

We're all home during our lunch break between classes. It's the big day. The rep for Penelope Hart is going to pick an outfit that she will wear during her world tour.

"Penelope is here."

I sit forward. "What?!"

Jane looks over the magazine in her hands. "How do you know?"

"I saw her." Dahlia sits down. Her blue eyes are bright with excitement, and she waves her hands around. "I was at University Hall and these two big guys in all black walked in. They caught my attention because they looked so out of place, and they sort of just stood there, scanning the room. I was a little creeped out at first, but then Penelope walked in, flanked by two more big dudes."

"What did she look like?" Daisy asks.

"What was she wearing?" I follow up before Dahlia has time to answer.

"Why would she come here?" Jane's brows pinch together.

Dahlia lets us attack her with questions before telling us every detail she remembers.

"I still don't understand why she would come. She has assistants that have assistants." Jane is the only one of us that isn't giddy over the news. I guess when you grow up in LA, celebrity sightings are just part of a typical day.

Dahlia and I jump up and down, clasping hands.

"We're going to meet her," I squeal. "This is so cool."

"I'm so jealous." Daisy sticks out her bottom lip. "Do you think your professor would notice if I tagged along?"

"I could tell her you're my model," I say after I catch my breath.

"We should go," Dahlia says.

My nerves ramp up. I'm going to meet Penelope Hart, and she's going to see the design I created just for her.

Dahlia, Daisy, and I grab our backpacks. Jane takes her magazine to the stairs.

"I think I'm going to skip my afternoon classes today," she says. "I have a headache that won't quit."

"Are you sure?" Dahlia asks her. "Maybe we'll bump into her on the way."

"I'm sure. Promise to tell me everything when you get back though?"

Dahlia nods.

"Good luck." Jane beams. "I hope she picks one of your designs."

Dahlia and I squeal some more.

The three of us walk to campus, chattering about Penelope. Jordan meets up with Daisy in front of the library.

"Penelope Hart is here," Daisy tells her boyfriend.

"Oh yeah? That's awesome."

"Want to skip class to hang outside of their classroom and catch a peek of her?" she asks him.

He chuckles. "I would love to, but we have a quiz today."

"Oh yeah." Her shoulders sag. "One of you needs to get picked, become best friends, and get us tickets."

"We'll see what we can do," I tell my cousin before she heads off with Jordan.

Dahlia and I link arms as we hurry to the art building. At the end of the hall, we pause and take a deep breath.

"I see what you mean about the big, creepy dudes standing guard," I whisper. Two giant forms fill the doorway.

They don't say anything to us as we pass by. Once inside, we see Penelope standing with Professor Richards and another woman, who I assume is her assistant or one of the many other people who work for her.

Dahlia and I share barely contained smiles as we take our seats. I can't believe it. Penelope Hart is here. At Valley. Standing in our design classroom like she's just a normal person. Well, a normal person with two guards at the door and two more hovering in the back of the classroom.

Her signature lilac hair is pulled back in a loose ponytail and she's wearing a baggy Fleetwood Mac T-shirt. Even casual, she'd be impossible to mistake. She has that look, that intangible thing, that makes people look twice.

The class is buzzing with quiet chatter. A few people are taking pictures with their cell phones, but no one approaches her. I think we all might be a little in awe of her. Or a lot. A whole lot.

At the top of the hour, Professor Richards steps to the front of the room. "I'm sure you've all noticed that we have a special guest today. Penelope is here to help pick the outfit she's going to wear on tour."

She pauses and the room is filled with applause. Penelope

waves as she walks up and joins Professor Richard. "Hey. Hi, everyone. I'm Penelope. I'm so glad to be here. Fashion is my second love, so I can't wait to see what you've made."

My pulse ticks faster. Holy crap. This is really happening.

Professor Richards gives us time to set up, and then she and Penelope start around the room.

It's torture waiting. Dahlia and I watch as they talk to each student. Penelope smiles and listens as they talk through the design. She appears nothing but gracious, but I can't tell anything about how she feels about the outfits.

"I think I might throw up," Dahlia says when Penelope gets closer to us.

"You'll be fine."

"What if I freeze or blurt out something weird like, 'Your hair is so pretty?'"

"Breathe," I say, taking her hand and squeezing. "She's our age and she hasn't been super famous for that long. Talk to her like you'd talk to me or Jane or Daisy."

"She dated the Prince of Luxembourg. She is not just like us."

I stifle a laugh. "Fair point."

Penelope steps toward Dahlia's table. I squeeze her hand once more. "Focus on the design. You've got this."

While she looks over Dahlia's jumper, I scan my dress and pick at imaginary lint. This is it. How many opportunities like this come around? Peaking at twenty feels melodramatic, but what if this is it?

Before my life can flash before my eyes in swatches and lace, Penelope and Professor Richards are walking toward me.

"This is Violet Johnson." Professor Richards stops at the side of the table to let Penelope move closer to the dress.

"This is stunning," she says as she bypasses me and runs a hand over the skirt of the dress. "Sorry. That was incredibly rude. I was distracted by this gorgeous dress." She smiles at me. A smile

I've seen on red carpets and magazine shoots. "It's nice to meet you, Violet."

"Nice to meet you too."

"Why don't you tell Penelope a little about the concept and inspiration behind your design," Professor Richards encourages.

"Well, my passion is dresses. I'm inspired by historical pieces. The layering and careful construction. I took those elements but made it more modern with the fabric choice and the shorter skirt in the front. I spent a lot of time listening to your music and looking through pieces you've worn before. I wanted to create something that could be photographed on the red carpet but that would be comfortable and fun enough for the stage. I know that it's not as wearable as some of the other options, but I had my roommate test it, and she was able to sing and move around in it."

"Your roommate is a singer?"

"Music major."

Her gaze stays on the dress as if she's taking in every detail. "It's costume meets red carpet. Gorgeous. I love it."

"Thanks." I finally take a breath.

"Why black?" she asks.

"You've done a lot of color. People won't necessarily expect it."

She finally pulls her attention from the dress to me. "I love it. I love the thought that you put into creating it."

"Thank you, Penelope." I get a little thrill saying her name out loud. I'm talking to freaking Penelope Hart.

She looks to Professor Richards. Weeks of effort and it's over just like that.

They go back to the front of the room after finishing talking with each of us.

Professor Richards looks at the clock on the wall. "You can clean your areas while we talk things over, but leave your designs out, in case we need a second look. Don't stress. We'll have an answer for you soon."

Don't stress? Ha!

Dahlia comes over to stand with me while we wait. "How'd it go?"

"Good. I think?" My heart is still beating rapidly in my chest. "How'd yours go?"

"She smiled a lot, but she smiled at everyone. At least I didn't say anything humiliating."

It feels like an eternity, waiting for Penelope to make a decision. They confer up front and then make another lap to get a second look. They pause a little longer in front of a few of ours, mine and Dahlia's included, but I still can't read anything on Penelope's face.

"I want to thank Penelope for being here in person today." Professor Richards angles her body, clapping, and we all join in.

"It was my absolute pleasure. I can't thank you all enough for the time and effort that you put into this challenge. It was not easy to choose, but one in particular caught my eye, and I think it would be perfect to close out my setlist on tour."

Collectively, the class holds our breath.

Penelope tips her head to the left of me. "Dahlia, I would be honored to wear that jumper. It's exactly what I was looking for, but somehow, even better."

My friend goes still next to me. Her eyes are wide, and she looks like she might pass out as our classmates stare at her with jealousy and admiration. Disappointment washes over me, but I can't dwell on it for long. I want Dahlia to know how much I support her. If it wasn't me, then of course, I wanted it to be her.

"You did it." I nudge her with my elbow. "She picked your design."

Chapter
THIRTY-TWO

Gavin

"I'M SORRY. I LOST TRACK OF TIME." VIOLET ENTERS MY room, dropping her backpack onto the floor.

"It's fine." I take a break from packing and sit on the bed. "I didn't think I was going to get to see you before we left. I sent you like a stalker amount of texts."

She walks over to me and stands between my legs. "I know. I just saw them. I forgot to turn my phone back on after class, and then I stopped by the bookstore to get some new sketch pencils. Then I was thirsty and went by the café to—"

I place a kiss to her lips, silencing her. "I'm just glad you made it. I have to be at the bus in half an hour."

She wraps her arms around my neck. "Oh no. I don't have enough time to make a glitter poster with your name and number on it."

"Next time." I widen my stance and pull her closer. "Tell me how it went. Was Penelope really here?"

"How'd you know?" she asks.

"People were talking about it all over campus."

"She was," Violet confirms.

"And?" I squeeze her. The suspense is killing me. I think I've been as nervous as her all day long. "Did she pick your dress?"

"No." She frowns, and then quickly replaces it with a smile. "But she picked Dahlia's, so it was the next best thing."

"Ah, shit. I'm sorry." I was so sure she'd win.

"It's fine," she insists.

"It's all right to be disappointed. You spent a lot of time on it."

"I'm trying really hard not to feel anything right now. I don't want to go home and make Dahlia feel weird. She should be celebrating and not worrying about hurting my feelings, which is what will happen if I walk in looking upset. She worked just as hard."

"You're a good friend."

She lets out a little sigh. "I'm trying."

"Are you going to be okay?"

"Yeah, I'm okay. I'm going to lock myself in my room tonight and let myself feel really crappy, and then tomorrow, we're going out to celebrate Dahlia, and I'm going to be her number one supporter. I am really happy for her."

"I know you are."

Her face lights up with a little of her usual sparkle. "Stop worrying about me. You're the one about to go play the most important game of your life."

"Thanks for reminding me." I chuckle.

She presses her chest to mine. "You are going to be great. I might even watch my first college basketball game."

"You pierce my soul, Violet Johnson." I place a hand over my heart as I recite the words from the *Persuasion* quote hanging above her bed and grin.

Her eyes flare with heat. "You keep talking like that and thirty minutes won't be enough time for me to kiss the crap out of you. You'll miss the bus, and your coach will be pissed, your teammates will hate you, and—"

I slant my mouth over hers and, as she'd put it, kiss the crap out of her.

Violet climbs onto my lap and straddles me. She tugs at the hem of my T-shirt and we break apart briefly, so I can remove it. She pulls her tank top over her head and then throws her arms back around my neck.

I think knowing we have a time limit and that we're going to be apart for days, maybe a week, has us both eager to make the most of every last second before I leave.

My hands roam down her back as she runs her fingers through the hair at the nape of my neck.

Somewhere in the brain I'm not currently using, I know I don't have time to get involved in a hot make-out sesh, but I slide the straps of her bra down anyway.

She leans back as I drop kisses to her collarbone. I palm her tits over the lacy material and kiss the top of her cleavage that's peeking out. Violet reaches around and undoes the clasp, making the material fall into my hands.

She pushes me back onto the mattress, stands and removes her skirt and panties.

Fuck, she's gorgeous. Every inch, from the top of her shiny black hair to her purple toenails.

Swift fingers hook into the waistband of my athletic pants. We push them and my boxers down together, past my hips, and Vi pulls them all the way off and tosses them into a pile with the rest of our clothes.

Before I have time to figure out what's happening, she's back straddling me. I groan into her mouth and tangle one hand into her long hair.

"Do you have a condom?"

I freeze and open my eyes to stare into hers. "Vi, we don't have to."

"I want to. Do you not want to?"

I cock a brow. "Of course, I want to, but—"

She steals my trick, kissing me to shut me up.

I know there isn't enough time for all the things I want to do, but I start by flipping us, so I'm on top. Her chest rises and falls with labored breaths.

"You're so beautiful." I run a finger down her neck, and she arches into my touch.

I kiss her shoulder, her elbows, all the way down to her ankles. I kiss her everywhere, except the places she wants. When I nip at her hip bone, she whines my name.

Chuckling, I link an arm under one of her legs and cover her pussy with my mouth. It happens so fast, she isn't prepared, and she cries out, her shoulders coming off the bed.

I tighten my hold as I lavish her in slow licks and soft kisses that have the hottest sounds escaping her lips. It isn't enough. Not for either of us.

I leave her, only long enough to get a condom and cover myself. "Are you sure?" My pulse races.

She nods and licks her lips. "I'm sure."

Eyes locked on hers, I push in an inch. Her lashes flutter closed and her mouth curves. I slide in slow, filling her completely. Her pussy is squeezing me so tight.

My lungs feel like I've run a marathon. I don't have space to breathe or think. Sweat beads on my forehead and my muscles burn.

"You feel so good." I bury my head in her neck and breathe her in.

I stay there, unmoving, enjoying the sensation of being connected to her this way until her nails softly rake down my shoulders. I pull out an inch, then two, and drive back into her.

Thirty minutes feels like enough time to do this a dozen times at the rate my body is reacting to hers.

"I forgot how big you are," Violet says, voice trembling.

"I love it when you whisper sweet nothings."

She laughs. "That was sweet?"

"Straight out of Jane Austen. I'm thinking of hanging it above my bed." I grin down at her.

"I don't think so."

"Are you sure?" I reach between our bodies and drag my thumb along her clit.

"I'm not even sure of my name right now."

She brings her lips up to mine. I move faster, eliciting more of those sexy as fuck sounds from her.

"I'm close," she says on a moan.

I pound into her as a tingling sensation works its way down my spine. Violet cries out as her orgasm hits, and I chase mine until I see stars behind my eyes.

I fall onto the bed beside her as we catch our breath. I changed my mind again. Thirty minutes isn't nearly enough time.

Noah yells from the hallway, "Five minutes, boys."

I get up and get rid of the condom. Violet stands and starts to dress, but I grab her around the waist to kiss her again before she tries to escape.

"You're going to be late."

"They probably won't leave me."

I can't stop touching her and kissing her. My dick is already growing hard again. I bite her neck and whisper, "Mine."

She giggles, and I keep going, dropping more little nibbles all over her body and claiming her.

"Time to go!" Noah yells.

"You have to go." Violet extracts herself from my hold and tosses my T-shirt at me. "Get out of here, boyfriend. I'll still be yours when you get back."

I bite her one last time. "To be continued."

Reluctantly, I get dressed. She does the same and then sits on the bed while I double-check that I've packed everything. Her smile hasn't dimmed, but I know she has to be bummed about the whole Penelope situation. She worked her ass off on that dress.

"I'm sorry about your design. You'll have other chances. Someday, people will be lining up to have you create a custom dress for them. I know it."

"Thank you."

I brush my lips over hers. I'm definitely going to miss the bus if I keep kissing her.

"Leonard!" Noah yells.

"I really have to go. I'll text you later."

"Good luck. I'll be watching."

"Oh yeah?"

"Did I not mention the celebration was at The Hideout? From the sound of it, half the university is going there to watch the game."

"You can take your glitter sign." I grab my bag, and Violet walks out with me.

We're already late, so I don't have time to kiss her again before Noah drags me away.

"Good luck," she calls as I jog across the street. Then adds, "To be continued."

We arrive at the Sweet Sixteen later that evening. The tournament sets up a buffet to feed us and then we meet Coach in the practice space they've designated for our team.

He gives us a quick pep talk before instructing us to shoot around to shake loose the nerves and stiffness from traveling.

No matter how many courts I play on, every time I step onto

a new one, I feel like I'm five years old, standing at half court and staring out into the crowd in awe.

We head up to our rooms early. We have a seven o'clock wakeup call and are nonstop with media, team and individual meetings, and practice to warm up and shake off the nerves before a six o'clock game. It's going to be hard to sleep tonight with all the adrenaline pumping through my veins.

I pull out my phone as I get off the elevator, our team's rooms are on the eighth floor, and send Violet a quick text. *Just getting to my room. Whatcha doing?*

She sends a picture of her in bed with some sort of cream on her face. She's holding her laptop up, so it's visible in the picture. I can't tell exactly what movie it is, but it's something historical.

I'm smiling and tapping out a reply, which is why I don't see the man standing in front of my door until I look up to check the room number.

I freeze. "Dad?"

"Hey, Gavin."

"What are you doing here?"

A few of my teammates are walking by, heading to their rooms on the same floor. They gawk at the sight of my father.

Dad lowers his voice. "Can we talk in your room?"

I let us inside. I hadn't expected to see him here. Not after I declined the father/son interview.

I flip on the light and grab a water from the fridge. Dad lingers in the doorway, shuffling from foot to foot uncomfortably.

"You wanted to talk, so talk."

This hotel suite feels too small for the both of us, and Noah will be back any minute.

"Big game tomorrow. How are you feeling?"

"Fine. We're ready."

"Oregon is quick. They like to rebound and run. And their defense is tough. You'll need to keep your heads and play good D to keep them quiet." He takes a step farther into the room.

"What do you really want?" I ask. My tone is bored, even though my pulse is racing. "You didn't come all the way here to give me pointers."

"You said no to the interview."

He waits for an explanation that I don't give him.

"You know, I wanted to be a doctor when I was a kid."

I shake my head. "No, I didn't know that. What does that have to do with you showing up here to try to convince me to do some bullshit interview that I don't want to do?"

Instead of answering me, he continues his jog down memory lane. "Your grandpa Leonard didn't want me to go to the NBA. When I got to high school and people started talking about college and beyond, I mentioned that maybe I'd like to play professionally. It was an off-handed comment, one I didn't really think was possible at the time. He went nuts. To him, basketball was fine as a hobby, but he didn't think it was a serious career. Too much risk. So he pushed me toward medical school. God, we must have had a million arguments about it my junior year. He'd leave those paper brochures for colleges with outstanding medical programs on my desk, and he stopped asking about my games. It built a lot of tension between us. I resented him for it. He was the only one not encouraging me to do this big, scary thing, and it made me feel like he didn't think I was capable of doing it."

Dad sighs. "I loved playing basketball, don't get me wrong. Maybe I would have gone to the NBA anyway, but I'm one hundred percent certain that, at the time, I did it just to piss him off. To prove that I was good enough because he didn't believe in me. Don't make the same mistake I did. Pick for yourself, not to punish me."

I swallow around a lump in my throat. "That's not what I'm doing. I'm not you."

"No. You're not."

The door to my room opens, and Noah steps in. When he sees my dad, his eyes widen. "Mr. Leonard."

"Hi, Noah." Dad puts on his fan smile.

"Am I interrupting?" Noah asks, gaze darting between us. "I can come back."

"No. We're all done here," I say.

Noah isn't an idiot. I'm sure he can sense the tension between my dad and me.

Dad's smile falls, but he adjusts it, then addresses Noah. "Good luck tomorrow."

"Thanks, Mr. L."

My dad goes to the door and then meets my gaze across the room. "The choice is yours, son, but make sure you're choosing from your heart. Chances like this don't come around a second time. The worst thing in life is to sit around asking yourself what if."

Chapter
THIRTY-THREE

Violet

F RIDAY NIGHT, THE HIDEOUT IS PACKED WITH VALLEY students on the bar side. It's standing room only, but we got here early to snag a table with the best view of the TV. I was on the edge of my seat at tip-off, but our team took an early lead, and Oregon hasn't been able to recover. Most people have stopped paying attention, but I'm still staring at the screen, eager for every glimpse of Gavin.

Jane snuck in a bottle of Malibu, and she and Dahlia keep disappearing to the bathroom to steal drinks from it, which means my friends are well on their way to being good and drunk. Or at least Dahlia is.

She comes back to the table, blue eyes lit with excitement.

"You look happy," I muse as she takes the seat next to me.

"I am." Her smile dims. "I'm sorry that my win is a loss for you."

REBECCA JENSHAK

"Hey, no. Don't think of it like that. We're on the same team. When you win, I win." I pause. "I'm not a sporty person, does that metaphor work?"

She nods. "Yeah, that was perfect. Maybe the sporty boyfriend is rubbing off on you." She bumps my shoulder with hers.

"Maybe it's my sporty roommate."

She wraps her arms around my shoulders from the side and squeezes gently. "Thank you. Seriously. You're amazing and I'm so thankful we found each other. You make me a better designer and push me to go out of my comfort zone. I never would have won this without you."

"Right back at you. I'm thankful for you too. I've learned so much from you. We're going to rule the fashion world someday."

"Definitely." She beams and sits back in her chair. "I feel invincible. I want to climb on the bar and dance or ask out the hottest guy in here." She pauses and looks at me. "Please don't let me. I know I'm drunk, but gosh, I just feel so good. I wish this feeling would last forever."

"Why can't it? You're generally fabulous."

"Well, for starters, I can't dance. And you know how I get in front of cute guys. My brain stops working."

"Then we should take advantage of this rare opportunity." I scan the bar area, looking for a potential target. Mr. Blue Steele is at the bar with guys that I assume are football players by their massive shoulders.

I stand and pull her with me.

"Okay. I wasn't being serious. Please don't make me get up on the bar. I'll be a viral video by the time I sober up." Nerves creep into her voice.

"No dancing on the bar. I want to introduce you to someone."

When we get to the bar, I squeeze in sideways between Felix and the person next to him.

"Excuse us," I say, and lean an elbow on the bar.

Felix glances over and then a slow smile tips up the corners of his lips. "Hey. Violet, right?"

"That's right."

"Your boy is looking good tonight." He motions with his head toward the TV behind the bar.

"He always looks good." I get distracted from my mission for a second as the camera pans to him. He jogs down the court, dribbling the ball between defenders.

Dahlia squeezes my hand. Right. Dahlia.

"Felix, this is my friend, Dahlia. She is on the Valley golf team and is an incredible fashion designer. Penelope Hart just selected one of her designs to wear on tour this summer."

"Is that right?" He shifts to give us more of his attention and aims a panty-melting smile right at my friend.

Dahlia opens her mouth, but no words come out, just a tiny squeak.

Oh no. This was a terrible plan. His smile even throws me a little off balance.

I lean into her for reassurance.

She still stares frozen at Felix's handsome face.

"Well, congrats." He lifts his beer toward her. "Can I buy you a drink?"

She shakes her head, sending the blonde strands around her shoulders

"Another time," I answer for her. "We're with some friends."

"Okay. Good to see you. When you talk to Leonard, tell him good game for me."

"I will."

His blue eyes slide over to Dahlia once more. "Nice to meet you."

I tug a still frozen Dahlia with me, and we slip back into the crowd of people.

"Are you okay?" I ask.

She starts laughing. So hard that she bends over and fights to catch her breath. I'm glad she's laughing instead of crying. Pretty sure that's the alcohol though. Like a good friend, I promise to retell the events of tonight with a much kinder lens than how it actually went down.

"Yeah, that was a good dose of reality."

"It was?"

Nodding, she smiles. "Even drunk and on top of the world, I could never talk to someone like him. Wow. I mean, wow." Her eyes widen.

"Come on. The game is almost over. Let's find the girls."

"Tonight was the best."

"It's not over yet." I link my arm through hers.

"It isn't?"

"No way. Sigma is having after hours. We're going dancing."

Valley wins the game by fifteen points. We hang out after long enough to see the after-game interviews. Gavin isn't among them, but they flash his roster photo on the screen as one of the top performers of the game tonight and do the usual spiel about his parents.

At the frat house, Dahlia and Jane head to the dance floor; Daisy and Jordan are outside sitting with some of his teammates, and I'm clutching my phone in one hand and waiting for Gavin to reply to my congratulatory texts.

"You again," Felix says as I nearly collide with him when I step out of the front door, where it's quieter.

"Hey."

"Lose your friend?"

"She's dancing inside. Sorry about earlier. She's shy."

"I get that."

I tilt my head and narrow my gaze. "You're shy?"

"No." He chuckles and runs a hand over his jaw. "But I have a sister that is."

"Oh." I glance down at the screen of my phone again.

"Are you going to the game Sunday?"

"In Texas?"

"Yeah, a bunch of the guys and I are driving."

"I don't know. I hadn't thought about it."

"I figured Gavin was begging you to come cheer him on."

"He's pretty focused on the games," I say, but a prick of embarrassment makes my face heat. My phone vibrates in my hand. "That's him."

"Later, Violet." He passes me and heads into the house.

Bringing the phone out in front of my face, I answer to an exhausted-looking Gavin. "Hey. Congrats."

"Thank you." He adjusts the hat on his head to give me a better view of his face. He looks like he's seconds from passing out. "Where are you?"

"Sigma. Jane and Dahlia are inside tearing up the dance floor."

"I'm shocked you aren't with them."

"Oh, I will be. I just wanted a quiet spot to talk to you first." I smile bigger. "You're going to the Elite Eight!"

"Yeah. I don't think it's sunk in yet. Too exhausted."

"I bet."

He leans back against the headboard of his hotel bed. "Noah's already crashed." He angles his phone to show me his sleeping roommate on the bed next to him.

"I assumed you'd be celebrating."

"Not yet. We celebrate when it's over. Coach has us on a strict schedule every night."

"What will you do tomorrow?"

"Practice in the morning after breakfast. We have the day to catch up on homework and turn in any assignments due, some of the guys are doing interviews and press, then we'll watch the other teams play, so we're ready for whoever comes next."

"Interviews, huh?"

"Not me. I bailed out of those."

"Why?"

"They wanted to do some Leonard legacy piece." His tone is

bitter and his features harden. It lasts only a few seconds before a little of his carefree demeanor returns. "I have a ton of homework anyway. It would really suck to retake Spanish next year."

"Are your parents there at the games?"

"My mom is in St. Louis."

"Oh right. They're still playing too. That's really cool that both of your teams are still in it."

"The coolest," he says.

He doesn't mention his dad.

"Hey, I ran into Felix tonight. He wanted me to tell you good game."

"Oh no, did Blue Steele win you over with his charm and good looks?"

"No." I laugh. "But he did mention that he and some of the guys are going to the game on Sunday."

Gavin nods.

"He asked if I was going."

"I knew it. He's hitting on my woman. Do not get in the vehicle with him, Violet. Promise me." He smiles, so I know he's joking.

"Do you want me to come?" It honestly never occurred to me that people would be traveling. I don't even know if there are still tickets, or how to get them. I'm basically clueless about all of it.

"Nah. Don't worry about it."

"I want to worry about it if it's important to you."

"It's just basketball." His expression is so blasé that I don't know what to make of it. "Baby steps for you, Vi. You just watched your first game on TV. Two hundred thousand fans cheering on all of us stupid jocks might scare you off for good. We're the worst, right?" A little of that bitter tone seeps back into his voice.

Throwing my words back at me hurts more than expected. I said it. I might have even meant it at the time, but things have changed. I'm not an idiot, I know basketball is important to him, regardless of what he says.

228

He yawns and sinks lower onto the bed. His eyes close. "I better go before I fall asleep on the phone."

I feel like crying or yelling and I'm not sure why, but I force my tone to remain even. "Congrats again. Get some rest and I'll talk to you later."

"Night, Vi." He hangs up before I can respond.

"Night," I say to myself.

I stand in the front yard of Sigma, replaying the conversation in my head. Eventually, I head back inside. Dahlia and Jane have retired from the dance floor and sit on a worn couch pushed back against the wall near the bathroom.

"Hey!" Jane lifts her arms to greet me.

I fall into the spot next to her.

"What's wrong?" she asks.

Dahlia sits forward with a concerned expression marring her pretty features.

I tell them about the phone call with Gavin, trying to repeat it word for word, so I can get their take on it.

"He probably didn't want you to worry about getting there," Jane reassures me.

"I don't know. It felt weird, like he didn't want me there."

"I think he just thought you wouldn't want to come," Dahlia says.

"Do you want to go?" Jane asks.

"Yeah. I do. He acts like it doesn't matter because he isn't going pro, but I know it's a big deal for him, and I want to be there to show him how much I support him."

"Then let's go," Jane says.

"He just told me not to." I can't decide if him telling me not to come is him trying to be considerate or if he's holding on to some resentment for the things I said when we were fighting. He has to know that I don't really hate all jocks, right?

"I think I screwed up," I admit to my friends. "All my grumbling about jocks."

"You were hurt," Jane says. "People say things they don't mean when they're hurt."

"That doesn't make it okay." I like him so much. All of him. And I want to be there to support him and this thing he loves doing. We'll never make this work if we're both holding on to things the other said or did in the past. And I think I just realized how much I want this to work.

"Dahlia, back me up," Jane says. "We should go to the game, right?"

"I love it when my family and friends are standing on the sidelines during a match."

"See?" Jane smiles proudly.

"But," Dahlia continues, "every player is different. There's a girl on my team who gets really nervous when her boyfriend comes to watch her play."

I tuck my phone into my purse. "It was a dumb idea anyway. Getting a flight or hotel is probably hard this late, plus tickets."

Jane stares down at her phone, thumbs flying over the screen. "Hotel prices are outrageous, but there's still availability."

"I don't think I should go. Wouldn't he be more pissed if I show up after he basically told me not to come?"

"No," Dahlia and Jane answer at the same time.

"I'll come with you," Jane adds. "It'll be fun."

I shake my head. "Thank you, but no. I'll watch the game here with you guys. Maybe we should have a little dress-up party at our place and watch the game."

"A red carpet would really improve basketball." Jane smiles. "I'm in."

"Are you sure?" Dahlia looks disappointed with my decision.

I fake a smile for their benefit. "Positive."

Chapter
THIRTY-FOUR

Gavin

I SMILE DOWN AT THE IMAGE ON MY PHONE. VIOLET'S holding a posterboard that says, *Leonard #31*. It's decked out in Valley colors and an explosion of glitter. It's from Friday before the game against Oregon.

Before I was an asshole and hurt her feelings. I know I did. I could see it as soon as I told her not to come to the game. And confirmed it by the fact we've barely talked since then.

To be fair, yesterday was a packed schedule, even though we had the day off, and Violet was probably nursing a hangover from being out with the girls all night.

I also had another run-in with my dad. He was at the game, and after, he made a point to come say congrats. The interaction lasted only a second, but it was long enough for the big news of the night to be us and not Valley U winning the game.

Instead of Noah or one of my teammates having their photo

splashed across the top headline, it's me and him. And it's such bullshit.

I pocket my phone and grab a basketball from the rack.

Today, the buzz of excitement humming through the arena is like nothing else. Coaches and players, media and fans. There is no quiet. Which is good because any time things get too quiet, the shit with my dad replays in my head and I feel like I'm going to explode. I keep waiting for the next moment he corners me or I get ambushed by a reporter, who pulls him into the interview without a heads up. I'm tired of putting on a show when the truth is, I don't know my dad and I can't figure out what he wants from me.

He didn't do the interview without me, which I guess makes me happy. To be honest, I'm just trying not to think about any of it too much. I want to get lost in the rhythm of my dribble and the practiced ease of the ball rolling off my fingertips.

There's an uncertainty in basketball. The best team doesn't always win. It's the best team on any given night. The pressure of the tournament has a way of making unlikely heroes and upsetting top-seeded giants. I don't know if we'll get back here next year, so I want to make every second count.

I told Violet it wasn't important, but the truth is, it's the only thing that's important right now. It's my sanity, and my team is counting on me, so I have to push past all the bullshit.

Coach comes in with a coffee in hand about thirty minutes before we're due to head into the locker rooms.

I rebound a ball near him, and he tips his head to indicate he wants to talk to me.

"How are you feeling? Nervous?"

"A little," I admit. "The size and noise of the crowd was intense Friday."

"It'll be worse tonight," he says. "I saw your dad. Any other friends or family coming tonight?"

"Some guys from school, I think. I'm not really sure. My mom is watching from St. Louis. They play again next week."

"I bet it's killing her not to be here."

"For sure."

"When you get out there for warmups, do a quick scan of the crowd. Get it over with, soak it in, let it freak you out, and then find some of your buddies in the crowd, a friendly face, whatever helps. When you're overwhelmed in the game, you know where to look to bring yourself back to the calm."

"Thanks, Coach." I start back onto the floor, but then stop and ask, "Do you miss it?"

His brows furrow.

I palm the ball and stretch out my arm. "This. Playing ball. The nerves and anticipation before a big game. All of it."

He nods slowly and a smile transforms his face, as if he's lost in the best of the memories. "For me, basketball was an outlet. It was family. I had some good times out there and I don't regret a single second of the time and sweat I left on the court, but no. This job gives me as much of that as playing ever did." He takes a drink of his coffee. "Besides, I was good, but the NBA would have chewed me up and spit me out."

A chuckle escapes my lips. I think he's being modest. I've seen the films. He was a great player. "It'd probably do that to me too."

"If you believe that, then it's a good thing your mind is already made up." His smile dares me to say I'm not as confident in my decision as I've made everyone believe.

I swallow thickly. "However it happened, I'm glad you ended up here."

"Thanks, Gavin." He nods toward the rest of the guys shooting around, dismissing me.

When we take the court for warmups an hour later, I do as he suggested. I turn in a circle, staring up at the thousands of spectators. Those nerves from earlier turn into adrenaline. God, I love this game. I love the energy that flows through me when I step out in my uniform, the test of my focus and skill, and the honesty of the sport. Genuine talent and hustle are what it takes, nothing less. You can't let up for a second.

I find my dad in the same spot as last game, sitting in a section across from the bench. He's wearing a Valley U T-shirt, hands clasped in his lap as he meets my stare. Someone next to him thrusts a paper and pen in his direction and he offers a gracious smile as he signs it for them.

Seeing him doesn't fill me with the calm Coach mentioned, so I continue looking around until I find Felix and a few other guys from the football team. Their seats are high up, but they stick out with their painted faces and bright yellow T-shirts that when read together say, VALLEY.

I keep searching, and it takes me a minute to realize I'm looking for her. Guilt coats my insides. I should have told Violet I wanted her here. I did. I do. I don't know why I didn't say that. Shit with my dad has my head spinning, but it's no excuse.

"Are you good?" Jenkins asks as he approaches me. I guess I probably look star struck, standing here staring out into the crowd.

"Yeah, I'm good. Did you see the football team?" I point.

Jenkins chuckles. "That's awesome."

"It really is." I hold up my wrist. "Ready to do this?"

"So ready." He taps his wrist to mine.

From the start, the game is fast-paced and physical. Gonzaga is tough. They put a full-court press on us and get away with a few sneaky fouls. We push back, but we're frustrated and off our game. That's how the turnovers start. One bad pass turns into a carry, and the next thing I know, we're down by eight in the first five minutes.

Coach calls a much-needed timeout to settle us down.

"Take a deep breath and let it go." He scribbles on the white board a play we all know by heart. "Take care of the ball. Push it down the court, get set up and pass it around the perimeter. I promise if you swing it around enough, someone will have a look at the basket. They're playing too tightly not to get caught a step behind. All right?"

We all nod our agreement.

"Let's go." He puts his hand up and each of us does the same, joining together. In unison we say, "Run 'em."

Noah inbounds the ball to me underneath the Gonzaga basket. Like they've done all game, they pick us up in a full-court press. I push the ball up the court and pass it off once I cross the half-court line. Jenkins holds the ball until we're in position, then passes to the right wing. Their defense is tight and grabby, the guy covering me is constantly holding my elbow or my jersey, anything to keep me from getting away from him.

I'm a step faster than him, though, and able to make a quick cut from the wing to the basket. Noah snaps the ball to me as defenders close in from two sides. I make a split-second decision that dumping the ball off to a teammate is riskier than going for it myself, so I take two dribbles, angle my body and jump above the defense to dunk the ball.

My legs are taken out from under me, and I come down awkwardly. The crowd explodes as I crumble to the ground. A tearing sensation rips through my left knee. *No. No. No. No.*

I curl into myself and cradle my leg. I think I cry out, but the noise in the arena is deafening. It's probably only a second before everyone realizes something is wrong, and then one hundred and seventy thousand people go silent.

Chapter
THIRTY-FIVE

Gavin

MY TEAMMATES CROWD AROUND ME. I DON'T LOOK at their faces, afraid I'll see my panic mirrored back at me.

The refs yell for my teammates to give me space, and trainers flank me on all sides. I drop my head back onto the wooden floor and spread out my arms, taking up as much space as I can and letting my body soak up this feeling of being on the court. I hadn't planned to say goodbye flat on my back, but I don't want to forget this feeling. The floor, the lights, the sweat dripping off me.

The noise filters back in slowly. The whispers in the crowd, the opposing coach calling his guys over, and a deep voice I know all too well slicing through the rest.

"Gavin!" my dad calls. I pretend not to hear him.

Someone must try to stop him because he adds, "That's my son."

He comes into view behind the trainers. That panic-stricken look I was trying to avoid slams into me.

"Did you hear a pop?" He leans over to get a better look at my leg.

I ignore him, so he asks it again.

The trainers help me sit up and then two of them take me by the arm, one on each side, to get me standing. The crowd claps as they help me off the court, and there's a golf cart waiting for me on the sideline. I lose sight of my dad until they're loading me onto the back.

"Gavin—" he starts.

"Go away," I yell at him.

"Don't be ridiculous. I'm your father. I'm going with you."

"No." I grit my teeth.

He takes a step closer.

"I don't want you here. Why can't you get that through your head? You don't get to play the father card when it's convenient for you. You are a shitty fucking dad. You were absent most of my childhood. Too busy sleeping your way through the ball honeys while Mom picked up your slack. We were fine without you. We didn't need you then, and I don't need you now."

He looks shocked by my outburst, and that's when I see the cameras aimed right at us.

The game continues, but they send me to the nearest hospital to take X-rays. Tommy comes with me, and my mom calls and says she'll be there as soon as she can get a flight. I think I tried to talk her out of it, but she wasn't having it and I didn't have it in me to put up much of a fight.

I'm scared. Knee injuries are the kind of things people don't come back from. What if this is it? My eyes burn. This can't be it. It can't be.

I'm lying in a bed in the ER, still in uniform, waiting for the doctor. Tommy paces beside me.

"Dude, relax."

He nods, sits in the lone chair by my bed. His leg takes up a bounce that makes his shoe squeak on the floor.

"Can you give me a minute? I want to call Violet."

Tommy stands quickly, looking like he's happy to have something to do. "Sure. Do you want anything?"

I shake my head. "I'm good."

Let's be honest, I'm terrible, but worse with him hovering over me.

He disappears out the curtain pulled around this small bed, and I let out a breath, but I don't pick up my phone from the table to call Violet.

She's probably still pissed at me. Has to be if she hasn't bothered to call or text to check in. Or maybe she didn't even watch the game, so she doesn't know. An image of the moment I went down flashes in my mind and I drop my head back onto the hard pillow.

I think about what Coach said earlier, how coaching gives him the same joy that playing did. Will that be true of me too? Will I be content holding on to this sport I love, with my entire being, by sitting at some desk writing stories about other great players? I thought I knew the answer when I made up my mind years ago.

My knee twinges with pain and I rub my thigh just above it. I don't know how long I've been back here, but it feels like hours. I'm irritated and impatient. The pain I can handle, but the unanswered questions threaten to swallow me whole.

The curtain rustles, but I keep my eyes closed, expecting Tommy. Maybe if he thinks I'm sleeping, he'll chill the fuck out.

"Mr. Leonard." I crack one eye to see a man in blue scrubs and a white coat. He doesn't look up from the clipboard as he continues, "I'm Dr. Scarella."

He asks me a few questions, all of which the trainer that brought me over from the game already told the nurse.

"Have they taken you for X-rays yet?"

"Yeah. A while ago."

He nods. He still hasn't looked up from that clipboard. "Let me see if I can track those down. Hang tight just a little longer."

"That won't be necessary." Another guy steps through the curtain with a tablet in his hand. "Hi, Gavin. I'm Dr. Chase. Sam, good to see you again." He nods to the other doctor. "I've got this one."

Dr. Scarella looks like he wants to argue, but only for a second, before he turns around and walks out.

My new doctor sets his tablet on the tray table next to my bed. His black hair has streaks of gray. He's wearing a striped polo and black slacks. He looks like maybe he stepped off the golf course or came from a board meeting, instead of the hospital floor.

"How's the pain?"

"Not that bad."

He raises both brows.

"It hurts, but I can handle it. Am I done?" It's the question that has been on a loop since I went down. Am I ever going to play ball again?

He slips into doctor mode, turning on the tablet and bringing up my X-rays. "I've ordered an MRI to get a better look at it." Pointing to the tablet, he continues, "You tore the patellar tendon and collateral ligament."

It hurts to swallow, to breathe. "Can you fix it?"

The smirk he gives me makes him look younger. "Of course, I can. That's why I'm here."

"And I'll still be able to play basketball at a college or professional level?" My heart races.

His confidence slips a bit. "Let's get an MRI. I'll have a better idea of exactly what we're dealing with."

"Dr. Chase?" I need him to be straight with me. I can't wait another hour not knowing.

"Knee injuries are tough. It depends on the damage, and I most likely won't have a definite answer until I'm in there."

I can't speak, so I simply nod.

"I'm going to put the order in for the test—" The rest of his sentence is cut off by chaos outside.

A woman is yelling. Dr. Chase and I both pause a second to listen. I can't make out her words, but she is pissed about something. That's probably the norm for the ER—screaming or crying. I feel like doing both.

"Gavin Leonard," she says my name, and I cock my head to hear her better. "I know he's here."

Without leaving, Dr. Chase pulls back the curtain. *Violet.*

I sit up. Her eyes are wild, and she stretches every inch of her short and petite frame to stand up to the much bigger nurse blocking her away and trying to calm her down.

"I'm his girlfriend. Ask him." She crosses her arms over her chest. I don't hear the nurse's response, but she doesn't budge, so I don't think she cares.

Violet scans the area again, obviously not giving up, and this time, her gaze widens when she sees me.

"She belong to you?" Dr. Chase asks with amusement lacing his tone.

I don't answer. I can't. My heart hammers in my chest.

Dr. Chase must decide she's not a threat because he holds up a hand to indicate that it's okay, and the nurse doesn't charge after her.

When she gets close, I see the tears in her eyes. She sets a large, rolled-up piece of paper on the end of the bed and comes to my side. Her gaze roams over my bum knee and then snaps back up to me.

"Hey." The single word scrapes my throat. I turn my hand, palm up, on the bed, and she laces her fingers through mine.

240

Chapter
THIRTY-SIX

Violet

"HANG TIGHT WHILE I ORDER THAT MRI." THE doctor taps the tablet on the rail at the end of the bed. "Hopefully it won't take too long."

As he leaves, he pulls the curtain to give us privacy.

"Fancy meeting you here," Gavin says, and attempts a smile. "How are you?"

"Been better."

He scoots over on the bed and tugs me to sit with him.

I hesitate. "I don't want to hurt you."

"The damage is done, baby doll."

"What happened?" I breathe him in as I climb in next to him and wrap myself around his middle.

"I fucked up my knee." He stills under me. "How did you get here so fast? Wait, how long have I been here?"

I lift my head to meet his gaze. "I'm sorry. We were running late. By the time we made it, you'd already left."

"You were at the game?"

"Sort of. When Jane and I got to our seats, I couldn't find you, so we didn't stay. I'm sorry. I know you said I shouldn't come, but I had to."

Sooo… turns out I wasn't positive about not coming. I spent all day yesterday feeling like a jerk for every mean thing I said about him, about basketball and the entire jock population, and I decided the only way I knew how to show him that I accept every part of him was to get on a plane and watch him do his favorite thing.

Only I messed that up too. I was in such a state of anxiousness about coming against his wishes that I left my purse, with my ID, at the house. Jane and I had to go all the way back home and then we missed our flight, which put us getting in later than we planned. I killed my phone by frantically checking the time and composing texts I couldn't bring myself to send. When we finally made it to our seats, Gavin was nowhere to be found. We spent another thirty minutes trying to figure out where he was. We overheard two guys behind us talking about the play that sent Gavin to the ground in what they described as a "nasty" fall.

So, we looked for him at the arena first. Not that we could get very far. Jane tried to bribe a security guard; it wasn't pretty. Eventually, she thought to call the closest hospital.

"I was looking for you," he says. "I hoped you'd come. I'm sorry I was an asshole."

"I get it. I have said some pretty awful things about you, your teammates, and the entire athletic community."

"Well, you didn't have the best intro to Valley jocks."

"That isn't true. Dahlia is amazing."

He laughs softly and then falls quiet again.

"Your dad is in the waiting room."

A small huff leaves his lips. "Always playing the part of the perfect dad when people are watching."

"I don't know your dad or all the things that have happened between you two, but he doesn't look like a guy who's out there just playing a part." He looked soberingly normal with his head in his hands, leaned over in a cheap plastic chair with all the other people waiting for news of their loved ones.

"He's probably pissed at me."

"Why?"

"I yelled at him in front of a bunch of reporters."

"What?"

Gavin looks embarrassed as he says, "I didn't know the cameras were on us. I just snapped."

I squeeze his hand. I don't know the right thing to say. His relationship with his dad is a complicated subject and he has enough going on at the moment.

"I'm sorry I was late. I was looking forward to waving that sign proudly for you." I nod to the glitter sign I brought from home.

He smiles again. This one lasts longer. "I'm just glad you're here."

A nurse comes to take Gavin to get an MRI and I head to the waiting room. Tommy is coming down a long hallway, headed my way, with a bag of chips and a cookie in one hand and a can of Coke in the other.

"Hi," I say. "Hungry?"

"I bought them for Gavin. I figured it was better than a 'Get Well Soon' balloon."

"They took him back for an MRI. Have you seen Jane?"

"No." He nods to a couple of empty chairs and we take a seat.

"Cookie?" He offers me the one that's supposed to be for Gavin. When I don't immediately take it, he says, "We might be here awhile."

"Thanks." I take it and break off a small piece.

"I keep seeing it over and over." Tommy's leg bounces as he

tears open the chips. "The angle was bad. He just crumpled to the ground. I've never seen anyone go down like that. And I never expected it to be him."

His phone makes a sound, and he wipes his hands and sets the chip bag on a table next to him before digging it out. "Valley won."

"That's great."

Tommy nods. "They had to. Gavin never would have forgiven himself if he thought his getting hurt cost us the game."

"I'm guessing he's out the rest of the season."

"At least."

"You mean this could be it? He could be done forever?"

He shrugs one big shoulder. "A lot of guys aren't the same after knee injuries."

A knot tangles in my chest and drops to the pit of my stomach.

Jane reappears as Tommy and I are silently staring at the wall, both lost in our own thoughts.

"I ordered food. It'll be here in thirty." She drops into the seat next to me.

"Thanks." I lean my head onto her shoulder.

"It's going to be okay," she says.

I hope she's right.

When Jane said she ordered food, she should have said she ordered enough food to feed an entire waiting room. The man behind the reception desk eyes us with annoyance until Jane takes him a carton of noodles and beef.

Guys from the team start to arrive, Coach Reynolds and his wife, and others that I assume are part of the team in some way. The mood has lightened. Everyone is worried, of course, but we eat and joke.

Only one person hangs off by himself. I scoop up what's left of the food onto a plate and walk it over to where Anthony Leonard sits.

His head is down, and he stares at the floor, completely lost to the rest of the room.

"Do you want something to eat?" I ask.

He looks up slowly and eyes the plate in my hand. "Thanks, but I'm not hungry."

I turn to flee, but he asks, "How is he?"

Something in how broken he looks compels me to answer him. "They were taking him to do an MRI. I don't know anything else, sorry."

He shakes his head. "I talked to Dr. Chase, but how is *he*?"

"Oh. I'm not sure."

I can tell he's displeased with my answer, but he just smiles and nods.

I set the plate down on a table near him, just in case he changes his mind about eating, and take a seat two chairs down from him. "I think he's disappointed and scared right now, but I'm not really sure. He didn't say a lot. You could go ask him yourself. You're family. I had to bulldoze my way in, but if you tell them who you are, they'll let you see him."

"He doesn't want me back there." He waves a hand. "Besides, he has his coach and his teammates and you."

"Sometimes we have to show up for people even when they don't want us to. He didn't want me to come to the game, but here I am."

"Why?" His brows pull together in question.

"I said some mean things. It's a long story."

He doesn't push for more of an explanation, but he keeps watching me.

"Is it true that he might not play again?"

"It's a tough injury to come back from." His mouth pulls into a tight line. "*If* he wants to play again, he'll probably have a long road ahead of him."

"If?"

He shrugs.

"Gavin loves basketball. He wants to play it off like it's not important, but he loves it. I think he's afraid people will always compare him to you, no matter what he does."

"He got his love of basketball from his mother. I wasn't around enough to take any claim on that."

I don't think it's that simple. I know that Gavin looks up to his dad, even if his anger and resentment overshadows it. "I don't know everything that's happened between you two, but you can't move forward if you're holding on to the past. If you and Gavin are going to have a relationship, you're both going to have to accept that."

"And if he can't?"

"Then at least you did everything you could." With that, I leave him to his thoughts.

Dr. Chase comes out a couple of minutes later, and after a quick chat with Gavin's dad, he lets Coach Reynolds know they've moved Gavin up to a private room and the guys can see him.

Jane and I hang back.

"I think I'm going to head to the hotel soon. Are you staying here tonight?" she asks.

"Oh. I don't know. I hadn't thought about it. I doubt they'll let me."

Mr. Leonard steps up to me and pulls a rectangular card from his pocket. "I talked to the nurses and Dr. Chase. He'll be here for at least tonight. They're bringing a cot into the room for you. If you or Gavin need anything, will you let me know?"

He extends the paper to me, his business card.

I take it with mixed feelings, but I know I will never call him without Gavin's knowledge. "Thank you."

With a nod, he walks away.

Jane stares down at the card. "You could probably sell his private number, or we could spam him with prank calls."

"I'll keep that in mind." Laughing, I slide it into my purse. "Go ahead to the hotel. I'll check in later tonight. What time is our flight tomorrow?"

"Whenever you want. I'll reschedule it."

"You don't need to do that."

She waves me off like it's no big deal.

"I will call you later when I know what's going on. Do not do anything until then."

"Okay." She gives me a one-arm hug. "Go play nurse to that sexy man of yours."

I wait until some of the team starts trickling out before I make my way to Gavin's room. He's sitting up in bed, left leg elevated on a foam pillow. Jenkins is telling him about something that happened in the game, and Gavin and the few guys that are left laugh.

"Okay, everyone. I think it's time for him to get some rest." A woman I hadn't seen steps forward from where she was hidden out of view. She's tall, with her dark hair pulled back in a low ponytail, and black jeans that make her legs seem never-ending. Gavin's mom.

Coach Reynolds spots me in the doorway and smiles.

"She's right. Time for us to go, boys." He squeezes Gavin's shoulder. "I'll come by in the morning. Try to get some rest." Coach gives him the same instructions Gavin's dad gave me, to call him if we need anything.

His teammates offer up fist bumps and well wishes, then file out, leaving me alone with them. My palms sweat and my heart races.

His mom starts arranging things around the room. She has a presence, a very intimidating one that makes me want to slink away. I had not planned on meeting his mom tonight.

"There you are," Gavin says when he notices me hovering in the doorway. "I wondered where you disappeared to."

I step in and smooth my hair behind one ear. "I wanted to make sure you had some time with the team."

Gavin's mom stops what she's doing and smiles at me. "You must be Violet."

"Yes, ma'am."

"I'm the Mom. Kelly. Nice to meet you."

"You too."

She picks up the ice bucket and then speaks to her son, "I'm going to get ice and track down your father. Has he been in since they got you to your room?"

Gavin doesn't meet her gaze as he shakes his head.

"Oh, uh, he left," I say. "Not long ago. He said to call if Gavin needed anything."

The disappointment on Gavin's face makes me wish I would have tackled and dragged his dad back here.

Kelly nods. "Well, he got Dr. Chase here, so that's something."

Gavin and I stare at her.

"What do you mean he got Dr. Chase here?" Gavin asks.

"Dr. Chase is the best there is. He's like the knee-whisperer of professional athletes. I don't know how your father got him here so fast, but I'm glad he did."

"I thought..." Gavin starts then trails off.

"You thought you just lucked into a great surgeon here?"

"Yeah, kind of." He shrugs.

"This was all your father's doing."

With that, she passes me and leaves the room.

I step closer to him and whisper, "I just met your mom. I'm kind of freaking out."

He laughs and runs a hand through his messy hair. He's out of his uniform now and in a T-shirt and shorts. "What? Why? You already met my dad."

"I know, but meeting 'the mom' is a big deal. And yours is particularly intimidating."

"She's the best." Gavin holds his arms out to me, and I go to him, sitting on the bed on his good side.

"You need to rest. I should go."

He ignores me and wraps his arms around me, pulling me closer. "We're having a sleepover. I got you a cot."

I laugh at the small, uncomfortable looking contraption squeezed in between the wall and his bed. "What a gentleman."

He hums. "I'm hoping you'll sneak into my bed after my mom falls asleep."

I snuggle into his chest as I laugh. "Wait, what?"

His chest shakes with his own laughter, and he points to the other cot across the room. "Did I not mention it was a supervised sleepover?"

"You definitely did not."

"Well, I'm afraid she isn't going anywhere. My surgery is scheduled for first thing tomorrow morning."

"Surgery?"

"Yeah." He blows out a breath. "Dr. Chase thinks it's the best option, and apparently, he's the best." He leans back against the pillows stacked against the headboard. "Hey, about the other night."

I shake my head. "It's okay."

"I was an asshole."

"It's okay," I say again. "We can talk about it later. You need to get all fixed up first."

"All right." He takes my hand. "What time do you leave tomorrow?"

"Early. Do you want me to change my flight? Nothing important is happening in class Monday." Or I hope not anyway.

"No. I'll be out of here tomorrow afternoon anyway. My mom is driving me back to school."

"That soon?"

"I'm only here tonight because Dr. Chase wants to do the surgery at some godforsaken hour. It's usually an outpatient procedure." He shakes his head. "It all makes sense now that I know my dad got him here. I probably would have had to fly back and meet with doctors, making it days or weeks before they could fit me in, so I guess I'm thankful."

I squeeze him a little tighter.

"I'm sure they're printing it in some paper right now. 'Anthony Leonard Hires Top Surgeon for Son,'" he says the last part like he's reading the news from a teleprompter. His voice changes again, this time to annoyed. "All for show and then gone without a word. I don't know whether to be happy or pissed anymore. It's all such bullshit."

I curl up next to him and he drops his chin to the top of my head. "But you're here and that's all that matters."

Chapter
THIRTY-SEVEN

Gavin

VIOLET HAS TO LEAVE FOR THE AIRPORT AROUND THE same time they're ready to take me down for pre-op. She looks as nervous as my mom.

"Jane is waiting downstairs. I will come over to see you as soon as you get back. You're going to do great." She squeezes my fingers, but I think she's reassuring herself more than me.

"Have a safe flight. I'll see you back in Valley tonight."

"Okay." She glances to see if my mom is looking and then presses a quick kiss to my lips.

I think it's hilarious that Violet's scared of my mom. I capture her with an arm around her back and deepen the kiss. She reciprocates for barely a second before pulling away. Her face is red.

As soon as she's gone, I sink back into the bed and blow out a long breath. "Okay, I'm ready."

Mom follows me as they wheel me out of the room and down the long, quiet hallway. "Violet seemed nice. Really pretty too."

"She is nice," I say. "And smoking hot."

The nurse laughs as Mom gives me a side-eye.

"Don't look at me like that. It's a compliment. Violet's great."

In the pre-op room, they get me all ready to go. Mom's phone is buzzing constantly as she stands next to the bed.

"Thanks for coming," I say. "Are your girls freaking out?"

"They'll be fine. The assistant coaches have it covered."

"I bet they're freaking out." They have a game tomorrow night. I think it's only the second time she's missed a game in all the time she's been coaching, and the last one was for Pop Pop's funeral.

She puts her phone away. "They're fine. And you're going to be too."

God, I hope she's right. My stomach is a mess.

"Good morning." Dr. Chase steps into the room, wearing scrubs that somehow make him look even less like the other doctors than the polo and dress pants he had on yesterday. He smiles when he sees my mom. "Kelly, it's good to see you."

I look between them. "You two have met before?"

"We traveled in the same circles once upon a time." She gives him her full attention. "Hey, Theo. How's Lexi?"

"She is doing great," he says. "Or so I hear. We got divorced about two years ago."

"I'm sorry. I hadn't heard."

He nods his appreciation and then steps up to the side of my bed. "Nervous?"

"Yeah." I swallow the lump in my throat. "But I'm ready."

I doze on and off as the anesthesia wears off. I have weird dreams where I'm shooting hoops with my dad in the driveway, something we probably only did a few times.

When I'm fully awake, I'm groggy, and my mouth feels like I swallowed cotton. Mom says Coach came by before the team headed back to Valley. My chest constricts as I think about them leaving without me.

I lie my head back and try not to fall into a self-pity spiral. Athletes get hurt all the time. I can come back from this. And if I can't, then I can still do what I planned and get a degree in sports journalism.

Mom takes a phone call and Dr. Chase reappears, this time dressed like he's heading to the country club.

He takes a seat on the end of the bed and angles his body to face me. "I already talked to your mom, but I wanted to stop in before I left to let you know the surgery went really well. I was able to repair both the patellar tendon and collateral ligament. A colleague of mine has an office in Valley. He's successfully rehabbed a lot of knees. Listen to what he says, don't slack off or push too hard, and I think you'll be dunking basketballs for many years to come."

The relief that washes over me makes me feel as light as a feather. My voice is gruff when I thank him.

"My pleasure." He stands. "If you have any questions or problems in the next week, give me a call. Your mom has my card. Day or night. Okay?"

"I will. Thank you again."

As soon as I'm discharged, they wheel me out to Mom's SUV. A couple of nurses are helping me into the vehicle when my gaze snags on a man across the parking lot. He's standing in front of a black SUV staring this way with a stuffed animal in his hand. A frog? An alligator? It's something green.

The guy looks kind of like my dad, but I'm probably still out of it. I don't know if my dad has ever bought me a stuffed animal or a toy that wasn't basketball-related in my entire life. I blink a bunch and try to clear my head as I stare harder, but a van drives by, blocking him from view before I can tell for sure, and then the nurses helping me step in front of me to say their goodbyes.

"Ready to go home?" my mom asks, putting the SUV in reverse.

"Ready."

As she pulls out, I look across the parking lot for the man again, but there's no one there.

Noah, Jenkins, and Tommy are at the door welcoming me home when Mom and I pull into the driveway of The White House.

They follow me as I crutch to the living room.

"Do you want some help up to your room?" Jenkins asks.

"Nah." I lower myself onto the couch. "I'm good here for a beat."

I think the pain killers are wearing off because my knee's screaming. Being in the car for six hours probably didn't help either.

Mom is a whirlwind as she comes in behind me with bags, and calls out instructions to the guys. Before I know it, I have a fresh ice pack, my pillow from upstairs, and anything else I might need is in reaching distance.

She disappears into the kitchen and the guys take seats around the living room.

"How'd it go?" Noah asks.

"Good, I guess. The doctor said I'll be able to play again."

"How long?"

"A few months, at least."

"You'll be good as new by the time the season starts in the fall," Tommy says with a chin tip.

"I hope so." I really, really hope so.

They have to head out a few minutes later to go to practice. It sucks to watch them go without me, but Violet arrives shortly after.

She drops her backpack on the floor and takes a seat next to me. "How are you feeling?"

"Tired, but happy to see you." I lean over until my shoulder touches hers.

"You should rest," she says.

"Help me up to my room?"

"Are you sure?"

"I want to sleep in my own bed."

My mom comes out of the kitchen and the two of them get me upstairs in bed.

"I'll bring up some food in a couple of hours," Mom says. "I need to run to the grocery store first."

"Thanks, Mom." She closes the door behind her.

"You should get naked and nap with me," I say to Violet. She's across the room, sitting on the edge of my desk.

"You need to get some rest."

"Sexy striptease to lull me to sleep?"

Laughing, Violet lies down next to me. "You're too much."

I place a hand on her thigh and slide my fingers under the hem of her dress.

"Your mom is downstairs." She pulls the dress down and bats at my hand.

"I missed you."

"I missed you too." Violet turns and snuggles into my side.

"How about just a little under the bra action?"

"To be continued," she says with a chuckle.

My eyes squeeze shut as I yawn. "I'm going to hold you to that."

For the next day and a half, I don't do much but sleep, watch movies with Violet, and play video games with the guys.

The team left this morning for the Final Four. It was hard to watch them go, but I smiled and wished them luck. Now I'm staring at my Spanish homework. It isn't due until the middle of next week, but I'm bored and restless. Violet has class all day, and Mom's been on conference calls with her assistant coaches and players. She needs to get back, I know she does, but she said she wasn't leaving until she made sure I had everything I needed here.

I've read the same paragraph at least three times when I hear voices downstairs. I toss the book to the end of the bed. Thank fuck. If that's Violet, maybe I can convince her to spring me from this room or to make out with me. Or maybe make out first and then spring me from this room.

"Gavin?" My mom calls from the other side of my door as she knocks softly. "Are you awake?"

"Yeah," I call back and adjust the pillow propping up my knee.

She comes in, but hovers near the doorway. "Feeling up to some company?"

"Definitely. I'm so bored."

"Good because there's someone here to see you."

"Who?"

She glances behind her and my dad steps into the room, carrying a gift bag.

Nobody speaks. I feel cornered and trapped, but also curious as to what the hell he's doing here.

"Are you two good?" she asks, looking between us.

I nod.

"I'll be downstairs if you need me," Mom says before leaving us alone.

Dad walks across the room, looking around and taking in my space.

"I like the artwork," he says.

"Violet brings a new one every day." I glance at them again— the posters that hang on every wall say things like, *Go Valley #31* and *Gavin Leonard MVP*. They're cheesy and covered in glitter, but they bring the biggest smile to my face every time she hangs another one up.

"What are you doing here?"

"I wanted to see how you were feeling, and I brought you this. You're too old for toys, but I didn't know what to get." He pulls something from the gift bag he walked in with and tosses it at me.

I stare down at the small, stuffed dinosaur. "It was you. You were at the hospital the day of my surgery."

He nods and stares at the floor. "I was there. Yes."

"Why?"

His head lifts, and his brows furrow in confusion.

"My season is over, maybe my career. There's no headline left that makes you look good."

"I didn't come here to fight with you about basketball. It's your future, do with it what you want, son. I just didn't want you to have the regrets that I do is all. But that's not why I'm here."

I'm not sure I believe him for all the pushing he's done before now, but I'm curious. "Okay, then why are you here?"

"Because I don't know you and I'd like to."

"What?" I'm so thrown, I can't stop the question.

A rough, sardonic sound leaves his lips. "When you're young, you think you have all the time in the world to do all the things you want to do, but it goes by so fast. I thought after I retired, I'd be able to make up for all the time I was gone. Instead, I realized we were strangers and you didn't need me. You had your mother, your routine; the two of you had created a life, a family, without me."

Anger builds in my chest. I start to tell him we had no choice, but he holds up a hand. "I'm not blaming anyone but myself. Your mother is an angel I never deserved."

"That we can agree on."

He glances at the floor.

"I don't understand you. You walk in here claiming you want to get to know me, and that Mom is an angel, but you spent my childhood using ball as an excuse to stay on the road and cheat on her every chance you got. You missed birthdays and school events.

I know more about you from reading the tabloids than I do from any conversation we've ever had. What kind of bullshit is that?"

"I know. Trust me, I know. I have spent the past year in therapy, trying to work through it. All I can say is I think I carried that need to prove myself and be seen as this hotshot pro-player that stemmed from my father's disapproval of me for most of my adult life. Pathetic as that is, I'm still struggling with it. I'm embarrassed that I let it overshadow everything else."

"And you still want to get to know me, even if I never touch a basketball again?"

"Of course."

"What if I can't forgive you?"

He looks up at the posters on my wall again before meeting my gaze. "I'd say I probably don't blame you. I'm not sure I'd forgive me either."

Chapter
THIRTY-EIGHT

Violet

I SMACK AT GAVIN'S HAND AS HE SLIPS IT UNDER THE HEM of my shirt. His calloused fingertips brush against my stomach as I switch out his ice pack for one that's fresh out of the freezer.

"You promised we could go to second base today."

"Not right now," I say through gritted teeth. I take a step back and his hand falls away. "Your mom is in the kitchen."

"I'm so bored." He tosses his head back on the couch.

"It's day three. You might need to find a new hobby." Since he got back to Valley, Gavin's been restless. The team already left for the Final Four, so The White House is oddly quiet.

"I don't need a hobby. I need you to take off all your clothes and straddle me."

Gavin's mom walks in as he's finishing that sentence. My face gets hot as I take another step away from her son, tempted to toss this warm ice pack at his head. I shoot him an annoyed glare, but he just grins.

"I stocked enough food to keep you fed for a day or two, at least." She's rolling a suitcase behind her. She stops and smiles at him from across the living room. "I wish I could stay longer."

"I'll be fine. Violet's a good nurse."

She laughs and her gaze slides to me. "I have a feeling she's going to be sick of you by the end of today."

"You wound me." He holds both hands over his heart.

She leaves her suitcase and goes over to the couch and leans down to hug him. "Behave yourself and take care of that knee. Ice, elevate—"

"I know. I know," he says. "I'm not going to do anything stupid."

She stares down at him like she still doesn't want to leave.

"Go," he smiles, "the Leonards need to represent at the tourney."

"I will check in before and after the game. Do me a favor and answer your phone when I call."

He picks it up from the cushion next to him and holds it in the air. "Got it right here."

She seems to relax a little as she starts for the door. "I love you. Call me if you need anything."

"Give 'em hell tomorrow." A spark of pride lights up his face.

She nods and lifts a hand to wave to me. "Bye, Violet. Thanks for looking out for him. If he gives you any trouble, let me know. I have a lot of dirt on him."

Laughter spills from my lips. "That sounds promising."

"You wouldn't," he says to her.

She heads to the door. "Behave yourself and we won't have to find out."

With another wave, she steps outside.

Gavin shakes his head and mumbles under his breath, "Can you believe that? My own mother is blackmailing me with pictures from Halloween like ten years ago."

I sit next to him on the couch. "Halloween pictures?"

He closes one eye and grimaces. "She didn't say that part, did she?"

"No, but now I absolutely need to see these pictures."

"Oh no." He slams his lips together tightly.

"Please?" I place my hands on his shoulders and swing one leg over, so I'm straddling him, but I keep my weight off him.

My hair falls into his face, and he brushes it back and then slides his hand behind my neck.

He shakes his head, still holding his mouth tight, but tips his head back so that our lips are millimeters apart. I close the distance. "I'll let you get to second base."

"You already promised second base as soon as my mom left, and guess what? She's gone."

His hands find their way back to the bottom of my T-shirt and glide up my skin. He goes straight for my bra, cupping me through the lacy material.

I sigh into his touch and lower myself until I can feel him hard beneath me. My body heats. Gavin holds me in place as he lifts his hips to create more friction between us.

He makes the sexiest, gruffest noise.

"I don't want to hurt you."

"Doesn't hurt," he says quickly.

"Would you tell me if it did?" I pull back to look at his face.

He gives me a sheepish grin.

I climb off his lap, and he runs his hands through his hair. Suddenly, he snaps his fingers in the air. "A blow job wouldn't hurt, eh? Or sixty-nine?"

I swear his eyes light up like he's just come up with the greatest idea ever.

My phone buzzes in my back pocket. I take it out and see an unfamiliar number. Normally, I wouldn't answer it, but I've had a lot of texts and calls from people checking in on Gavin.

"Hold that thought," I say, and then bring the phone up to my ear. "Hello?"

"Violet?" an older woman's voice asks. Familiar, but I can't quite place it.

"Yes," I say hesitantly.

"It's Professor Richards."

Gavin's hands roam freely while I'm distracted.

"Oh, uh, hi."

"Sorry to call, but I didn't have a chance to catch you after class."

"It's okay."

I shoot Gavin a wide-eyed look and mouth, "my teacher."

"Am I in trouble?"

She laughs softly. "God, no. I have something I wanted to talk with you about. Can you stop by my office tomorrow afternoon?"

"Sure." My mind spins with possibilities.

"Perfect. I have office hours from one until five, so just pop in when you have time."

"Okay. See you then."

I hang up and stare at my phone screen. "That was my professor. She wants to meet with me."

"About what?"

"She wouldn't say."

"Interesting." He hooks one long finger into the center of my bra and tugs me closer to him.

"Bad news. I have to go to class."

He groans.

"Jordan is on his way over, and we're all coming over later to watch the game on your giant TV."

"His boobs aren't as nice as yours." He leans down and bites one through my T-shirt.

"Later. I promise." I brush a kiss over his lips. "Get some rest and take your medicine in an hour."

Me, Daisy, Jordan, Dahlia, and Jane all go over to The White House to watch Valley play in the Final Four. It's a close game, but ultimately, Valley loses by five points. Gavin looks as disappointed as his teammates walking off the court.

We're all quiet as he stares ahead at the big screen in the media room.

"Tough loss," Jordan says. He tips his beer toward him. "Hell of a run though."

Gavin nods. "Next year. We'll get 'em next year. Both of us."

It's the first time he's mentioned playing again, except for in the broadest terms of the doctor saying it was possible.

Our friends stay only a few minutes longer before they say their goodbyes. It's late and I help Gavin back upstairs by letting him use me as a crutch.

He pulls his shirt over his head and gets into bed. I lie down beside him.

"I'm sorry about the game." I rest my hand on his bare chest.

He covers my hand with his. "It's all right. Kansas is tough. I won't be surprised if they win the whole tournament. Plus, my mom's team is heading to the championship. The Leonards are still representing."

"Your mom is kind of a bad ass."

He chuckles softly. "That she is."

"I'm sorry," I say again. "You'll get there next year."

He lets his head fall to the side and meets my gaze. He looks like a thousand thoughts are running through his mind.

"What?"

"This injury, not being able to play, it's made me really stop and reconsider what I want."

"And?"

"I can't imagine giving it up for good. It's only been a few days and I'm already going out of my mind."

"Maybe it gets easier or it's harder right now because you didn't get to finish the season."

"Maybe." He scoots closer. "My dad stopped by yesterday."

"Here? When?"

"While you were at class." He sighs. "He told me he wanted to get to know me, that he regretted not having a relationship with me sooner."

"Wow. And you kept this to yourself all day. Why?"

"I've been going over it and over it, trying to mesh his version with mine to make sense of it all."

"And?"

"I'm still pissed at him, and I'm not sure I trust him, but I think I have to forgive him. I don't want to be the guy harboring daddy issues in my fifties, ya know?"

I press a kiss to his lips. "I'm proud of you."

He grins. "I've also been thinking I might not want to cross off the NBA as an option just yet. I'm not saying I definitely want to play professionally, but I think I should at least give it some real thought, try to separate it from the shit with my dad."

His words don't match the hesitant look on his face.

"What is it? Why does talking about maybe playing in the NBA make you look like you want to throw up?"

"I don't want to be any version of him. Regardless of if I forgive him, I don't want to follow in his footsteps."

"How do you mean?"

"My dad cheated on my mom for basically their entire marriage. It fucks with you, you know? It's hard not to look back at all the things he missed and wonder if he really couldn't make it or if he was choosing other people over his family. I want to get married someday and have kids, but not if I'm going to end up like him."

"You aren't. You won't."

"My entire life, people have compared me to him. If I had a

dollar for every time someone said I was the spitting image of him, had his skill with a basketball or that I was destined to follow in his footsteps, I could buy my own private island."

I sit up so I can really look at him. "You are not him."

"I cheated on you," he says softly. "I can make all the excuses I want about being drunk or not remembering it, but I did it. I'm capable of that."

"You made a mistake. I forgave you."

"Did you?"

"Yes. Truly. You are an incredible guy. And I'm sorry that I made you feel weird about who you are and this thing that you love doing. It was just easier to hate on the entire jock population than admit I was in love with someone that didn't want me."

"I wanted you." He traces my bottom lip with the pad of his thumb. "I fucked up, but I have always wanted you."

Gavin places a soft kiss on my lips and then his gaze snaps back up to meet mine. "Wait, did you just say you were in love with me?" He cocks his head to the side. "Past or present tense?"

"Past *and* present tense."

He kisses me and then speaks against my lips. "Hey. Let's play a game."

"A game? Now?"

"Mhmm. Two truths and a lie."

"Okay." I give him a tentative smile.

"Number one, I have the hottest girlfriend alive."

"Two, I can't imagine my life without you."

"And three?" I ask.

"I have been in love with you since the night your sandal broke, and I carried you to your dorm."

My heart threatens to burst in my chest. "Which one is the lie?"

"None of them." He grins. "They're all true."

The girls and I go to University Hall together Friday morning for coffee before classes. We're sitting at a table near the front doors when a big guy wearing all black enters.

I nudge Dahlia with my elbow. "Doesn't that look like one of the guys that was with—"

"Penelope," we say in unison as the pop star steps in behind him. Her lavender hair is up inside a ball cap that's pulled low on her face and she's wearing baggy clothes, but it's most definitely her.

"Guys," I whisper, "that's her. That's Penelope."

"Penelope Hart?!" Daisy's voice lifts, and Penelope glances our way.

I offer a small wave.

She starts toward us and Daisy squeaks next to me, "Oh my gosh. Oh my gosh. She's coming over here."

"Hi! Dahlia and Violet. It's good to see you." She lowers her voice. "I'm trying to blend in, but the muscle with me makes it nearly impossible."

Daisy grabs my leg under the table and squeezes.

"Penelope, these are our roommates, Daisy."

She waves at my cousin.

"And—"

"Ivy?!" Penelope's face breaks out in a smile that makes her look younger and more like a normal girl our age, instead of a superstar, as she looks at Jane. "Oh my gosh. I haven't seen you since—"

"It's *Jane*," my friend says.

"Wait. You two know each other?" I ask, studying Jane carefully.

Jane fidgets with the lid of her coffee. "I think we met once at a party back in LA."

266

Penelope looks between us, brow furrowed and mouth slightly open.

"Right," she says the word slowly. "Yeah, that must be it." Penelope stares at her a beat longer before her gaze slides to me. "I am so happy I ran into you."

"Me? Why?"

She nods quickly. "I cannot stop thinking about that black dress."

"Oh, uh, thanks."

"I have this award show next month, and I was hoping you might consider letting me wear it. I know it isn't a world tour stage, but there's a red carpet and the show is televised."

"Do you mean the MTV Awards?" Daisy asks. My cousin's blue eyes are wide with shock.

"You know it." Penelope smiles.

Daisy nods slowly. "I think everyone knows it."

"I'd let you wear that dress to the grocery store if you wanted," I say honestly.

She laughs. "Professor Richards has all the details and my contact information. She said she'd pass it along and set up a time next week to do a fitting with both of you."

That explains why she wanted to meet later today.

"Don't you need to get back to LA?" Jane asks, her tone is borderline hostile.

"Jane!" Dahlia admonishes. "Sorry. She had too much caffeine this morning."

"It's okay," Penelope says, "I do need to get back soon. My agent is having an aneurysm that I haven't already returned, but I like it here. College is cool."

The four of us share an amused look. Well, three of us. Jane is still sort of glaring at Penelope.

"This is incredible news," I say. "You are going to look amazing in that dress. Thank you."

"Thank *you*." She looks to Dahlia. "Thanks to both of you."

She pulls the Valley U hat down farther over her eyes. "I better get out of here before my luck runs out. Bye."

"Bye," we return, staring after her.

When she's gone, I turn to Jane.

"You know Penelope Hart?" I ask.

"Know is a stretch." Jane waves me off.

"Why would you not mention that?" Dahlia elbows her.

"I guess I forgot."

"You forgot?"

We all stare at her.

"It was forever ago." She shakes her head. "Someday I'll tell you about all the celebrity run-ins I've had, but right now, we need to focus on the important thing here. Penelope is going to wear your dress. This is amazing."

She's right. It is amazing. "I'm shocked. Did that really just happen?"

"It really happened," Dahlia says. "We're going to dress Penelope Hart!"

Chapter
THIRTY-NINE

Gavin

AS THE CAMERA PANS TO FOLLOW PENELOPE WALKING down the red carpet, Violet and Dahlia jump up and down. I've never seen my girl so happy. She hits me with a smile that makes the world feel simple and good, and then lunges at me, throwing her arms around my neck.

She's a whirlwind of excitement. I stumble, and she freezes, wide-eyed. "Are you okay?"

"Fine." I steady us. "You're just stronger when you're all amped-up on fashion."

"She's wearing my dress. Penelope Hart is wearing my dress." If her voice gets any higher, she'll be able to communicate with animals.

"I saw. She looks great. Congrats, baby."

She squeals and bounces, rubbing her body all over mine in the process.

"You look pretty great too," I murmur, leaning down and attempting to kiss her. She's a moving target, but as soon as my lips cover hers, she melts into me. Being on the receiving end of all that enthusiasm has me ready to throw her over my shoulder and run upstairs. Metaphorically, of course. I'm not quite up to running stairs yet.

The knee is better. I'm off my crutches and in physical therapy. I don't know if I'll be ready by the time the season starts next fall, but that's my goal. I want that NCAA championship. After that? I'm still not sure. I know it involves the girl next door. She doesn't hate my guts so much anymore and I'm going to do everything I can to keep it that way.

"I'm so happy for you." Dahlia comes over to my girl. I let her go, so the two of them can hug again.

We're in the media room for the big event. All her roommates and a few friends from her fashion design class are here to watch Penelope strut down the red carpet in Violet's dress. There's a party outside for her, too—the biggest of the year. That was Tommy's doing. I think he's trying to win over my girl. He's still a little scared of her.

Felix steps into the doorway and tips his beer in my direction. "What's going on?"

Nodding toward the TV, I say, "Penelope Hart. She's wearing one of Violet's dresses tonight."

"That's awesome." He glances at the screen.

It really is. She's so talented. It blows me away.

"Felix!" Violet greets him.

"I just heard the news. Cheers to you." He lifts his drink.

"Thank you. Done any recent modeling?"

He smirks. "Busting my balls?"

I chuckle and pull her into my side.

Felix moves his attention to Dahlia, who seems to have turned to stone right in front of us.

"Hey, Dahlia," he says. "How are you?"

Her blonde hair bounces around her shoulders as she nods. She opens her mouth like she's going to respond, but it takes another three or four bobs of her head before she does. "Hi. Okay. I mean, great."

Felix takes a step closer to her, and she looks panicked. "When is Penelope wearing your dress?"

"It isn't a dress," she says, sounding a little more confident, but her face turns red. "It's a jumper, and this summer."

"On her *worldwide* tour," Vi adds.

Dahlia blushes harder.

"Let's go dance." Jane rescues Dahlia and tugs her friend out of the theater room. The rest of us follow behind.

Vi and I are the last to step out into the yard. I swing our joined hands between us.

"Need to sit?" she asks.

"Offering to do a lap dance?"

She rolls her eyes and shoots me a playful smile. A few empty chairs are abandoned next to the fence, so I take one and pull her to sit on my good leg.

The music is pumping. People are laughing and having a good time. Vi sways to the beat as she watches her friends.

"Go."

"But what about you?"

"I need a fresh beer anyway."

"Why didn't you grab one on our way out?" Her eyes twinkle with humor.

"I didn't need one then."

Laughing, she presses a quick kiss to my lips and then rushes off.

The kitchen is as packed as the rest of the house tonight. Someone made Jell-O shots and the little cups of colorful gelatin laced with alcohol take up the entire island. I grab a couple of beers, so I don't have to come back any time soon, and then stack up as many shots as I can for Vi and her friends.

I'm heading back out when Bailey steps in front of me.

"Hi, Gavin." She smiles at me and eyes all the booze in my hands. "Woah, someone is planning on having fun tonight."

"Bailey," I say coolly as I try to pass her.

"Let's do a shot." She places a hand on my forearm and closes the distance between us.

"I don't think so."

"Violet's busy. She won't mind."

The fact she knows where Violet is, tells me everything I need to know about how calculated this little interaction was.

I look her dead in the eye and smile. She reciprocates and tips her head to indicate we should go inside.

"*I* mind." I try to push past her again.

Her grip tightens and a smirk twists her lips. "Come on. Don't be like that. I'll let you do anything you want to me."

"I'm with Violet, and even if I weren't, I'm not interested, Bailey. Not now. Not ever."

"Whatever." Her body stiffens. "You probably can't even get it up or you'd pass out like last time."

I start to walk away but then her words sink in. "What did you say?"

"I said you probably can't even get it up."

"The other thing," I grit out. "You said I passed out. Before or after we hooked up?"

She says nothing and my blood boils. "Answer the damn question, Bailey. Did we or did we not sleep together?"

"Not yet," she purrs and tries to step into my space.

I hold up a hand. "But we were in bed together." She'd been fully naked, and I was mostly there. I don't remember getting to her dorm or anything that happened after, but it didn't look good.

"I told you it was Violet's bed. You were so drunk, you would have believed anything I said."

"So you and I didn't do anything?" I ask again, to be sure I'm following correctly.

She rolls her eyes. "No. You were going on and on about Vi all night. It was obnoxious. Seriously, she isn't that great. You passed out as soon as you hit the mattress."

"Are you fucking kidding me? You just let me think that we hooked up? Why?"

She shrugs. She fucking shrugs.

Something snaps inside of me. My head tips back in a laugh that's part hysteria and part relief. "Get the fuck out of my house, Bailey."

I leave her without another word and cross the yard to get to my girl.

Vi sees me when I get close and dances toward me. Her brows pull together in concern as she studies my face. "Are you okay?"

I know I'll tell her eventually, but not tonight. Tonight is about celebrating her. "Never better."

"O-kay." A slow smile spreads across her face. "Then are we drinking to black out tonight?"

"For your friends." I hand her the stack of Jell-O shots and then loop my arm around her waist. "And to answer your question, fuck no. I want you to remember every dirty thing I'm going to do to you later."

Her eyes darken. "Maybe we should take a quick party break."

I fight back a chuckle. "Sounds like an excellent idea."

We cut through the crowd, and I chase after her upstairs to my room. We're both laughing and out of breath. She stands in the middle of my room, looking so gorgeous. I can't believe she's mine.

I linger in the doorway, just staring at her.

"What?" she asks, confused because I still haven't moved.

"I love you so fucking much."

A coy smile tilts up the corners of her mouth. "I love you too."

She turns and walks to the window. I finally step fully into the room and close the door behind me.

She gasps. "My car is blocked in!"

I wrap my arms around her from behind. She's right. Cars line both sides of the street, including her driveway.

"Good thing you're not going anywhere tonight."

She spins on me and gives me a haughty glare that takes me by surprise. "You're the worst, Gavin Leonard."

A slow smile replaces the glare.

I place an open-mouth kiss to her shoulder and then bite lightly. "The absolute worst."

Chapter
FORTY

Violet

Two weeks before Junior Year

"I'M SO GLAD YOU AND GAVIN GOT BACK TOGETHER." Jane drops onto a lounge chair on my right and slides on a pair of red, heart-shaped sunglasses. "Access to this pool is a definite perk. If you're going to break up with him, please wait until this heat wave passes."

Daisy, on my other side, hums her agreement. "It's almost as good as the tree house."

Dahlia laughs. "You only like that tree house because it's where you and Jordan have sex nonstop."

My cousin blushes. "It's not the only reason I like it."

"Better enjoy the pool now," I say, letting my eyes fall closed, "because once classes start up, it won't be nearly this quiet or as relaxing out here.

Only two weeks left of summer until the fall semester starts. The girls came back early to settle into the house and hang out. I missed them so much. I saw Daisy a couple of times this summer with our families, but Jane and Dahlia were both too far away. Jane went back home to California for the break and Dahlia spent most of her time off traveling. She entered some golf tournaments, went with her family on vacation to Italy, and then saw Penelope Hart in concert, VIP-style, so she could watch with thousands of others while Penelope wore the design she created. Dahlia said the show was incredible.

But the really incredible part is that Penelope posted a stage shot of her wearing Dahlia's jumper on all her social media accounts (it was SO gorgeous by the way!) raving about how much she loved it. My friend has a new glow since she's been back. She's always been amazingly talented, but I think she just might be starting to believe it for herself.

Daisy spent the summer between Flagstaff with her family and visiting Jordan in Phoenix. They are the cutest. Every time I think Jordan can't possibly make her any happier, he proves me wrong.

And me, well, I spent my summer vacation falling more in love with the boy next door. Gavin stayed in Valley to continue his knee rehab, and I went home to see my family and lounge around the pool. We planned to visit each other on weekends, and maybe take a trip somewhere together. But, well, things didn't exactly go according to plan.

I did go home, and he did come to see me, two weeks after I left. He met my parents (I think my dad likes him better than he likes me. Kidding, but seriously, it's possible.) and I showed him all around my hometown. It was great. Then it was over. Far sooner than either of us wanted.

Gavin left early on a Monday morning, because he had to get back for a physical therapy appointment, and an hour later, I packed up and followed him. Life is better when he's around. I still got to spend my summer by the pool, at The White House, and we drove up to Phoenix a few more times so that my parents could see me (at least I think it was me they were excited to see).

All in all, a great summer. But I'm glad my friends are back. This morning we woke up and decided a day of swimming was in order. The basketball guys have camp this week, so the pool is all ours in the mornings.

"Oh my gosh, Vi. Did you get a tattoo?" Jane's voice snaps me to attention.

I follow her line of vision to the mark on my hip.

Her brows rise in question and Daisy and Dahlia sit forward to get a better look.

"You got a tattoo?" Dahlia asks.

"No. It's pen." I run my finger lightly over the infinity symbol and heat creeps down my neck. "Gavin drew it."

"Ooooh." A small burst of laughter leaves Daisy's lips. "That's what these are."

She grabs my wrist and points to the inside of my bicep where he wrote *I love you*.

A dozen more mark up my body in places my friends can't see.

"What can I say, he expresses himself better with a pen in hand."

"And when you're naked?" Jane asks with a grin.

"Precisely."

"I got a tattoo," Daisy says, casually.

We all look at her with shocked expressions.

"Really?" I scan her body, looking for ink, but don't see anything.

"Where?" Dahlia asks.

My cousin lifts the pinkie finger of her left hand. It's so small I can barely make it out.

"A stick man?"

"A stick *woman*. It matches Jordan's. When we link pinkie fingers, they kiss."

"Just when I think you two can't get more adorable," I say through giggles.

The four of us are still laughing when Gavin walks out the

back door. He's in workout clothes and pulls the sleeveless T-shirt over his head before he sits on the end of my chair.

He hits me with a smile that makes my insides tingle. "Hey, gorgeous. Enjoying the pool?"

"Hi." I sit up and wrap my arms around his neck. He's warm and sweaty, and his hair is wet and curls up at the end. "We are. Your pool is a real selling point. I'm not allowed to break up with you until winter."

He grunts before pressing a hard kiss to my mouth and then nipping at my bottom lip.

"Are you going to swim?"

"Maybe. I need to shower first." He brushes his lips over mine more softly this time.

"I could use a shower," I murmur against his mouth. "Someone got pen all over me."

"Yeah. I had to explain to the guys why my back says, *Touch and Die*." He swivels to show us his back where I did, indeed, write those words.

"Did it work?"

Instead of answering me, he kisses me again.

"How's the knee?" Dahlia asks him.

He extends his left leg. "Better. Not one hundred percent yet, but I'm getting there."

He's worked so hard this summer with physical therapy and light workouts. Who knows? I might go watch my first basketball game at Ray Fieldhouse this year.

"Shower with me?" he asks quietly, so only I can hear.

My heart races and my core aches. I don't know how it's physically possible to be so turned on in such a short amount of time. *And* in front of my friends.

"Be right there."

He nods and gets to his feet. "Later, ladies. Enjoy the pool and I restocked the hard seltzer. That oughta get me to at least next summer?"

"We'll consider it," Jane says through a smirk.

"'Preciate it." He winks as he leaves.

"Pool access and free booze," Jane says. "Yep, I'm really glad you two worked things out."

"Me too." I watch as he goes inside. A year ago, I never would have believed it were possible. Life is funny that way. Always surprising me.

"Go," Dahlia says, nudging me, "but don't ditch us all afternoon."

"I won't." I scramble to my feet. "Do you want me to grab fresh drinks on my way back?"

"Definitely." Daisy shakes her can. "Hurry. I'm almost out."

I do hurry, but only because my body is vibrating with need. Upstairs, I hear the shower going and head straight for the bathroom. The door is cracked open, and I linger outside for a second. I have a constant fear that I'm going to walk in on one of his roommates. None of them ever closes the door.

"Gavin?" I ask tentatively and push it open an inch wider.

Fingers wrap around my wrist and tug me in. Before I realize what's happening, my boyfriend has me pressed against the now closed bathroom door.

Naked Gavin is a glorious thing. I only get to appreciate it for a second before his mouth crashes down on mine.

"Missed you." He practically growls the words before his tongue tangles with mine, leaving me unable to respond.

There isn't anything to say anyway. He knows I missed him too.

Logically, I know that at some point we'll likely move out of this phase where we can't get enough of each other, but we're so far from that now it feels like a lifetime away.

While pressing me into the wooden door, Gavin kisses down my neck. He makes quick work of untying my bikini top and tossing it to the ground. Then his lips are skimming over my breasts. He lavishes me in kisses, and I thread my fingers through his thick hair and tug.

Last night, he drew petals around my nipples to make my

boobs look like flowers. That was right before he drew the infinity symbol and told me he'd love me forever. Sweet and sometimes silly, that's Gavin. And oh, so sexy.

His mouth covers a nipple, pulling a happy groan from me. He lifts one leg, encouraging me to wrap it around him, then his long fingers dance around the edge of my swimsuit bottoms. He slides one digit under the spandex material and inside me. I moan as I arch into his touch, silently asking for more.

"You're so wet, baby. You must have missed me too."

"Always."

He drags his thumb over my clit. I whine in protest when his hand falls away, but he drops to his knees in front of me and covers me with his mouth.

Steam billows in the bathroom. I feel like I could float away with it as my first orgasm jolts through me. This summer has been a master class on getting each other off, and Gavin is an eager, attentive student.

Then again, so am I.

And Gavin always likes to get off the first time inside me. I step into the shower, letting the warm spray pelt my skin. He steps in behind me and pulls the curtain closed.

I turn to face the wall and bend over. Another thing Gavin likes—to take me from behind.

He guides the head of his dick to my entrance and slowly pushes in. I hold my breath as I enjoy the sensation of him filling me up. If I'm honest, this is how I like it best, too. Although, there aren't a lot of ways I don't like it with Gavin.

"You're so damn beautiful and amazing and mine, Vi. I'm so lucky that you're mine."

He reaches around to circle my clit as he moves in and out of me at a steady pace. Neither of us will last long like this. Quick and explosive, and frequent, that's more our style.

And I wouldn't have it any other way.

Epilogue

Gavin

"**A**RE YOU SURE YOU DON'T WANT TO COME WITH US?" I ask my wife as Jordan tosses my camping stuff in the back of his truck. Austen holds both our hands, and we swing our son between us.

"Tempting, but Daisy and I have big plans of watching TV and ordering takeout."

"And sleeping in," Daisy adds.

I lean forward to kiss Violet, stopping an inch from her lips. "Who is going to protect me from the bears and other wild animals, or keep me warm in my sleeping bag?"

"Did you say bears?" Emily asks.

Ah, shit. I glance down at the four-year-old girl clutching on to Daisy's leg.

My son stands a little taller as he drops my hand to take Emily's. "Don't worry. My dad is bigger than anything out there."

Austen is only three months older than Emily, but he's been her protector and confidante since birth. They're more like brother and sister than second cousins.

A smile tugs at my lips as I give the little girl with blonde ringlets a reassuring wink.

Daisy squats down to hug Emily, and then our kids race off toward the truck.

"She'll be fine," I promise a nervous-looking Daisy as she watches her daughter climb into the back of the truck after Austen.

"I know," she says, but she doesn't sound convinced. "She's going through a phase where she's scared of everything."

"We'll keep a close eye on her."

"Thanks, Gavin." Daisy follows after our kids, and I hang back to say bye to my wife.

"See you on Sunday." I steal another kiss. Nine years of kissing her whenever I want, and it never gets old. "To be continued, Mrs. Leonard."

She and Daisy stand at the curb and wave us off as we head on our annual camping trip. This has become our yearly tradition. One weekend every summer, up in the mountains, catching up and unwinding. It's changed over time. Different locations and different people. Sometimes Violet and Daisy have come along, other times, they haven't, especially when Austen and Emily were babies. And these days the cooler is filled with as much juice as it is booze, but I look forward to it all the same. Occasionally Jenkins and Liam even make the trip.

Two hours later, after a stop for lunch and another to pick up food and ice for the weekend, we arrive at the campsite. A familiar vehicle, *mine*, catches my eye. As I look closer, I see some of my buddies and teammates. I glance over at Jordan. "What's going on?"

"Happy birthday, man." He opens his door and hops out. "Welcome to the dirty thirties."

Scanning the site, I find Violet and Daisy staring at the truck.

"Did you know your mom was coming?" I ask Austen.

One side of his mouth tugs up at the corner. He has the same lips as his mom, the bottom one is just a little bit fuller and always sticks out. "She said it was a surprise."

I get out of the truck and walk toward my sneaky wife.

She meets me halfway with a smug smile. "Fancy seeing you here."

"What is all this? My birthday was months ago."

"I know, but you were busy, and we didn't get to properly celebrate."

"Oh, we celebrated."

Her cheeks flush. We brought my thirtieth in with a bang. Lots of them.

"We did, but your friends wanted to do something since a lot of them didn't get to see you." She laces her fingers behind my neck. "You're really surprised? I thought for sure you'd figure it out. I had to look away every time I lied about not coming."

"You are a spectacularly bad liar, but I had no idea. This is amazing. Thank you."

"Welcome." She drops her mouth to mine in a quick kiss. "Lots of people want to say hi to you."

"They can wait." I pick her up and slant my mouth over hers.

"Gross," Austen mutters. "Are you two going to do that all weekend?"

Laughing, I pull away and set Vi on the ground.

"Yep." I scoop him up and lift him onto my shoulders, and the three of us head to the campsite.

My mom sits in a camping chair, and next to her is Dr. Chase, with one hand resting on her thigh. He stands when I get close, and we shake hands. "Good to see you, Gavin. Congrats on the season."

"Thanks. Good to see you too."

I set Austen down. My mom pulls him into a hug first and then me. Dr. Chase, or Theo as I've been instructed to call him a million times, stays close, watching my mom with a lovey grin on his face.

They got married last year after dating for several before that. I like him, but more importantly, I like the way he treats my mom. She's never seemed happier.

"I can't believe you're here," I say to them as we watch Austen run off to his mom.

"We aren't staying the night, but we wanted to come by and say hi." She places a hand on my scruffy face. She hates the short beard I've grown. "Your dad is coming by later too."

"I don't know how you guys pulled this off." My gaze drifts to all these people. They had to drive long distances or hop on a plane to be here. I spot Liam from afar and he lifts a hand in a wave.

"This was all Violet," my mom says. "You found a good one."

"The best." She and Austen are attempting to set up the tent. It does not look to be going well. The woman can design and sew a dress in minutes, but she's still hopeless outdoors. She's still doing it, too. The designing part, I mean. She's worked on movie sets and created custom gowns for celebrities. She just started her own clothing line, primarily dresses of course.

"I better go help," I tell my mom. "I'll be back."

I get stopped on my way, first by Liam and then Jenkins and Noah. Some of my NBA teammates are here, too, and I introduce everyone. It wasn't an easy road, but thanks to Dr. Chase (I mean Theo) and a lot of hard work in rehab, I battled back from the knee injury, played my senior year of college, and decided to go pro.

My dad was happy. Though I think he truly might have been either way. Our relationship is better than it's ever been, but I won't lie, sometimes a reporter asks me a question about him or compares me to my dad in some way and my hackles go up.

But then I go home to my wife and son and remember that I get to decide every single day to be the husband and father that I wanted.

"Need a hand?" I ask when I finally reach them.

"I think we got it." Vi blows out a breath and steps back.

"Should we try it out?" I nudge Austen, and he scrambles inside, all too eager. He loves camping. He even has a tent in his room where we often find him hiding away with a book.

The three of us sit in the middle of the tent. Austen explores the small space while I wrap an arm around Violet.

"What do you think?" she asks.

"That I love you. That I'm damn lucky. That this tent used to seem a hell of a lot bigger."

A small laugh escapes her lips, and she leans forward to kiss me.

"And that life with you... definitely, not the worst."

PLAYLIST

- "10 Things I Hate About You" by Leah Kate
- "No Romeo" by Dylan
- "F U Anthem" by Leah Kate
- "Dirty Thoughts" by Chloe Adams
- "As It Was" by Harry Styles
- "Thousand Miles" by The Kid LAROI
- "Figure You Out" by VOILA
- "Friends" by Emma Lov feat. Loote and Jordy
- "Friends Don't Fuck" by HAVEN
- "Lean On Me" by Cheat Codes feat. Tinashe
- "Misunderstood" by Xuitcasecity
- "Guess That's Love" by Ryan Mack
- "Touch Me There" by Emma Holzer
- "FMRN" by Lilyisthatyou
- "Parents" by Riley Roth
- "First Class" by Jack Harlow
- "Sunshine" by OneRepublic
- "Party 22" by Lilyisthatyou
- "Riptide" by The Chainsmokers
- "Water Under the Bridge" by Adele

Also by
REBECCA JENSHAK

Campus Wallflowers Series
Tutoring the Player
Hating the Player

Campus Nights Series
Secret Puck
Bad Crush
Broken Hearts
Wild Love

Smart Jocks Series
The Assist
The Fadeaway
The Tip-Off
The Fake
The Pass

Wildcat Hockey Series
Wildcat
Wild about You

Standalone Novels
Sweet Spot
Electric Blue Love

About the
AUTHOR

Rebecca Jenshak is a *USA Today* bestselling author of new adult and sports romance. She lives in Arizona with her family. When she isn't writing, you can find her attending local sporting events, hanging out with family and friends, or with her nose buried in a book.

Sign up for her newsletter for book sales and release news.

WWW.REBECCAJENSHAK.COM

Made in the USA
Coppell, TX
28 May 2023